A WILD SURGE OF GUILTY PASSION

"Ron Hansen has written a mordantly funny, vividly compelling, and irresistibly readable chronicle of the twenties."

—Joyce Carol Oates

"Mr. Hansen is a master of historical fiction. . . . Not since his brilliant *Mariette in Ecstasy* has Mr. Hansen so convincingly entwined sexuality with fate. This novel reads as breathlessly as a tabloid—that is, if a tabloid were well-written."

—John Irving

"No one writing today is better at re-creating the past than Hansen."

—James Lee Burke

"*A Wild Surge of Guilty Passion* is by turns blackly comic, irresistibly seductive, and implacably devastating. As a tour of the Seven Deadly Sins, it's pretty much unsurpassed in recent literature."

—Jim Shepard

"In using crime as the basis of his new novel, *A Wild Surge of Guilty Passion,* Ron Hansen joins a distinguished group of writers for whom it has served as an imaginative platform: Sophie Treadwell, James M. Cain, Raymond Chandler, and William Styron."

—*The New York Times Book Review*

"A gripping, entertaining novel."

—*Los Angeles Times*

ALSO BY RON HANSEN

Fiction

Exiles
Isn't It Romantic?
Hitler's Niece
Atticus
Mariette in Ecstasy
Nebraska
The Assassination of Jesse James by the Coward Robert Ford
Desperadoes

Essays

A Stay Against Confusion

For Children

The Shadowmaker

A
WILD SURGE
OF
GUILTY PASSION

A NOVEL

Ron Hansen

SCRIBNER

New York London Toronto Sydney New Delhi

SCRIBNER

A Division of Simon & Schuster, Inc.

1230 Avenue of the Americas

New York, NY 10020

First Scribner paperback edition July 2012

SCRIBNER and design are registered trademarks of The Gale Group, Inc., used under license by Simon & Schuster, Inc., the publisher of this work.

For information about special discounts for bulk purchases, please contact Simon & Schuster Special Sales at 1-866-506-1949 or business@simonandschuster.com.

The Simon & Schuster Speakers Bureau can bring authors to your live event. For more information or to book an event contact the Simon & Schuster Speakers Bureau at 1-866-248-3049 or visit our website at www.simonspeakers.com.

Designed by Akasha Archer

Manufactured in the United States of America

10 9 8 7 6 5 4 3 2 1

Library of Congress Control Number: 2011005571

ISBN 978-1-4516-1755-9
ISBN 978-1-4516-1756-6 (pbk)
ISBN 978-1-4516-1757-3 (ebook)

To Bo

A
WILD SURGE
OF
GUILTY PASSION

ONE

ART EDITOR SLAIN

She woke to a slow thudding on her bedroom door. She was Lorraine Snyder, aged nine. She'd wasted Saturday night with her parents at their friends' card party and she'd gotten home only after two o'clock Sunday morning. It was now just over five hours later. March 20th, 1927. She fell asleep again, and then she heard a louder thudding and her mother called in a muffled way, "Lora. Lora, it's me."

She got up, slumped over to the door, found it mysteriously locked from the hallway, and opened it with a skeleton key that was hanging on a string.

Ruth Snyder was lying on the hallway floor in a short green satin nightgown that was hiked up to her thighs. She'd been softly drumming the door with her head. White clothesline was wrapped many times around her ankles, and her wrists were tied behind her back.

Lorraine screamed, "Mommy! What happened?" She knelt to free the man's handkerchief that gagged her mother's mouth, and she heard Ruth say, "Don't untie me yet. Go over and get Mrs. Mulhauser."

Harriet Mulhauser was filling an electric coffee percolator from the kitchen tap when she heard the front doorbell ring. The pretty blonde girl from across the street was there on the porch, still in her sailor pajamas and slippers. Wide-eyed and frightened and breathless. "My mother needs you," she said.

Mrs. Mulhauser found a Snyder house that seemed to have been ransacked, with sofa cushions on the floor, curtains yanked down, and books and silverware strewn. Upstairs she found Mrs. Snyder helplessly lying on the south end of the hallway floor, still tied up. As Harriet knelt to unknot the ropes, Ruth told her in a frantic, disjointed way that the house had been burglarized. She'd gotten whacked on the head by a giant Italian thief and she'd fainted. She had no idea what happened to Albert. Would Harriet check to see if he was all right?

Mrs. Mulhauser looked to the north end of the hallway, where the door was ajar. She felt it improper to go into a bedroom with the husband still in it, and there was something too eerily quiet there. She even thought she smelled something foul. She sent Lorraine to get her husband.

Louis Mulhauser was in his gray wool church-service suit and getting the Sunday *New York Times* from the front sidewalk when he saw the Snyder girl running to him.

"We need you," she said. She was crying as she took him by the hand.

The Snyder house had been constructed by the same real estate firm and was just like his. Upstairs, Mrs. Snyder was still on the floor and sagging into the hug of his wife. Yard-lengths of clothesline were at Ruth's bare feet. Although her face was not wet, she made crying sounds.

"Look in on the mister," Harriet solemnly said, and turned Louis with a tilt of her head.

Louis went alone into the master bedroom. Clothing was scattered and the contents of upended drawers were heaped on the floor. A jewelry case seemed to have been looted. There was a strong chemical smell and Albert Snyder was in his flannel nightshirt and lying mostly on his chest in the twin bed closest to the door. His head seemed arched back in agony and was turned away from the entrance. His wrists were tied behind him with a white hand towel, and his ankles tied with a silk necktie. A .32-caliber revolver was beside his back; his flipped-open wallet had been flung near a bureau. Mr. Mulhauser sidled around between the twin beds to see a horrible, florid, lifeless face that still seemed to be straining away from a chloroformed blue bandana of the sort that farmers used. Albert's head had been gashed more than once and his pillowcase was sodden and maroon with his drying blood. Worms of chloroformed cotton plugged his nostrils and a fist of chloroformed cotton bulged from his mouth. And a gold mechanical pencil had been used to twist a tourniquet of picture wire so tight around his neck that it furrowed into the skin.

When Louis Mulhauser exited the bedroom, Ruth Snyder was still lying on the floor and snuggling Lorraine as she petted the girl's hair. "It's bad," he said. "I'll go call the police."

"Oh *no!*" Ruth screamed. "Albert! Darling!" She seemed to want to go to her husband but Lorraine could feel she was holding back and she finally just stayed as she was and squeezed her daughter even closer. The girl had never heard her father called "darling." He was not the darling kind.

Mr. Mulhauser hurried downstairs to the foyer telephone and found George Colyer, a friendly widower in his late sixties, letting himself in. Colyer's house was just behind the Snyders' corner home. Colyer said, "I saw you with the girl and figured something was wrong."

"Albert's been killed."

"Oh my gosh!"

Mr. Mulhauser spoke to the police and then, as Mrs. Mulhauser took Lorraine across the street to the shelter of their home, he and George Colyer lifted up Albert's lovely wife and helped her into Lorraine's bedroom, the one farthest from the murder.

A soft rain was falling when the first policemen got to the address and found a cream-yellow, green-trimmed, two-and-a-half-story Dutch Colonial house that faced west on the corner of 222nd Avenue and 93rd Road in Queens Village, New York, about fifteen miles east of midtown Manhattan. The tawny front yard was just six feet deep, a large and still-leafless elm tree stood between the front sidewalk and the curb, and behind the house was a sparrow bath that Albert had helped Lorraine create with a saucepan on a post. The first-floor north wing held a sunroom and what was called a music room because of its player piano, and the south wing contained the dining room and kitchen. Just south of that was a trellis archway woven with wisteria vines and the free-standing one-car garage that Albert had carpentered himself.

Upstairs in the northern master bedroom was the victim, Albert Edward Snyder, a muscular, sandy-haired magazine editor in his midforties, of slightly below-average height and just under two hundred pounds. Because of the chaos in the house and the extreme thoroughness of the killers, the Queens policemen immediately construed the crime as an assassination rather than a break-in that went awry. The policemen told Mrs. Snyder nothing about Mr. Snyder's condition and noted that she didn't seem curious about it. Homicide and burglary detectives were summoned and soon the house was filled with scowling men, including journalists, fingerprint experts, and a police photographer with a Graflex camera.

Mrs. Snyder went into the bathroom to cleanse her face with

Noxzema, brush her teeth with Ipana, and fix her marcelled and very blonde hair. But she told a policeman she was there because she had a horrific headache. Dr. Harry Hansen, their family physician, was called to treat her, but he could find no skull contusion or swelling so he just gave her some Bayer aspirin and left.

With a handshake, a solemn man introduced himself to Mrs. Snyder as Assistant District Attorney William Gautier. He'd been called to the scene because he lived just a few blocks away. Stiffly offering his condolences for her loss, but not admitting that Albert was dead, he interviewed Ruth for fifteen minutes and found she'd married Albert Snyder in 1915. He was thirteen years older and the art editor of *Motor Boating* magazine, handling page layouts and a half-dozen freelance illustrators.

"Could there have been a motive other than burglary?" he asked. "Could anyone have been seeking some particular document or article?"

Ruth said she had no idea why the burglars seemed to have searched the house so thoroughly. She wasn't aware of secret papers or anything Albert could have hidden. Why?

"The house has been turned upside down," the assistant district attorney said. "It's like the burglars were rummaging, not stealing. Like they were tossing things to give the *appearance* of burglary, when in fact murder was their sole intent."

Ruth felt sure Albert had no enemies, though she recalled that at a card party three weeks earlier he'd accused a stocky guy of stealing his wallet and its seventy-five dollars. The guy was named George Hough. A lot of fun but he could be loutish. About thirty years old. And last night, Ruth told Gautier, again in the home of Milton and Serena Fidgeon on Hollis Court Boulevard, and again at a card party—contract bridge, which she was lousy at—Albert got very drunk and ornery and there was another altercation, and George had told Ruth that he'd "like to kill the Old Crab." But of course, like she said, there had been a great deal of drinking and he was probably just fuming.

She told Gautier that she and Albert were asleep when she heard a hallway floorboard squeak. She thought it was Lorraine and went out to see if she was okay, but suddenly Ruth's throat was seized by a giant man who hit her hard over the head. She'd never seen the man before. Looked Italian, with a wide, black mustache. She then heard another man shout something in a language she couldn't understand, but maybe it was Italian, and she was about to get hit again when she fainted. She recalled nothing else from that time until she recovered consciousness around seven thirty that morning.

No, she wasn't sure where George Hough lived. She guessed New Jersey since he talked about New Jersey a lot. She thought he mentioned he was staying in the Commercial Hotel in Jamaica that night because there were so few trains that late.

She was asked if she owned things of high value, and she told Gautier there was a jewelry box that ought to contain some rings with precious gems, gold and silver brooches and bracelets, a magnificent pearl necklace, and four-carat diamond earrings. And she'd hung a fox stole and a mink coat in the foyer closet. And she thought Albert generally carried a hundred dollars in his wallet.

"Why is there a handgun in the house?"

"Al got it last year because of that guy who stole radios."

The so-called Radio Burglar had killed a policeman and had just been executed in Sing Sing. Assistant District Attorney Gautier closed his notebook, again offered his sympathy, and sent detectives to interview Mr. M. C. Fidgeon on Hollis Court Boulevard, to seek out George Hough in Jamaica's Commercial Hotel, and to find George's brother, Cecil, who lived, Ruth thought, in Far Rockaway. And then he invited in a gum-chewing stenographer to record Mrs. Snyder's statement.

Ruth smiled as she told the girl, "I was a stenographer once. At *Cosmopolitan* magazine."

Some neighbor ladies hunched at the front porch vestibule peering in, and when a policeman came to shoo them away, he was told a handsome stranger in fine clothes was seen prowling around the Snyder house one night about two weeks earlier, and also there was a feebleminded boy of nineteen who lived with his mother a few blocks away and he'd been caught peeking into first-floor windows. And Creedmoor Psychiatric Hospital was just a half mile to the east.

The policeman thanked the ladies for the information and crime reporters ran with that gossip in their initial stories.

Dr. Howard Neal, the Queens County medical examiner, got there within the hour and established that Albert Snyder was indeed dead, probably six hours gone in fact; then he waited for the assistant district attorney to finish with Mrs. Snyder and exit Lorraine's bedroom before Dr. Neal invited himself in and carefully shut the door.

She was willing to get out of the green satin nightgown for his examination, but Neal told her that wouldn't be necessary. She seemed to him a healthy, very attractive, voluptuous woman with ice-blue eyes and blonde hair. Her lilting, velvety voice was so fetching that he found himself leaning toward her as she spoke.

She told him she would be thirty-two in one week, on March 27th. She'd invited sixteen friends to a Saturday birthday party. Albert, she said, was forty-four. She said she fainted often and she had a tricky heart. She wondered if she had epilepsy like her late father.

"Worth checking out," he said. "But I'm only here relative to the crime."

She claimed again that she'd been almost strangled and hit over the head by a burglar, but like Dr. Hansen, he could find no contusions of the skull, no bruising of the throat, no injury of any kind. She said the attack probably occurred around two thirty in the morning, that she'd then "conked out," and that she woke up five hours later, gagged and with her wrists and ankles tied with clothesline.

"Had you been drinking?"

She shook her head. "I have a hard time handling alcohol. I get sick."

"Had you been sexually molested?"

She hesitated, then said, "No."

"Are you a smoker?"

"No."

"Was your husband?"

"Cigars sometimes. Why?"

"It helps the police."

She got a worried look.

"You fainted?" he asked.

"Yes."

"And were out for five hours?"

She nodded, but uncertainly. And then she smiled with perfect teeth in a perfectly lovely way, as if she'd just noticed how handsome and intriguing and gallant he was. With a softer tone that he crazily thought of as smooth and sweet as butterscotch, Ruth said, "You seem extra curious about that."

And he found himself wanting to help her out. "Well, it's unprecedented, Mrs. Snyder," the medical examiner said. "You faint, you fall down, blood flows into your head again, and you generally wake up within five or ten minutes."

She had the look of a child learning. "Still, that's what happened."

"And then what?"

She said she'd scooted along the floor to get help from Lorraine.

Dr. Neal found no chafing on the skin of the wrists or ankles where the presumably snug clothesline bindings had been. And he was surprised to find that yard-long lengths of quarter-inch rope had been wrapped four times around the ankles as if she were a movie damsel in distress.

"Are there any more questions?" she asked.

And now it was he who was defensive. "Yes," he said, "but not from me."

Seeming about to swoon, Ruth said, "I have to lie down now. I'm emotional and exhausted."

The head of the investigation was New York City Police Commissioner George V. McLaughlin, a hale, hearty, fashionably dressed Irishman of forty, who would soon leave elective office to become a banking executive with the Brooklyn Trust Company. He got upstairs just before noon and peeked into Lorraine's room to view Mrs. Snyder just as Dr. Neal was leaving.

"She's a looker, isn't she?" McLaughlin said, and Dr. Neal seemed embarrassed.

Walking into the master bedroom, the medical examiner showed McLaughlin how a blunt instrument had caused two lacerations above the right ear on Albert Snyder's head and a laceration on the skull near his cowlick. A hand or hands had caused seven abrasions on his neck as he was choked; he seemed to have been socked in the nose; he was suffocating on chloroform; and common picture wire had been used to strangle him.

"So what actually caused his death?" McLaughlin asked.

"The choice is yours. Either suffocation, strangulation, or even blunt-force trauma. The assailants were thorough."

"A lot of wasted effort if you just want to kill a guy. And the loaded thirty-two-caliber on the bed. Why would burglars leave a gun behind?" And then McLaughlin looked at the photographer. "You get all your shots?"

"Heading downstairs now."

McLaughlin waved in the coroner's men to collect the victim, told the policemen in the room to scour it and make an inventory, and then he followed the photographer downstairs.

Albert Snyder's cadaver was sheeted, carried downstairs, and laid onto a gurney that was rolled out to a hearse belonging to the Harry A. Robbins Morgue on 161st Street in Jamaica. Hundreds of Queens residents were out there, watching the Robbins men haul Mr. Snyder away.

A photographer had climbed high up the front yard's elm tree with a Kodak box camera and was taking pictures of Ruth answering over and over again the same questions. And a journalist roved among the horde in the yard collecting anecdotes about the Snyders. He found a twelve-year-old boy heading to church who remembered hitting a baseball that crashed through the Snyders' kitchen window, and Mr. Snyder had run out of the house after him, crazy with rage, chasing him inside his house and spanking the boy with his big hands in front of the boy's frightened father. And George Colyer told the journalist that all the neighbors liked Ruth because of her great love of fun and laughter. "But she's a cut below Snyder. He was a fine fellow. You just couldn't help but admire him." Colyer hesitated before he judged it tolerable to state, "I would have to say they were mismatched."

Mrs. Josephine Brown, Ruth's mother, was a practical nurse who had worked Saturday night and Sunday morning in Kew Gardens, caring for an invalid in his apartment at Kew Hall. She was a tall, sour, regal widow in nurse's whites, a brown woolen cloak, and owlish spectacles. She seemed genuinely upset by Albert Snyder's death, and once she'd gotten over the sorrow and tears she spoke frankly if formally in the metronomic cadence of a Swedish immigrant. She gave her maiden name as Josephine Anderson and said she also had a son, Andrew, who lived in the Bronx and was two years older than May.

"Who's May?" McLaughlin asked.

"Oh, I'm sorry; Ruth. We named her Mamie Ruth when she was born, but she decided she was May when she was grown some. We all of us got so used to that we never gave it up when she changed again to Ruth. And now I hear the men calling her Tommy."

"Why's that?"

"Oh, I guess she's one of the boys, like they say."

The police commissioner asked Mrs. Brown to go with him upstairs to the middle bedroom she slept in, just above the front porch vestibule and just south of Albert and Ruth's room. She was asked if she noticed anything different. She saw an empty quart bottle of Tom Dawson Whisky on the floor between the white Swedish chiffonier and her pink velour reading chair and she said she had no idea how it got there. And Albert's electrician's pliers seemed to have been shoed underneath the twin bed.

"Would your son-in-law have been working with pliers up here?"

"Oh heavens no. Albert respected my privacy. Even looked away when he walked down the hallway."

"Could you give me an idea of what kind of man he was?"

Seeking to say nothing ill of the dead, she told McLaughlin only good things about her son-in-law: that he was smart and artistic, fond of classical music, strong and handy and industrious, a good provider and avid sportsman with lots of hobbies and with a hearty, infectious laugh. But he was hotheaded and older than his age in his habits and customs, and Ruth was, after all, still vital and young.

"Was there marital discord?" McLaughlin asked.

Ruth's mother frowned. "My English ain't so good sometimes."

"Your daughter and Albert. Were they unhappy?"

"Oh, just like most folks."

McLaughlin felt confident she had nothing to do with the murder so he just called the invalid she cared for in Kew Gardens, heard Mr. William F. Code confirm that the nurse had been there the whole night, then walked Mrs. Brown across to the Mulhausers' to be with the granddaughter. But before leaving the neighbor's home, McLaughlin guided Lorraine into a parlor. Sitting left of her on a davenport sofa, he went over her memories of the card party Saturday night and the chaos on Sunday. Because there were no other children at the party, she said she'd just read *Motion Picture* magazines alone or with her mother while the grown-ups played cards. There was yelling at the party, but Daddy always got that way when there was drinking. She fell asleep in the car going home and couldn't recall getting into bed, it was so late and she was so tired. And then she found her mother on the hallway floor and all tied up that morning.

"Was your bedroom door often locked at night?"

She shook her head.

"Was it your mother who locked it?"

"I guess so," Lorraine said. "She was the one who took care of me."

"And not your father?"

She shrugged. "Daddy's always busy with things."

McLaughlin noticed she used the present tense. She'd not been told. "Are they happy with each other, your mommy and daddy?"

"I don't know. They're always arguing."

"Will you tell me again what your mother said when she was found?"

She told him.

"Would you hazard a guess as to why your mother wouldn't want you untying her hands and feet? And why she had you get Mrs. Mulhauser first?"

Lorraine gave it some thought and said, "She wanted a grown-up to see how she was."

"And why would that be?"

"Because it was important."

"Important to whom?"

"You. The police."

"Clever girl," McLaughlin said, and gently patted her left knee as he got up.

On the first floor of the Snyder home, burglary detectives found Chambly silverware, a Lalique vase, and some Baccarat crystal of value, but winter coats had been yanked pointlessly from their closet hangers and the floral chintz sofa cushions seemed tossed. Even a seascape oil painting signed by Albert Snyder had been lifted from its hook and sailed across the room.

A crime reporter asked, "What could these guys have been looking for?" And another answered, "My wife finds pocket change under the sofa cushions every time she vacuums."

On the kitchen table, Scotch whisky filled a water glass that was so gummy with fingerprints it hardly needed graphite dusting. And a dollar bill was beside it like a bartender's tip. The shoes of reporters kept whanging into the pots and pans and cutlery that were strewn on the kitchen's linoleum floor. The southern door out to the garage was not jimmied and the front door and storm windows had been locked, so it seemed the assailants had been let in. And in a pinkish seashell ashtray there were half-finished Sweet Caporal cigarettes. A detective said, "Weren't exactly covering their tracks, were they?"

The first and second floors of the house were feminine in their interior decoration, with little sign of a male presence, but upstairs in the attic there were old furniture pieces, boxes of Christmas ornaments and odds and ends organized and labeled in Albert's block printing, and also an overstuffed chair and a chrome pedestal cigar ashtray situated in front of the dormer storm windows, the right one still wedged out so his cigar smoke could escape. On the floor was the book *Deep Sea Fishing and Fishing Boats* by Edmund W. H. Holdsworth, 1874.

Albert's other domain was the basement, where Detective Frank Heyner found a highly organized workshop with a home-made liquor still, a rack of fishing rods and reels, a sanded rowboat that seemed intended for priming and painting, a Johnson outboard motor, and a laundry chute that would let clothing from upstairs fall into a hamper. There Heyner found a bloodstained pillowcase. The overheating in the house indicated the furnace had been stoked with coal an hour or two before sunrise. Looking inside the furnace, he found only the French cuff of what he guessed had been a fine shirt but was now just ashes. And finally, in a box of tools, the detective found a brand-new five-pound sash weight that eased the lift in frame windows. Coal ash had been sprinkled on it, but blood could still be detected. Heyner collected the evidence.

Upstairs that afternoon, Police Commissioner George McLaughlin was called to the telephone in the foyer. An investigator visiting the home of Milton C. Fidgeon told him that Ruth's story checked out. Milton's hand had gone to his forehead and he had to sit down when he heard the news of the homicide. The party giver had said Albert could be cantankerous, "a complex guy," but he was also fun-loving and good company. The Snyder family had arrived so early on Saturday that Fidgeon had joked, "Have you come for dinner?" Cecil Hough was Fidgeon's brother-in-law, as was, of course, George Hough, Cecil's kid brother. Also at the card party were Mr. and Mrs. Howard Eldridge, neighbors from down the street. Fidgeon recalled the incident three weeks earlier in which Albert claimed that George Hough stole his wallet and seventy-five dollars, and he'd thought, "It is pretty small business to accuse a party of friends of such a thing." But last night's scene was not as nasty, just a flare-up between two hot-tempered men.

Was it possible that George Hough could have been angry enough after Saturday night to kill Albert?

Completely and utterly impossible, Fidgeon told the detective.

The policemen who'd been upstairs in the Snyders' master bedroom found McLaughlin and handed him their inventory. Recorded on the list were the front page of the Italian newspaper *L'Arena,* a gold Bulova man's wristwatch in plain view on the floor, the gold Cross mechanical pencil used to twist the picture wire tight, a fine muskrat coat wrapped in paper and hidden deep in the closet, other unremarkable clothing, and a jewelry box that seemed to have been emptied. But to be thorough, the police had tipped up Mrs. Snyder's mattress and found some rings, earrings, and necklaces tucked underneath it. And on the floor near Albert's mattress was discovered an ascot or necktie stickpin bearing the initials "J. G."

Albert Snyder's former fiancée was named Jessie Guischard. She'd died of pneumonia before they could marry and his mourning never ended. The stickpin had been a gift to Albert from Jessie but the investigators, significantly, didn't find that out until later and instead guessed the initialed stickpin flew free from the intruder's necktie as Albert was being murdered. J. G., they thought, was their first solid clue concerning the killer's identity.

Seeking the names of friends and associates, a man from the Fourteenth Detective Bureau in Jamaica slid open the middle drawer of a Windsor desk in the sitting room and found Ruth's Moroccan leather address book. Written in it were the names, addresses, and phone numbers of fifty-six people, but the detective was interested in only the twenty-eight men. He happened to know two of them, Police Patrolman Edward Pierson, of the 23rd Precinct in the Bronx, and Peter Trumfeller, a friend from the Jamaica precinct.

Handing the address book to Deputy Inspector Arthur Carey, head of the homicide squad, the detective said, "We can clear one name at least. There's no way Trumfeller could commit a crime this half-assed."

Because of the heat in the house, Carey had taken off his jacket and was rolling up his sleeves. "We *are* looking at real amateurs, aren't we?"

Another burglary detective had already delivered to Carey a cardboard container of canceled checks. When he thumbed through them, he discovered weekly twenty-dollar checks made out to the Prudential Life Insurance Company. "That must be a lot of life insurance," Carey said.

"They probably got special riders on the policy," the burglary detective said.

"Like what?"

The detective shrugged. "Airplane crashes. Railway accidents. Double-indemnity stuff."

The deputy inspector flicked through some more canceled checks and found one for two hundred dollars that was cashed by H. Judd Gray. Judd Gray's name was also in the address book. Arthur Carey went up to Lorraine's room to wake and interrogate the widow.

Waiting for a minute at the doorway, Carey saw the pretty woman was lying on her side but only trying to sleep, for he noticed she was squinting cautiously in his direction from the slightly opened corners of her eyes.

Entering the room, he asked, "How are you feeling, madam?"

She seemed to pretend to moan. "I feel cried out," she said. Watching him seat himself in a chair, she sat up in Lorraine's bed and crossed her forearms over her too evident breasts.

"I'm trying hard to understand why burglars would ransack your house," Deputy Inspector Carey said.

Ruth seemed strangely puzzled, as if she'd done something wrong. "What do you mean?"

"Just that it doesn't look right."

"How can you tell?" She seemed not to recognize she was giving much away.

"We see lots of burglaries," Carey said. "They aren't done this way."

She glanced at Lorraine's night table and found a pack of Wrigley's Juicy Fruit gum. She unwrapped a stick and gauged the inspector's expression as she slowly and seductively pushed the gum between her pouting lips and into her pretty mouth. His glum face had not changed. She chewed.

"Are you aware of what happened to your husband?"

She seemed to shrink a little. She held a hand over her eyes as if crying. "He's dead."

"Well, I've been asking around and nobody told you that, and you never even questioned the medical examiner. Was he shot, was he injured, was he okay? Wouldn't a wife want to know for sure if he was murdered or not?"

She gazed at him in a pitying way. "You have how many detectives in this house?"

"Sixty or so."

She sneered. "Call it female intuition."

"Fair enough," Carey said. "Let me begin with the first thing this morning. You wake up from *a faint* and find yourself gagged with a man's handkerchief, your wrists and ankles tied with clothesline."

She tentatively said, "Yes."

"And you slithered along the hallway from in front of your room to your daughter's, here, opposite the bathroom?"

She gave him a look like *What's the big deal?*

"Why not get help from your husband?"

"Lorraine's room was just down to the right."

"But your own bedroom door wasn't three feet away."

"A mother's first worry is for her child."

"Was it you who locked her door in the night?"

"I forget."

"Because that was a good idea, wasn't it? That's why the giant Italians couldn't get to your daughter."

She just stared at him.

Arthur Carey could see she was clamming up and would give him little more about the morning, so he changed the tone and topic. "What was your husband's salary at *Motor Boating* magazine?"

"One hundred fifteen dollars a week."

"And what was your household budget?"

"I'm not sure what you mean."

"How much did he give you for groceries, gas and electric, incidentals?"

"Eighty dollars."

"Each week?"

She nodded. She seemed proud, even chipper, to be on such familiar terrain.

"And you carry accident insurance on your husband's life, yes?"

"Of course."

"How much?"

"A thousand dollars," she said.

"But what is that, just two and a half months' salary? Was that enough?"

"Well, it *was* just a thousand. I forgot that we changed that." She ultimately said there were in fact three policies, that the first was for one thousand dollars and that Albert had added another for five thousand and yet another for forty-five thousand dollars. All in November 1925.

"With which company?"

"Prudential."

"I'm just curious. I haven't bought much insurance myself. Were there any special provisions to the policies?"

"Like what?"

"I heard of this term 'double indemnity.' Have you heard of that? I hear it means an accidental death, even a homicide like this, pays double the amount on the face of the policy."

"We had that."

"All of the policies?"

"On just the last."

"The forty-five-thousand-dollar policy?"

She agreed.

"Wow," Arthur Carey said. "I'm doing the arithmetic in my head. You've got the one policy for a thousand and the one for five, and you get double the forty-five, so that's ninety-six thousand dollars?"

She shrugged. "I guess so."

"Your husband would've had to work fifteen years for that kind of money!"

"But isn't that the point of insurance? To give your family years of security if something horrible and awful and unexpected happens?"

"Couldn't agree with you more," the deputy inspector said. "Albert must have cared a lot for you and Lorraine."

"Albert was the ideal husband and father," she said.

Police Commissioner George McLaughlin strolled in and slouched against a wall, just watching Ruth, his hands in his suit pants pockets.

"We have your address book here," Arthur Carey said, "and I'd like to read off some men's names."

"Why?"

"Humor me," he said, and began with a florist named Abrams. He'd gotten through five more names, including Milton Fidgeon and then Harry Folsom, a hosiery salesman, when he hesitated a little and said, "Judd Gray." Both Carey and McLaughlin saw Ruth flinch.

"And who's he?" Carey asked.

"Sells corselettes," she said. "Have you heard of the Bien Jolie brand?"

"I'm not up on those things," Carey said.

"Well, go on," Ruth said.

"You know Judd Gray pretty well?"

"No, not really."

Reminding Carey, George McLaughlin quietly said, "J. G."

"Wait a minute," Arthur Carey said, and he opened the cardboard container of canceled checks. "I'm fairly certain I saw that name Judd Gray before. Oh yeah, here it is." The deputy inspector lifted up a canceled check with a masculine signature on the back. "To H. Judd Gray, for two hundred dollars. Isn't that your handwriting, Mrs. Snyder?"

She examined the check. She nodded. "Mr. Gray is a traveling salesman for Bien Jolie. He has a lot of food and hotel expenses and his company, Benjamin and Johnes, was late in repaying him, so I helped out with a temporary loan."

"And did he repay you?"

"Certainly."

"Wouldn't two hundred dollars be a lot to loan a man you don't really know?"

She was flustered. "Who said I didn't know him?"

"You did," George McLaughlin said. "Half a minute ago."

"I have no idea where this is going."

"We do," George McLaughlin said. "And we know where you're going, too."

"The Jamaica precinct house," Arthur Carey said.

"I can't leave here."

"You have to."

"But I'm ill."

"You look fine to us."

She teared up. "I've lost a husband," she cried. "You ought to be sympathizing with me. You ought to be looking for the killers."

"We just have some more questions to ask. But at the precinct."

And just like that her mood changed. "All right," she said, and in fury flung aside Lorraine's blanket as she got out of bed. She then gripped the hem of her green satin nightgown and wriggled it up over her head so that she was stunningly naked in front of the men. She was blonde *there* too. She defiantly smiled at their guilty fascination and uneasiness and then strode down the hallway to the room of Albert's murder, where she taunted the shocked policemen at the crime scene by ever so slowly getting into her undergarments and dress.

At the Jamaica station house Ruth Snyder was escorted past the glaring group of the Fidgeons, the Eldridges, and the Houghs, including the loutish George with whom Albert had skirmished. She was seated in an interrogation room, where she was grilled for several hours, with each interrogator making wilder suppositions and claiming evidence he didn't yet have. Still, she impressed the commissioner as "a woman of great calm." She never requested a lawyer. She requested only food and sleep. And so she was given an Italian restaurant's dinner of spaghetti, salad, and garlic bread, and was permitted a half-hour nap on an office sofa as McLaughlin interrogated the guests who'd played contract bridge with Albert on Saturday night.

Right after that Commissioner George McLaughlin gently shook Ruth awake and introduced her to Detective Lieutenant Michael McDermott, who'd "be just listening for a while." And then the commissioner asked, "Mrs. Snyder, is it true that you often stay out all night?"

"Well, I don't know about *often*."

"Who with?"

"With my cousin, Ethel Anderson. Call her and ask."

"She married?"

"She *was*. To Edward Pierson." And then, as if it confirmed her veracity and reputation, Ruth commented, "Eddie's a Bronx patrolman."

McLaughlin turned and McDermott took the hint, heading out of the office to telephone the officer and order him to Jamaica. McLaughlin faced Ruth again. "We've been told that last fall you went on a tour of Canada without your husband."

She frostily said, "Who told you?"

"Women at that card party."

"Anything wrong with that?"

"I just need to know who went with you."

Ruth was tentative. "Mr. and Mrs. Kehoe."

McLaughlin jotted the name down. "You have a telephone number for them?"

"No."

"How about an address?"

"Somewhere in Brooklyn."

She was lying; he'd counted at least three tells in her face. McLaughlin laid his pencil down in frustration and walked out of the office, and Ruth just sat there alone, stewing, for half an hour.

Around eleven o'clock Detective Peter Trumfeller peeked into the room and smiled as he said, "Why, hello, Tommy!" Trumfeller was a wide and happy man with slicked-back hair and windburnt cheeks. He owned a 1925 Ford T-bucket roadster convertible and she'd once cruised with him in it, her scarf and hair fluttering, all the way to West Point and back.

Ruth smiled at him in relief. "Oh, are you coming to take me home to Lorraine?"

Detective Trumfeller walked in and held his hand tenderly to her cheek. She turned into the hand and kissed it as tears filled her eyes. She was getting up to go as his other hand roughly forced her down. Like a lover, the fat detective bent over to find her right ear and say in hushed tones, "These guys know when you're lying, Tommy. They've gone through this hundreds of times and you, you're just a rookie. They know your stories are all baloney because nothing fits together. You're torturing yourself with lies. Just go ahead and tell the truth and get the elephant off your chest."

Ruth was stiff in astonishment and then she lifted the handkerchief in her lap and touched it to each pretty eye. "I'm so very tired," she said, but only as if she'd had a hard day tilling the garden. "Where's the police commissioner?"

Detective Trumfeller escorted Ruth past the still-glaring card party to the head man's office. It was just past eleven o'clock. Cigarette smoke hung from the ceiling. Lieutenant McDermott shook out another Pall Mall but just let it lie on his lip as he watched Ruth walk in. Commissioner McLaughlin swiveled in his creaking oak chair and immediately hung up the black telephone earpiece when he saw her.

She smiled. "Please accept my apologies for keeping all of you up so late."

The police commissioner jerked his head toward a straight-backed chair and Peter Trumfeller scraped it over for Ruth to regally sit on.

She softly said, "I don't think I can stand any more questioning."

McLaughlin nodded toward McDermott and said, "Mac's been talking to your cousin Ethel's estranged husband."

"Eddie," she said, as if saying it made her happier.

"Well, Eddie says you've got a boyfriend." The police commissioner twisted around and got a notepad from McDermott, and held the notepad up in front of Ruth's face. The name "Judd Gray" was printed on it. "Was this the man who killed your husband?"

She sighed. "Has he confessed?"

McLaughlin lied and said Judd had indeed confessed; then he invited a stenographer to record their conversation, instructing Ruth so she could make the stenographer's job easier. "We'll begin with your name and intent," he said.

"My name is Ruth May Snyder," she said, "and I want to make a full and truthful statement about the death of my husband, Albert Snyder."

The police commissioner coached, "'And I understand that anything I say may be used against me.'"

She said that.

The headlines for the front page of the *New York Times* had been firmly set by then: "GIRL FINDS MOTHER BOUND" and "Woman Tells of Quarrel at Card Party and of Strangers in House." Page two carried the headline "ART EDITOR SLAIN," but that was the last time an account would focus on Albert Snyder. It was Ruth who fascinated.

TWO

VERY PRETTY

She told them she could not recall when she was first introduced to Judd Gray, but she could, in fact, recall everything: the fierce sun at noon, the torrid heat shimmering off the streets of Manhattan, the horns of jockeying Model T taxicabs, and the shrill whistles of white-gloved police directing the traffic on Madison Avenue. It was June 1925 and inside the hosiery shop there was a faint chemical smell and a gray tin fleur-de-lis ceiling and giant fan blades shoving hot air around as a pretty hairdresser friend named Kitty Kaufman flirted with a stocking salesman named Harry Folsom and Harry joined the flirtation with lame jokes and flattery.

"Are you girls hungry?" Harry finally asked.

Kitty was Jewish and fetching, with hazel eyes and coffee-colored hair combed over to the left like a surge of ocean, and she wore a form-describing silk dress that hinted it could slither off. She was beyond the likes of Harry Folsom but she was ten years married and flattered by his attentions. She gave Ruth a *Shall I?* glance. Ruth snapped her Wrigley's Juicy Fruit gum and shrugged.

"Hey, you gotta eat," Harry said.

"I guess," Kitty said. She sought affirmation, but Ruth couldn't have cared less. She'd inserted a hand inside some fine silk hose that seemed dark as Coca-Cola. She held it up to the full glare of sunlight.

"Ruth, you keep those McCallums," Harry said. "Seriously. My gift. Look lovely on you. And join Mrs. Kaufman and me for lunch."

"You're very kind," Ruth said, as if he wasn't.

Kitty focused on Ruth in that *Say yes* way, seeming not so much attracted to him as to the fact that she still seemed attractive.

"Where?" Ruth asked.

Harry folded his gift of McCallum hosiery in a paper bag and became doggish in his eagerness. "How about Henry's Swedish restaurant? Cooler there because of the ice. Thirty-sixth Street, east of Sixth Avenue. My treat."

"Smorgasbord," Kitty said. "You get to have whatever you want."

"Rarely true," said Ruth.

Exiting the shop, Harry slanted on his Borsalino hat and inserted himself between the friends so his hands could ride both their backs in their stroll.

The façade of Henry's Restaurant was a cool, seawater green, and green were the lampshades inside, the cold tessellated floor, the fake ferns and nasturtiums and trellis. Ruth's late father was from a fishing village in Norway, and Josephine was from a fishing village in Sweden, so she'd grown up with the foods now laid out on cracked ice in Henry's Restaurant: cold dishes of salmon, herring, lox, whitefish, ham and mustard, jellied pigs' feet, and hard-boiled eggs. And elsewhere the hot dishes of Swedish meatballs, roasted pork ribs, matchstick potatoes covered with cream, stewed green cabbage, onion and sprats, and beetroot salad in mayonnaise. But Harry Folsom first wanted to slake his thirst, so he ushered them to a booth he called "his" and ordered three Clicquot Club ginger ales from a fat waiter named Olaf, who returned with highball glasses that were just two-thirds filled so there would be room for the first-rate London gin that Harry stirred in from his flask. After hearing Harry's old pun on his name as he offered them a "fulsome toast," Kitty joined him in swiftly finishing the highball and then ordering another, and Ruth just watched them, fascinated by Harry's heavy exertions at courtship and Kitty's schoolgirlish agreement to be wooed. Harry's left arm wedged its way around Kitty and he angled toward her, even whispered a few endearments, but he seemed increasingly nervous in his awareness that he was entertaining two women and if he lost one's interest he'd perhaps lose both.

And that's when his right hand flew up in a roundhouse wave and he called, "Why, it's Henry in Henry's! Hey Judd, join us!"

Ruth turned to see a solemn, handsome man in his early thirties hanging his straw hat on a peg. He was short but trim, athletic, and dapper, with owlish, round, tortoiseshell glasses; flannel-blue eyes; and walnut brown hair so wavy it seemed corrugated. His highly polished brown shoes were probably Italian, his tan Brooks Brothers suit seemed so unwrinkled it could have been bought just that hour, and his chin was square and manly with the deep almond of a dimple. She turned to face Kitty and smiled for the first time that day as the gentleman walked over. She smelled his spice cologne as he shook Mr. Folsom's hand and was invited into the booth.

"I'm fit only for a solo," he said. "I was just going to gobble a bite and get back to the office." He spoke with the lulling, tranquilizing baritone of radio broadcasters.

Imitating a pout, Kitty said, "But Ruth's feeling left out."

Judd Gray looked down and found a gorgeous Scandinavian

woman of thirty frankly staring at him with thrilling blue eyes that flashed with so much light she seemed candled. Even on such a hot day, a wintery, gray fox fur was flung over her shoulders and she wore a dark cloche hat over her very blonde hair. She was dressed in a navy blue, filmy fabric that betrayed the full, round breasts that were unfashionable in those first days of the boy look. Judd was good with scents and noted she'd chosen Shalimar lilac perfume for the day.

"If I'm not intruding," Judd said.

Ruth smiled and said, "Please do."

His thigh slightly touched Ruth's as he sat and she let hers stay as it was. His closeness to her made his handshake awkward as he affably said, "Hello there. I'm Judd Gray."

"I thought your name was Henry."

"It is in the birth register," the hosiery salesman said.

Judd explained, "I'm formally Henry Judd Gray but I just use the initial H. Harry likes to flaunt his detective work."

"So it's Judd," Kitty said.

"My friends call me Bud."

Ruth smiled again. "So many choices!"

"I haven't one for you yet."

"Mrs. Snyder," she said. "Ruth."

Imitating her, Kitty said, "Mrs. Kaufman. Karin. But they call me Kitty." She shook his hand. "She's also called Tommy."

Judd grinned. "Oh. Are you a tom-boy?"

"Kitty calls me that because my friends are mostly men."

"And why's that?"

She said with that silky caress of a voice, "Oh, who knows? I guess because they're so safely predictable in some ways. And unpredictable in others."

Harry called out, "Olaf! A ginger ale for Mr. Gray."

"Me too," Kitty said.

Seeing Ruth's highball glass was still full, Harry called out, "Three," and finished his own. And then, out of nowhere, Harry hiked up Kitty's calf as high as his chest. "Wouldja look at the shapely ankles on this gal?"

Kitty just laughed and swatted his hands off. Judd was sure, then, that these were fast "delicatessen" ladies, and he looked at Ruth so intently her face got hot. "You're very tan," he said.

"We just got back from a weekend sailing on the Atlantic."

"We?"

"The husband, me, and the baby." Ruth looked at his nicely manicured left hand. "I see you're manacled too."

Judd glanced at his gold wedding ring. "Almost ten years now. Isabel. And I have an eight-year-old. Jane. She'll be nine in August."

"Mine's seven. Lorraine."

"Oh. You said 'baby.' I was imagining a child—"

"The size of a shoebox?"

Judd laughed, and the ginger ales were served, again two-thirds full and with a spoon. Harry screwed off the cap on his hammered silver flask. "Shall I?"

Judd shoved his highball glass forward. "Homemade?"

Harry filled the glasses. "Certainly not, old fellow! Shipped from the Beefeater distillery by way of our friends in Canada."

Judd lifted his glass. "Well, here's to the Eighteenth Amendment."

Harry rejoined, "And may Congress prohibit sex just as effectively."

Kitty giggled, and Harry gave Judd a lewd wink.

Ruth angled her head. "Are you employed, Mr. Gray?"

Harry told the ladies, "Judd sells for Benjamin and Johnes."

"Sells what?" Kitty asked.

"The Bien Jolie line," Judd said. "Corselettes and brassieres.

I handle the retailers in eastern Pennsylvania and upstate New York. Our corporate offices are just a stone's throw from here—Thirty-fourth and Fifth."

Harry's hand heavily fell on Ruth's as he said, "And I'll make sure his office gets you anything you want, sweetie. How about it, Bud?"

Judd felt forced to say, "Always glad to be of service."

Kitty already seemed tipsy as she asked, "What kind of fella sells corsets?"

Judd told her, "A fellow who's fond of the female form."

Ruth smiled. "You must get asked that question a lot."

"Oh, did that sound practiced?"

Kitty asked what "Bien Jolie" meant.

"'Very pretty,'" Judd said.

Kitty frowned. "Isn't that *très jolie*?"

"Aren't you the smart one," Harry said, and grabbed her torso more tightly to him. Because of the heat, she wriggled away.

"I haven't any French," Judd said. "But I'm told the *bien* makes the *jolie* more intense."

"Like 'very, very pretty'?" Ruth asked.

Judd grinned. "Like you."

Ruth shied from the sultry pleasure of his gaze.

"And flattery like that is why he hauls in five thousand dollars a year," Harry said.

Kitty gasped. "Five thousand dollars! Jeepers!"

"It's just a number," Judd said, and noticed Ruth's interest. Judd noticed, too, that Ruth still had not lifted a glass with them, that her first iced drink was sweating onto the homey blue-and-white checkered tablecloth. "Are you a teetotaler, Mrs. Snyder?"

She seemed demure as she said, "I just pace myself. There's nothing worse than a full day of drinking, then waking up next to some guy and not being able to remember how you met or why he's dead."

She shocked them into raucous laughter and the fat waiter took that as an invitation to finally take their food orders. But Harry Folsom noted that the four of them seemed to be having so much fun together that they all should flee the torrid city and head up to his shady porch in New Canaan, Connecticut. Mrs. Kaufman liked the idea, but Judd excused himself to go back to work, and on a glancing hint from Kitty, Ruth said she wanted to catch the train to Queens Village.

Exiting the booth, Judd asked, "Are you taking the Long Island line?"

Ruth said she was.

"I'll walk you to Penn Station."

She said nothing as they strolled west to Seventh Avenue. Looking at their reflections in the shop windows, Judd noticed that she would be at least two inches taller than he even without high heels. But she was glamorous, too, and the gin had made him zesty and loquacious, so as they walked down to 33rd Street, Judd filled the silence with chatter and facts about Pennsylvania Station. Did she know it took up seven acres and was the largest indoor space in America? And the enormous waiting room? Judd had heard it was inspired by the Roman Baths of Caracalla.

She seemed amused. "You know a lot, don't you?" It did not seem a compliment.

"I have no idea why I'm so nervous around you."

She wryly said, "Well, I'm 'very, very pretty.' Any man would be."

Walking through the grand entrance, Judd noted for Ruth the Corinthian columns, and then the huge clock framed by a pink granite pair of sculpted females. "Day" was fully dressed in the flowing drapery of ancient Greece and was carrying a harvest of giant sunflowers, while "Night" was shaded by a shrouding cape she held over her head and she was naked from the waist up, the firm breasts inspiring some men there to become clock watchers.

"That's Audrey Munson," Judd said. "She was the highest-paid model in New York. All the great sculptors used her. You can find her everywhere in the city. And she appeared in moving picture shows, fully nude. *Inspiration* was one. And *Purity*. She was breathtaking. But a doctor she knew crazily murdered his wife to have Audrey, and at first the police suspected her of conspiring with him. She was finally cleared, but the gossip was devastating. She changed her lodgings to Mexico, New York, near where I was born, in Cortland, and tried to take her own life by swallowing bichloride of mercury tablets."

Ruth was concentrating hard on what he'd just said. "She's still alive?"

"But no longer right in the head, I'm afraid."

"I feel so sorry for her."

Was that where he was steering with that story? Sympathy? Judd wondered if he just wanted to use the word "nude" in Ruth's presence.

"She *is* beautiful," Ruth said.

"Like you," Judd said.

In a gesture that was both friendly and condescending, Ruth patted his cheek. "I have to go," she said, and was off to a one o'clock train heading across the East River to Queens and Jamaica Station.

Writing later of their first meeting in his penciled memoir, *Doomed Ship,* Judd claimed Mrs. Snyder was vague in his reveries then, that he remembered only *the charming good nature, the winsome personality, and the soft gray fur slipping so gracefully from one shoulder. I realized that a frank, sincere character lurked behind that radiant and healthy loveliness.* But there was no anticipation of ever seeing Ruth again.

That June afternoon, H. Judd Gray filled out an inventory sheet and a hefty expense report for his last sales trip, skimmed through a stack of mail, stood in front of the office's floor fan to scan the factory information on the new pink Bien Jolie corselettes that would be introduced in August, and, feeling chipper, jokingly chatted with founders Alfred Benjamin and Charles Johnes just to show his face. And then he took a southbound train for the short haul to East Orange, New Jersey, and his brick Craftsman bungalow at 37 Wayne Avenue, and to the emotional starvation of his sane, successful, monotonous life.

Scott Fitzgerald would name the twenties "the Jazz Age" and note that it "raced along under its own power served by great filling stations full of money." Wealth began to seem available to anyone then. Chrysler was founded. Scotch Tape was invented. The first-ever motel opened. RCA's shares were soaring in price and the stock market itself was high-flying due to an optimistic and gambling middle class that had formerly bought only Liberty Bonds.

The five boroughs of New York City constituted the largest city in the world, and the fifty-seven-story Woolworth Building at 233 Broadway was the earth's tallest skyscraper. There were thirty-two thousand speakeasies, and hard liquor could be found for sale even in dry cleaners and barbershops.

Calvin Coolidge was president, a man so dour, orderly, and parsimonious that he was joked about as "the nation's shopkeeper." Whereas in the fall of 1925, New York City would elect as its mayor the flamboyant, debonair Jimmy Walker, who flouted the laws and flaunted the high life in a way that overworked laborers fancied they could one day.

Madison Square Garden, home of the New York Americans hockey team, was under construction on Eighth Avenue between 49th and 50th streets on the former site of the city's trolley barns. The New York Giants and four other teams joined the National Football League. Rochester's Walter Hagen was the world's finest professional golfer and winner of the 1925 PGA Championship. Because of a lingering illness caused by tainted bootleg liquor, Babe Ruth was having his worst season as a Yankee, and the team would finish next to last in the American League despite having a rookie named Lou Gehrig at first base.

George Bernard Shaw won the Nobel Prize in Literature. The Grand Ole Opry premiered in Nashville. The fiction best-sellers included *The Constant Nymph* by Margaret Kennedy and *Arrowsmith* by Sinclair Lewis. *The Great Gatsby* was a financial disappointment. The hit movies were *Ben-Hur,* starring Ramón Novarro, and *The Phantom of the Opera,* starring Lon Chaney. Al Jolson was onstage in *Big Boy,* George Gershwin's *Lady, Be Good* was still running, and Louise Brooks was still just a half-naked chorus girl in *George White's Scandals* at the Apollo Theatre, where the seats went as steep as $4.40.

Judd Gray treated six clients from Albany to *Scandals*'s twenty-seven scenes of hoofer solos; juvenile skits; songs by the Williams Sisters, Richard Talbot, Helen Hudson, and Winnie Lightner; and seemingly hundreds of George White Girls high-stepping in oth-erworldly costumes by the Russian fashion designer Erté. The Elm City Four sang "Lovers of Art" as the spotlights played over stiffly posed girls in flesh-colored bathing suits that made them seem nude statues. And in a gala ending, the girls of the chorus wore only, as one scandalized reviewer put it, clothing "from the neck up and shoes down."

Even Albany's lingerie buyers were shocked, while Judd him-self was mostly offended that each glass of White Rock seltzer his party ordered as set-ups cost him a full dollar, and regular tap water cost him two. But when he got home to East Orange, there was a nightlong fray with Isabel over Judd's entertaining clients at such a risqué revue, and in a fury over his wife's condemnations, he stormed from the house for an earlier, July departure to eastern Pennsylvania.

Half a week later, after a hectic round of the ladies clothing stores, he'd toured the Crayola factory in Easton and purchased a box of school crayons for little Jane, then poked around the city farmer's market, marveling at how the weathered growers silently stood behind their cases of fruits and vegetables with no effort to sell them. No exaggerations, no conniving or entertaining, no sentimental manipulation, just frank presentation of goods. And immediately he felt overwhelmed by his own unimportance.

Judd returned to the Huntington Hotel and the front desk clerk handed him a letter. At first he thought it would be from his wife, a continuation of the quarrels and humiliations of the night before he left. But it was a penned letter from Queens Village that had been forwarded from his office.

Dear Mr. Gray:

We met at Henry's Resturant with my hairdresser friend and Mr. Harry Folsom a few weeks ago. I would like to buy as a gift your Grecian-Treco Classic Corset for my mother Mrs. Josephine Brown. I have used a measuring tape and she is 38" up top, 30" at the waste, and 40" around the hips. (Excuse my frankness, but your used to such female intimacies I guess.) Would you be so kind as to send it please to: 9327 222nd Avenue, Queens Village, New York? I have inclosed a blank cheque which amount you can fill out for the undergarment plus shipping and handle-ing.

I so enjoyed meeting you and hope to do so again.

Ruth Snyder

"also known as" Mrs. A. E. Snyder

Even the childish misspellings delighted him. Judd filled out an order form that he sent to his secretary, then tore up the check. And he found himself dwelling on *I so enjoyed meeting you and hope to do so again.*

Albert Snyder rented a gray saltbox cottage and a sleek, two-masted yawl for their July vacation on Shelter Island. Another editor at *Motor Boating* magazine found him a sailboat berth at the Shelter Island Yacht Club on Chequit Point, and when he wasn't on the water with the yawl, Albert made himself a hearty regular at the yacht club, slumping with highballs and new friends in the stout wicker rocking chairs on the piazzas overlooking Dering Harbor, gladly accepting invitations for deep-sea fishing and helping out like a mate on the boats, even agreeing to race his yawl in the August regatta.

Ruth and Lora stayed to themselves, hunting seashells and clams on the shore, reading children's books together in the Adirondack chair under the wide shade of the hemlock tree, finding a beach far away from the crowds where they could swim in their matching Jantzen tank suits and mobcaps until the knitted black wool became too heavy for them to freely stroke and they would fall back on sand as warm as toast and giggle over nonsense rhymes as the hot sun dried them.

Each evening when Albert got back to the cottage, all three of them would dine outside in the cool air, barbecuing fresh corn on the cob and filets of the fish he'd caught, and Ruth would watch him laughing with Lora in his white Top-Siders and white flannel trousers, and he would look every inch a yachtsman and seem so manly, dashing, and fun to be with that Ruth felt she could fall in love with him all over again.

On July 24th, 1925, she got a sitter for Lora and the couple celebrated their tenth wedding anniversary at a nightclub on North Ferry Road. Ruth gave him Shutz prism binoculars; Albert gave her a French, floral-beaded, silk evening bag with a matching compact. She kissed him and told him he had excellent taste; he agreed. Albert was in his white dinner jacket, drinking martinis in the 1920s formula of half gin and half Martini & Rossi vermouth, and as soon as he finished one he'd shield his bottles from fellow diners and the waiters as he mixed another. Because he was deaf in his right ear, she sat to his left, but still he sometimes seemed not to hear her. She noticed again that his tawny hair was receding from his temples, that his jacket was getting tight on him, that he wasn't fat but had the broad shoulders and fullback torso of a man who ought to have been half a foot taller. The orchestra was playing songs the Paul Whiteman Orchestra popularized: "Rhapsody in Blue," "Somebody Loves Me," "Linger a While." She wanted to dance; Albert didn't. The sun that had tanned him had also tired him. She filled his silence by mentioning a friend she'd just made on Shelter Island and how her husband, a Wall Street stockbroker, would be racing in the regatta with a ketch just like theirs.

Albert glanced up. "But that's impossible, isn't it, Ruth?" And in the overly calm, patronizing tone he used for all his instructions, he said, "A ketch cannot be like a yawl because they are *dissimilar*. A ketch is a sailboat with the same mainmast, yes, you are so very right to notice this, but it is rigged aft with its mizzenmast stepped forward of the rudderpost. A *yawl's* mizzenmast is stepped abaft the sternpost."

"And blah, blah, blah," she said.

Albert lifted up his martini. "But how can I expect you to know these things when you take so little interest in my hobbies?"

"Oh, are they hobbies? I thought they were just chances for you to yell at me."

Albert sipped the martini, slanting a little off balance even though he was sitting, so that his free hand had to hastily seek the chair cushion. "You and your disappointing education," he said. "You give me so many opportunities for—what is it?—*keen* and *pitched* correction."

"You know everybody is ignorant, it's just the subjects that are different."

Albert sneered. "With you there are not subjects, there are *chasms*."

She felt her mouth tremble. She looked away as her vision blurred.

"Are those tears?" he asked. "Aren't you used to my teasing by now?"

She felt his hard, callused hand fall onto hers and she turned. "You hurt my feelings, Albert."

"Oh posh. You're too sensitive."

She swiveled away from him and watched the orchestra's handsome crooner hold on to the microphone and face her with a smile as he sang "What'll I Do."

August was the month when women retailers from cities like Utica, Ithaca, and Binghamton visited Manhattan for a first look at the fall fashions and to fill out order sheets, a job that Judd Gray generally put off until the morning after he'd affably dined with them and escorted them to hit movies like Charlie Chaplin's *The Gold Rush* or revues like *The Garrick Gaieties* and then on to nightclubs like the Monte Carlo and Frivolity Club in Manhattan. Benjamin & Johnes even got him a room in the tony Waldorf-Astoria, just a block away on Fifth Avenue and 33rd Street, so he would have the freedom of entertaining without having to deal with railway schedules and his wife's worries about his drinking.

On Saturday, August 8th, Judd would be treating a gang

of Pennsylvania buyers to a fashion show and gala called Très Parisien, featuring the clothing designs of Jean Patou and Coco Chanel, but on that Friday night he was just going to have room service and finish reading P. C. Wren's *Beau Geste*. But there was a note for him at the Waldorf's front desk:

I'm footing the bill for some friends at Zari's. Will you join us? Informal, of course. Harry Folsom

Despite his weariness, Judd changed into a fresh shirt and gray flannel suit and took the Waldorf's elevator down. *Adventuring,* he thought.

Zari's restaurant was filled when he got there at eight. Electric fans whirred in slow semiarcs as he handed his fedora to the hat-check girl. All the wooden pillars and floor and furniture in Zari's were cherry. At the far end was a stage with a twelve-instrument orchestra playing jazz above wide round dining tables that held parties of eight and a gleaming dance floor that was gradually gaining post-dinner couples trying out the fox-trot. Rectangular tables with white linens, rose electric candles, and chairs jacketed in red chintz were under overhanging mezzanine galleries on three sides of the great room, each gallery with more round dining tables and railings hung with cascades of ivy. And it was up there that Judd saw a grinning Harry Folsom wildly swinging his right arm to get his attention and probably yelling his name out over the music.

Judd took the circular staircase up and was introduced to Harry's dinner party of two fat older men who seemed to be Rochester retailers in silks and hosiery; their female companions, whose day jobs were in Harry's Madison Avenue shop; Harry's homely wife, who glared at Judd as if he'd done something wrong; and Mrs. Albert E. Snyder in white pearls and an Alice-blue frock, prettily sitting with her elbows on the white linen and her fingers interlaced under her chin. She was still tan from her Shelter Island vacation and scented with Le Lilas perfume.

As Judd was shaking hands with the diners, Harry said, "We've already eaten, but I'll get you a menu. We're drinking screwdrivers." He whistled to a waiter and ordered for his friend a menu and a highball glass of orange juice and cracked ice.

The orchestra began playing "It Had to Be You," and one of the girls said, "Oh, I love this song! Can't we dance, please, Harry?"

"Excellent idea," Harry's wife said, getting up just as Judd was sitting. And after Harry handed on his flask, the whole dinner party, except for Mrs. Snyder, hurried downstairs.

"I seem to have occasioned a stampede," Judd said.

"Well, I hate to eat and run, myself."

Lacking a rejoinder, Judd dully asked, "How are you?"

She grinned. "I'm paralyzed with happiness." And she indeed looked at him as if there was no one in the world she so much wanted to see.

"You're a very pleasant surprise for me, too. Harry's note didn't mention you."

"Well, he's not a detail kind of guy."

"Your mother. She liked the Grecian-Treco corset?"

"Oh, I don't know. We don't chat about our underthings like we should. But thank you for the gift."

"Anytime," he said, and found he meant it.

A highball glass half-filled with orange juice was delivered and Judd stirred in vodka from Harry's hammered silver flask as he ordered a Shrimp Louie salad for his dinner.

Ruth's golden hair was equal to the fiery chandelier hanging near them, and her stunning, ice-blue eyes were checkered with its light. He felt he would have been content to just fill the night gazing at her, but in the practiced way of a lady's escort, he peppered her with questions about her upbringing.

She said she was born in a four-room apartment on Morningside Avenue and 125th Street in New York City. Her father, Harry

Sorenson, adopted the last name Brown when he emigrated from a fishing village in Norway. Josephine met him on Coney Island. Harry was a sailor then but became a carpenter who was often out of work because of a host of illnesses and epilepsy, so Josephine supported them as a practical nurse. Really a part-time housekeeper and sickroom attendant. Ruth graduated from Public School 11 at age thirteen and soon was hired by the New York Telephone Company as a relief operator. She was too young for the job but the guy in charge became enchanted by her voice. She went to night school at the Berg Business Institute on 149th Street. She was certified as a stenographer and could type sixty-five words a minute, some of them not misspelled. "You can't really be interested in all this."

"But I am," Judd said. "It's fascinating." A line from Laurence Sterne came to him: *Courtship consists in a number of quiet attentions, not so pointed as to alarm, nor so vague as not to be understood.* His highball glass was again half-filled with orange juice by the waiter and Judd completed it with vodka. "Say, I'm having a capital time," he said.

"Me too. You're a good listener."

"Would you like a drink?"

"Nah. Intoxicants don't agree with me. But I love seeing everyone else having a good time."

Slouching in his dining chair, he got his cigarettes out of an interior coat pocket and clumsily lit one.

She cocked her head like a child as she asked, "What kind?"

He exhaled gray smoke and faced the front of the package for her. "Sweet Caporals. I got hooked on them at fourteen when each pack carried a baseball trading card."

"And weren't there 'Pretty Lady' cards before that?"

Sheepishly grinning, he said, "Well, yes. I guess I got hooked on the *cards* at six."

"And thus was a job in lingerie begun."

Seeming embarrassed, he said, "So tell me how you met your husband."

She said she was a secretary at the Tiffany Commercial Art Studio and was instructed to contact an art editor at *Cosmopolitan* but mistakenly placed the call to the art editor at *Motor Boating* in the same building. Albert was the lout who yelled that she'd interrupted him and she must be very stupid and just kept screaming insults until she hung up. But then she was called back and he was a changed man, apologetic and funny and suave, with a faint German accent. "Are you as pretty as your voice?" he'd asked. And he invited her to the magazine's offices on West 40th Street. She was hired that afternoon as a stenographer, proofreader, and copyist in the secretarial pool shared by *Motor Boating, Cosmopolitan,* and *The American Weekly*. It was July 1914. She was nineteen years old. Soon Germany was involved in the Great War, and Albert changed the spelling of his last name from Schneider to Snyder, "as if that would fool anyone." She was warned that he was a womanizer. But she dated him anyway, for he was cultured and educated, a manly connoisseur with a degree in art and graphic design from the famous Pratt Institute. And if he was hot-tempered and thirteen years older than she, and his favorite things to do, like fishing and sailing and going to the symphony, bored her to distraction, he also seemed the father she'd never had: a good provider who was vital and sensitive and very involved in her life. On Ruth's twentieth birthday, Albert gifted her with a box of chocolates and she discovered inside a little jewelry box and a one-carat diamond solitaire fixed on a golden ring.

Ruth dangled her left hand in front of Judd's intent and myopic stare, his owlish round glasses lifted up to his forehead so he could inspect the jewel.

"Lovely," he said.

"I had lots of misgivings, but I said finally yes to getting hitched. Mostly because I wouldn't have given up this goddamned ring for anything once I had it on my hand."

His Shrimp Louie had arrived, and he'd finished it as she talked. And now he poured the final inch of Harry's vodka as a waiter took the dishes and cutlery away. She glanced over Judd Gray's shoulder to find Harry Folsom there, loosening his tie, his hair a wreck and his face flushed with sweat. "Are you kids going to join us on the floor or are you just going to make goo-goo eyes all night?"

"Are you up for it?" she asked Judd.

Harry intervened. "Up for it? The guy's . . . What's that fancy word, Judd?"

"Terpsichorean?"

"That's him."

Ruth was lost. Judd got up, the vodka tipping him off balance, and took her golden-ringed hand as she rose. He slurred, "Terpsichore is the goddess of dancing and choral song."

She smiled. "How flattering for you to be likened to a goddess!"

His hand friended her back in a foretaste of waltzing. "Harry means well," he said. "We all do."

She loved dancing and Judd could do them all: the fox-trot, tango, Castle Walk, even the Charleston and American rumba, which he taught her there on Zari's floor. Held by him, she felt the knotted muscles of his back, the jump and bunch of his upper arms, the shift of his deft thighs against hers. She liked it that she was taller than he. She could smell his hair and hair tonic and just a hint of his cigarettes. She grazed her nose on his neck. She asked, "Is that aftershave?"

"Eau de Cologne," he said. "Jean Marie Farina's fragrance. Worn by royalty throughout Europe."

"Albert wouldn't dream of smelling like anything but hand soap."

"Well, it comes with the territory. Selling women's undergarments."

"And being a clotheshorse?"

Judd fell back so she could see his face and the hurt he was faking. "But I'm not that, I'm just 'tailorish.'"

"Anything '-ish' isn't good."

Corny as a yokel, he said, "And yet you rav-ish me."

"I was thinking 'fiendish.' And 'piggish.' Like my husband."

Judd laughed. "Is he as bad as all that?"

She swayed with him, feeling his genteel lead, and saw Harry in a hoofing four-step and frowning with jealousy over the head of his wife. Still eyeing Harry, she tilted her head to Judd so intimately that her mouth fluttered his ear like a kiss as she confided, "We had to cut our Shelter Island vacation short. Albert was caught necking with a yacht club wife and got slugged by her husband."

Judd jerked his head away, his face rucked with vexation. "But that's *awful,* Ruth!"

There was something tricky in her wet eyes. Was she lying? She nodded like a shamed unfortunate and huddled into his masculine symmetry to say, "I was so humiliated. Lora and I left that afternoon and Albert came later with his tail between his legs. We haven't spoken in days. And then when I was on my way here, his first words were to accuse me of having an affair." A hot tear slid down her cheek and she wiped it with the flat of her hand. "And then he said he marveled that he'd stayed with me for so many years and said any man who wanted me was welcome to have me. And other hateful things."

Judd held her in a fatherly way. "Oh, Ruth. I'm so sorry."

She eked out, "It's okay." She tucked her head against his neck and noted Harry Folsom's wild jealousy, Mrs. Folsom's scorn. She'd

not noticed that the orchestra was playing "What'll I Do." She laid
her hot cheek against Judd's gray flannel shoulder and sang along
with the girl in the evening gown onstage.

Around ten, the girls from the Madison Avenue shop left Zari's and
got on an uptown bus, and the out-of-town retailers joined Harry
Folsom and his wife in their Packard for a jaunt out to Hyman's
nightclub on Merrick Road in Long Island. Ruth hurt Harry's
feelings by saying she wanted to call it a night, as did Judd, and they
shared a taxi to his hotel at 33rd Street. She'd walk to Pennsylvania
Station from there.

She shifted uneasily on the taxi's bench seat. Seeing his curiosity, she explained, "The fabric hurts my sunburn."

"But haven't you been in the sun all summer?"

She seemed embarrassed for some reason.

"I have my golf clubs in my office and a jar of sunburn cream in
the bag. Would you like it? We're very close."

The Benjamin & Johnes offices were in a twelve-story building
on the corner of Fifth Avenue and 34th Street. There was a gruff
night watchman who thought Judd was up to no good, but then
all Judd needed was the elevator up and his Schlage key for the
entrance.

She said, "I feel like a child on an escapade."

Judd hung his fedora on a coat rack as he insisted, "We're
not doing anything wrong." Switching on one bank of overhead
lights, he tilted with drunkenness as he walked ahead of her
down a herringboned oak hallway to a fundamental office of four
paired desks, one shared telephone, a stack of Benjamin & Johnes
catalogues, a persuasive store mannequin of the female torso, and
pinned-up *New York Times* advertisements for Bien Jolie undergarments. Judd failed to notice Ruth shutting the Venetian blinds

as he unzipped the pouch on a khaki, leather-trimmed golf bag monogrammed HJG. He stood up again with a jar of Dr. Bunting's Sunburn Remedy, a Baltimore product that would soon be renamed Noxzema.

She asked, "What's in it?"

Lifting his spectacles, he focused hard on the jar's ingredients. "Camphor, menthol, and I think it says eucalyptus."

Shyly, and with just a hint of a smile, she asked, "Will you put it on me? I can't reach."

"Certainly," he said, and fell over into a goofy bow.

"I have to take off some things."

"Oh." And then with recognition, "Oh! I'll go out." But first he pulled open a door on the right pedestal of his desk, fetched a bottle of Canadian whisky, and carried it out in his right arm's crook. Judd fell back into a secretary's chair just outside the office, unscrewed the whisky cork, and took a long swallow, liking the scald in his throat, and forgetting why he was there. Some minutes passed and he fought sleep. He twirled in the oak chair to see the city lights and hunched over to find the moon. And then he heard her call, "Okay. I'm ready."

She shocked him by standing in his office with her lovely back and rump revealed, very naked and very tan where her bathing suit failed to cover her, very pink wherever the skin was newly discovered by the sun. Without rotating, Ruth said, "I have no idea what I was thinking. I was hurt and mad and I rented a motorboat at Jones Beach and steered it far out to sea and it was hot so I took off all my clothes and just floated."

Judd could only stare at her fine body for half a minute, stunned and aroused by its beauty. He tried to seem both fastidious and jaunty in case he was misinterpreting the moment. "You poor thing," he finally said. "You're fried." His hands were shaking as he took hold of the jar of Dr. Bunting's Sunburn Remedy and spooned out a glob with his fingers. He hesitated before he reached out and touched the hot skin of her left shoulder blade.

"Ooh!" she said. "Icy."

Softly applying it, he felt the stirring of an erection, and he looked down with satisfaction at her firm, round rump. "Remember me talking about that famous sculptor's model, Audrey Munson?"

She turned her head slightly left. "Yes."

"You're as breathtaking as she was."

"Well, of course. I'm *bien jolie*."

"Oh, right. We've established that, haven't we?" His healing hand had reached her waist and he hesitated again before going farther. "May I?"

She shuddered as if she were sobbing.

Ever cautious, he said, "I'll stop."

"Don't," she said, and she turned. Even with hot tears trickling down her face, she was electrifying. She held his cheeks in her hands and said, "It's your kindness. You're so, so kind, Judd! No man has ever been that way to me; not my father, not Albert—just the opposite."

She fretfully watched as he hesitated at the foreign threshold of unfaithfulness, and then Judd took the initiative and kissed her and she held his head so that he couldn't jerk away, her soft, full lips seeming ravenous for his, her full breasts pillowing against his chest. And then she let him retreat a little. She smiled. "I have been wanting to do that since I first saw you. I knew you'd be a good kisser."

"You're so gorgeous, Ruth. I hadn't the daring to even dream—"

She kissed him again and lifted his left hand to her right breast. He cupped it in a measuring way and then squeezed its cushion. "You're so much larger there than Isabel."

She smiled. "You like?"

He hunched to revere it with a kiss and took the blunt pink nipple in his mouth, sucking it hard until he smacked. And then he straightened. "Shall I take off my clothes?"

Shyly, she said, "Yes, please."

With his wife he'd get naked in a hidden way so he'd not scare her with "his thing," but as he was turned away and getting out of his gray flannel trousers, Ruth squirmed against him from behind and reached around to grip him in her palm. She tenderly jerked him erect, and he held still, tottering with intoxication, a slave to the pleasure of her hand, and sighing out, "Oh, you're amazing, Ruth."

She stepped around to the front of him and knelt. "I have wanted to do this, too." She took him in her mouth and her head moved frontward and back. She'd stop now and then to back away and examine his cock as if just looking gave her joy. And then she said, "Don't come yet," and flicked her tongue a last time before standing and walking over to his desk and slouching back on her forearms with her thighs receptively wide. "Have you been with your secretary here?" she asked.

"I haven't had sex with anyone but my wife. And certainly not here."

She grinned. "Good."

"Shall I kiss you down there?"

"Oh, that's all right. I'm ready."

"Shall I pull out?"

She pouted. "No. I like the seed inside me."

Judd walked into her and sneered a little as he entered the soft and velvety caress of Ruth. She wryly gasped with false wide eyes as if he were enormous, and he smiled as he jammed himself in and out, holding off as long as he could, and then feeling his semen lash out of him with such force he loudly cried, "Ah!"

She petted his head as he fell against her in exhaustion and feebly kissed her ear and neck. She cooed to him, "Oh yes, there's my good boy. My Loverboy. I have such a nice place for you to visit."

His heart was hammering as he said, "I haven't felt this way. Ever."

She whispered, "You will, Judd Gray. Whenever you want."

And he smiled. "I so enjoyed meeting you and hope to do so again."

THREE

MR. & MRS. GRAY

She got to Queens Village just before midnight on Friday. All the lights were still on in the house. She walked through the foyer and dining room to the kitchen, found the cellar door wide open, and heard the finale to Beethoven's *Fidelio* playing on Albert's Victrola in the attic. Because the baby would be sleeping, she didn't call to him, but ascended the staircase and saw Albert was kneeling next to their clawfoot bathtub and gently lowering a steaming, three-gallon copper kettle of beer wort into a foot of ice water. His white shirtsleeves were rolled up to his elbows. A hank of sandy brown hair fell over his forehead. She asked, "What are you brewing now?"

Albert glanced up at her. "I lucked onto some Saaz noble hops. I'm making a fine Pilsener lager." He dipped a thermometer into the wort and watched the temperature gradually change. "Was the moving-picture show good?"

"Lots of action. Douglas Fairbanks in *The Three Musketeers*."

"Was the plot impossible to follow?"

It was his standard complaint. "Not really."

"And how's your nutty cousin?"

"Ethel's fine."

"I have to get this down to forty-five degrees," Albert said.

She went into Lorraine's room, kissed the sleeping girl's cheek, and she woke. "Mommy?"

Ruth petted Lora's straw-blonde hair and softly whispered, "Hey there, lovergirl. I'm home. Sweet dreams."

On Saturday afternoon, Judd found a table for five clients at the gala that followed the Très Parisien fashion show, but he was too woozy with shock and guilt to stay. Each greeting and jibe seemed to carry an undercurrent of irony, as if his friends and associates detected his adultery, his coveting of another's wife, and were grandly pretending to forgive him. At last he felt he needed his family more than sales commissions, and he offered a hurried good-bye in order to catch a train for New Jersey and his Craftsman bungalow in East Orange.

His house was havoc's opposite and contained very little of him. The *Vanity Fair* and *Success* magazines he'd left scattered on the cocktail table had been overcome by *Radio Digest* in his absence. The Tiffany floor lamp he'd shifted for his reading was now reestablished to its seemingly fixed position. His high school mandolin was probably in its scarred case in the closet; the lid on the Priest upright piano was locked. And installed on the yielding, purple mohair sofa was his mother-in-law, Rebecca Kallenbach, whom he called Mrs. K. She'd divorced her husband, Ferdinand, a lithographer, just before Judd married Isabel, and she increasingly seemed to find her ex's vices in her son-in-law. But now she was involved in crocheting a chair cushion as she listened to "Every Morn I Bring Thee Violets" on the phonograph, and she failed to notice his entrance.

But little Jane was at the dining room table in a yellow sundress, furiously coloring an apple orchard on butcher paper with the box of Crayolas he'd bought her in Easton. He softly laid a hand on her chocolate-brown hair as he said, "Hello, sweetie."

She failed to look up. "Hi, Daddy."

"Whose farm is that?"

"It's imaginary."

"Who's that stick man standing way off in the distance?"

Jane frankly said, "You," and his fathering heart felt stabbed.

"I *have* been gone a lot, haven't I?"

Unprompted, Mrs. Kallenbach snidely offered, "Oh, we manage to get by without you." She pulled red yarn taut with her hooked needle.

Isabel walked out of their spic-and-span kitchen, drying her hands on her apron. She forgot to smile as she said, "Hi, Bud. You're home early."

"I had enough."

She kissed him and wrinkled her nose at the hint of railway whisky. "Smells like you had plenty."

"And so it begins," he said.

Judd Gray was sixteen and in the rigorous college preparatory course at William Barringer High School in Newark, intent on attending Cornell medical school. He was president of his high school fraternity, chairman of the Dance Committee, a Newark high schools sports reporter, manager of the basketball team, and in spite of his scrawniness, the quarterback on the football team. Yet he was high-strung and giddy around girls; he thought they could read his dirty mind. And then he met a considerate, pious, slender, solemn, not-pretty brunette named Isabel Kallenbach, of

Van Siclen Avenue in New York City. She had a too-prominent nose and a jutting chin and he initially dated her out of chivalry and pity. His first and only sweetheart, Isabel married him in November 1915, when he was twenty-three and she twenty-four. Because of pneumonia, Judd had been forced to quit high school in his senior year, and when he was healthy again he took a job in his father's jewelry factory, and then became a jewelry sales-man, serving as a volunteer for the Red Cross during the Great War though he'd wanted to join the Army. His grandfather was an investor in the Empire Corset Company and offered Judd the greater freedom of a job with that firm, and later, in 1921, Judd shifted over to Benjamin & Johnes. And Isabel became a devoted but dowdy housewife, finicky in her cooking and cleaning, priggish, overweight, acting ever more disgraced by his job in lingerie sales, and in reaction given to wearing frowzy dresses and farmerish shoes.

"We're having meat loaf and fresh sliced tomatoes," Isabel said from the kitchen, verging on disgust as she added, "And you're having your Scotch first, I suppose."

Judd fetched his bottle of Johnnie Walker from the dining room sideboard. "Wouldn't do without it."

Mrs. Kallenbach would later state for journalists that she was "very close" to her son-in-law and hardly ever saw him drink, but she watched Judd flee into the back yard with his liquor and stri-dently called, "You have broken the law, buying that!"

"I'll have to get rid of the evidence then!" he yelled back.

Judd sat in the Adirondack chair with the Johnnie Walker and a glass in the high bluegrass of the yard he'd need to mow. He brooded as he remembered how as a boy in his teens he used to go outside in Newark and sit on a wicker settee between his father and mother, holding their hands, watching the poetry of a sunset. And now no one in the East Orange house seemed inclined to sit with him in the twilight that his mother called "the gloaming," and he felt hurt and wronged and liable to do anything.

Writing of that Saturday evening later, he stated he was *surging with remorse, self-condemnatory, lashing myself with feverish contempt one minute, then remembering Ruth's tenderness, her loveliness, the next. My thoughts would go back and back again to her. Then regrets and that inner turmoil of a conscience that was burning hot with shame.*

Judd maniacally used his reel mower on the lawn at sunrise, washed his purple Hupmobile with its sporty black roof and black fenders, then took a bath and drove the family to Trinity Presbyterian Church in South Orange. Jane went to Sunday school, Isabel and her mother found their usual pew, and Judd took his familiar place in the choir to sing "When Morning Gilds the Skies," "O Gladsome Light," and "Jesu, Joy of Man's Desiring." And, as if word was out about him, he heard a sermon from Reverend Victor Likens on a passage from the Gospel of Mark: "And he said, That which cometh out of the man, that defileth him. For from within, out of the heart of men, proceed evil thoughts, adulteries, fornications, murders, thefts, covetousness, deceit, lasciviousness, an evil eye, blasphemy, pride, foolishness: All these evil things come from within, and defile the man."

Scorching himself for his hypocrisy, Judd made a secret oath that he would never have sexual congress with Mrs. Snyder again, and right after that he visited his mother, Mrs. Margaret Gray, in West Orange, alone.

She was a frail, dignified, courtly woman whom he adored almost to the edge of weirdness. Welcoming him as if he were long lost, she hugged him close and rocked with him, saying, "Oh, my Bud! My darling boy!" She then gave him a grilled cheese sandwich and Coca-Cola and hovered over him as she gladly watched him eat. She said Bud looked exhausted. She wondered if dresses could get any shorter. She inquired of Bud if Mrs. Kallenbach was giving him anything for her share of the room and board. She said, "Don't let her walk all over you." Bud asked if she had any jobs that needed doing, but she only ordered him sternly to get his family and go on a nice vacation somewhere.

Judd did, as always, as he was told and called Alfred Benjamin at his home, then left Mrs. K to her needlework and motored across Long Island with Isabel and Jane to an ocean-view inn in Sagaponack for Jane's ninth birthday and a week's vacation, the three of them swimming in the Atlantic surf and hollering from the cold, or horseback riding in jodhpurs and English saddles on the white sand roads linking villages there. Alone he went to the public golf course with his hickory-shafted clubs, his argyle sweaters and plus fours, his flailing, uninstructed swing. And at night there was fine food and dancing and games of bridge.

Because Isabel and Jane hated having the vacation end, but Judd was required in the office, he booked them for another week; left the Hupmobile Eight with his wife, who'd just learned to drive; and took a jitney into the city on the third Monday in August.

And he was walking into Rigg's Restaurant on 33rd Street for ham and eggs when he ran into Harry Folsom as he was leaving. The hosiery man tarried long enough to wedge around in his mouth with a toothpick as he said he wasn't a kid anymore and he was through with wild parties, through with the hangovers from bathtub gin, and for sure he was through with fast women. "They can't keep secrets, you know."

Judd tried to act shocked. And because Harry's chocolaty eyes had the solemn, baleful look of a hound, Judd asked, "Are you in the doghouse?"

"Not in, under. Whatever's on the doghouse floor, that's my roof."

"Because of?"

Harry lit a Raleigh cigarette. "Dames. What else? I have been ordered by the Mrs. not to talk about it."

Hoping to seem merely conversational, Judd asked, "Say, have you heard from Mrs. Snyder recently?"

Harry tweezed a shred of tobacco off his tongue. "Well, she's not getting along with the old wet blanket at home, is all I hear. I know Albert, too, through bowling. Have you met him?"

"No."

"Solid guy, fine artist, but sort of a stick-in-the-mud. She's not the right girl for a killjoy like him. Anyways, I'm not going to take either one's side. But I guess there's another friend gone."

"Which friend?" Judd asked.

"Al, of course," Harry said, as if Judd were dense. "You don't abandon a doll like that."

Abandonment, Judd thought. *That's what it was.* "I have a hard time fathoming how anyone could treat such a lovely woman so badly."

Harry's stare was long and interrogatory, and then he got out a postcard invitation from his vest pocket and handed it to Judd. "Are you aware of this 'Bon Voyage' party? Hosted bar and everything. Some big fashion-month shebang." And he added dismissively, "You're supposed to look *nautical.*"

"Are you going?"

"Nah. I'm through with shebangs, too." And then he winked. "But *you* should definitely go."

Waiting for him in his Benjamin & Johnes office were retailer inquiries, order forms, an announcement from the Club of Corset

Salesmen of the Empire State, a notice of an increase in dues from his Elks lodge, and three neatly typed letters lacking a sender's name or return address. The first, dated Tuesday of last week, read:

Dear Judd,
Hate to bother you on the job but I have no one in whom to confide, no one but you to whom I can unburdun myself and speak of my troubles, my husband's neglec, our night after night of arguments, Albert's cruellty toward our baby. Won't you see me for lunch sometime? We can just talk.

Judd slit open another that was postmarked on a Wednesday evening:

Dear Judd,
I have been investigating an Ursuline convent for Lora to get her out of this din of inequity Albert has created. She could learn and be safe and far away from a father who has no regards for her. But I cannot bare to part with her. She is all I have of love and happyness.
*   I feel certain I could get a job in business. Selling stocks and bonds maybe. I need financial advice, your smarts. Oh please won't you call me? Orchard 8591. Each night I pray, "Dear God, give me back the past." I would do so much so different. You have shown me all that is possible.*

The final letter was postmarked on Saturday:

Dear Darling Mr. Gray,
You must think I'm some loon since you haven't answered. Please accep my apologies for the desparate tone of my letters. They would certainly scare me if I were a man! I have not

wanted to call your office for fear people there will talk, and
that would be distructive. I have no other expectations beyond
speaking to you since I value your intelligence and mastery
of situations. Won't you call when Al is gone? Eight in the
morning to 6 at night. Orchard 8591. We can meet at Henry's if
you'd like to.

Judd did nothing.

Earlier, in 1924, Albert Snyder had felt certain his wife was having
an extramarital affair. C. F. Chapman, the publisher of *Motor*
Boating magazine, recommended Albert initiate actions for a
divorce and forced him to leave their offices on West 40th Street
to have a conversation with Judge Nathan Lieberman, a New
York state assemblyman and a high-paid Broadway attorney. The
judge reviewed New York's divorce laws with Albert, urged him
to hire a private detective to find proof of Ruth's infidelity, and
then introduced him to an ex-cop named Jacob Sanacory. She was
investigated for a week, and at its conclusion Sanacory wrote Judge
Lieberman, "We have incontestable evidence on this man's wife."
And that same afternoon Sanacory telephoned Albert to say, "She's
in your house with a guy right now."

Albert stood in the front yard with the gumshoe and vaguely
heard a Brooklyn voice and Ruth's giggling in Lorraine's bedroom,
but though Sanacory got his camera out and egged Mr. Snyder to
hurry inside, saying they needed a photograph of the lovers in fla-
grante delicto, Albert hesitated. "And then what?" he said. "End
it? She's an adequate mother and domestic. With Root I can at least
be sure that the house and the girl are being taken care of."

Sanacory shook his head as he went off, and Albert sat on the
front porch for a full hour, inventing ever-bloodier ways to destroy

the diddler's face. And then he did not even do that. "I could have done a lot," he told C. F. Chapman, "but I would have had to be in love."

Soon after that the Snyders established an unspoken accommodation: Albert would ignore Ruth's nights out or counterfeit an acceptance of the lies she told, and she would affect a nonchalance about him.

And so it was that in August 1925, both of them could be going out on the town, but alone. Thursday was Albert's night for duckpin bowling in his Flatbush summer league, so he came home from work earlier to get his six-inch ball and high-top bowling shoes. But he also took a bath and changed his shirt and necktie.

Ruth carried in a stein of his Pilsener as he hunched toward the dresser mirror and tied a Windsor knot. She got his royal blue Jacquard from the closet tie rack and said, "She'll like you better in this one."

Albert frowned. "I have no idea what you're talking about." But he tugged the plaid necktie off and took the Jacquard from his wife. "So what are your plans?"

She told him Josephine was staying home and could watch the baby, so she was going out with Ethel. "She wants to see that new Rudolph Valentino movie. *The Eagle*?"

Albert swallowed some beer and said, "I have no idea why you females swoon over that foolish, effeminate *Italian*."

"Could it be we find manliness overrated?"

"Well, it's like they say. Women have the last word in any argument. Anything the man says after that is the beginning of a new argument." Admiring himself and tying a Windsor knot in the Jacquard, he said, "I'll be late."

And she said, "Me too."

✑ ✑

Judd rented a skipper's hat from a costume shop and avoided Mrs. K at home as he collected his blue cashmere blazer and white flannel slacks, then telephoned Isabel and Jane at the inn as he tanked up with a full glass of Scotch and got back to the city for the Bon Voyage party on a sultry August night. It was being held on a three-masted schooner moored on the East River. Judd held up his postcard invitation and was whistled aboard the schooner by a security guard who was pretending to be a naval petty officer.

Walking up the gangplank, Judd encountered perhaps a hundred nautically costumed guests in the fashion business gabbling and laughing underneath the hanging ship's lanterns and taking weenies, canapés, and Taittinger champagne from waiters attired like seamen. Judd was greeted by a buyer for Bloomingdale's and hugged by a buyer at Macy's, but there were few others he knew. The haute couture models—who were then known as mannequins—strutted around the schooner to parade the finest of the fall designs, but no lingerie was on display and he did little more than feel the fabric and inquire if one girl was wearing a Bien Jolie. She was not.

A gaudy flag of sandwiches and hors d'oeuvres had been laid out and he filched a few. And then he saw Ruth there, far off near the prow. Alone and dismally staring at him, but glamorous in a filmy, lyrical white evening gown encrusted with fiery little beads that were like dewdrops. She saw he'd seen her and she became demure, glancing away.

Judd noticed a few men watching her, getting up the courage to approach, and he stole two tulip glasses of champagne from a passing tray and affably strolled over.

"Hello, Ruth. You look exquisite."

She smiled. "Really? I'm feeling self-conscious in this fashion crowd. I have no idea what the fall styles are."

"Hemlines up; higher waistlines; straight silhouettes." He held out a champagne glass but she shook her head, so he drank it down and handed it on to a waiter. "How'd you get in?"

"I still have friends at *Cosmopolitan*." She squinted beyond him. "I was expecting Harry—he invited me, too."

"I guess I'm his stand-in."

"Well, you're quite an improvement." She shyly glanced down. "You got my ravings?"

"Oh, they weren't that. I couldn't reply because I was on vacation in Sagaponack that week. And then when I got back I was swamped with work."

She faced him solemnly as she said, "And you were feeling guilty. You worried about your hoity-toity reputation, and you wondered if you'd lose Jane if your wife found out about us."

Judd laughed in a high-strung way, but she seemed to find nothing funny. She looked him flush in the eye. Ruth's were intent and glistening and electric, and he felt cowed by them. "So," he said. "You can read minds."

"Aye-aye, *Captain*."

Judd instantly felt foolish for his skipper's cap and finished his second glass of champagne. And then he leaned on the starboard railing and gazed out at the scraps of moonlight writhing on the night of the river. "I haven't been able to rid myself of you, Ruth. All I have to do is shut my eyes and your gorgeous face and figure are there. I find myself just wanting to say your name aloud. There was a time when my office phone rang and I imagined how glad I would be to hear your lovely voice in the earpiece."

Just as Jane would often imitate his stance and manner, Ruth crossed her forearms on the railing, and she leaned slightly into him, giving him some of her weight in a delicacy of acknowledgment. His hand slid around a waist far more taut than his wife's.

Judd continued, "I felt ashamed of myself for our fornication and my disloyalty to Isabel, and I was too much a coward to call you or agree to see you because I find you so irresistible I couldn't govern my emotions or good behavior. But now I feel ashamed of my disloyalty to *you,* to the joy you give me." He twisted his head to her. "I'm crazy about you, Ruth."

"I have a yen for you, too," she said. But she retreated from the railing and hurried aft so hastily in her high heels that he was forced to scurry like a terrier to catch up. "Don't talk," she warned, and he honored that caution as they strolled the deck.

Judd looked out at a ferry slowly churning up the East River toward the Sound, the swift traffic and glittering lights of the Queensboro Bridge, the flicker and iridescence of the city skyline overlooking all the racy adventures of a sultry August night. She seemed not to notice the tribute of masculine stares as she walked past. There were glints of moonlight on her tears.

She finally recited sentences that seemed lifted from *Romance* or *True Story* magazine. "I have stayed up late just recalling how I fell in love with you at Zari's. With your sweetness, your sympathy, your interest in me. My life has become intolerable, Judd. All the happiness that I have lacked for years is now completely lost. Albert calls upon my body only for his own needs. But I indulge him because then I can fantasize that it's you, my Loverboy." She was crying but she was trying to smile as she turned to him. "Are you aware I'm yours? Really, do whatever you want with me. I'll run away with you. Anything."

There was some hooting festivity near the mizzenmast as five half-naked showgirls from *Earl Carroll's Vanities* were wickedly introduced by the acidic celebrity Peggy Hopkins Joyce, who was then thirty-two and on her fourth wealthy husband. Joyce was saying in an aside, "You know, I sometimes lie awake in the afternoon—because we do not generally rise before two—and I gaze at Gustave in the other bed and *My* God, I think, *whatever made me marry* that?"

There were gales of laughter, but Ruth just said, "She's hitting too close to home."

And Judd asked, "Shall we go?"

She nodded.

Judd hailed a horse-drawn carriage for a romantic ride to the Waldorf-Astoria on Fifth Avenue and 33rd Street. She wanted to kiss him out there in public but he primly insisted, "We cannot lose our heads."

She noticed the green patina of the hotel's oxidized copper roofing, and Judd told her it was called verdigris.

She asked, "Have you heard that expression 'Ignorance is bliss'?" Then she smiled as she held up a shushing finger to his lips.

She admitted she'd never been inside the neighboring, brownstone, Victorian hotels that the Astor family had joined into one. The famous George C. Boldt, who was said to have invented the modern hotel, had retired as general manager and was replaced by a gregarious Norwegian woman whose name, Jorgine, had been Americanized to Georgia. She'd talked with Judd before, and she grinned as she said, "Hey, sailor. What ship?"

Judd took off his skipper's hat and said he didn't believe she'd met his wife, introducing Ruth as Mrs. Jane Gray and signing the register that way.

Walking up the staircase, Ruth whispered, "Aren't you feeling naughty?"

"Deliciously so," Judd said.

She looked down and said with amazement, "This carpeting is soft as a sponge!"

"John Jacob Astor called it the most luxurious hotel in the world. Of course, that was thirty years ago."

She grazed her fingers along the flocked wallpaper, then stooped to praise a tazza urn on a hallway credenza. When they reached their room, she fondled the silken draperies, the tapestried furniture, and the woven fabric on the wide bed. She flipped off her high heels and flopped down on it and smiled. "The springs don't creak!"

"Were you excruciatingly poor as a child?" he asked.

She seemed to take that as an insult. "Was I too dizzy?"

"Oh no, darling. It just makes me feel so good to give you things you haven't had."

Ruth crooked a finger inside the front of his belt and pulled him to her. "Ditto," she said.

But then the field of force shifted and he said, "My turn," as he lifted Ruth to her feet so his clotheshorse hands could deftly undo and tease off a hushed waterfall of jeweled white evening gown. In the still-new flapper fashion, she wore nothing underneath but a garter belt and silk stockings, and she liked his shock at her sudden nakedness and the frank wolfishness of his gaze as it seized information of her body. With a faint groan of veneration, Judd fell to his knees in front of her to unfasten each stocking and tug it free while offering tickling, reverent kisses to her inner thighs, her calves, her feet. "Sit," he said then. "Lie back."

She took off the garter belt and did so, and watched the city's flashing lights affect the Waldorf's ceiling as she heard him taking off and folding his glasses, and then Judd was kneeling again and widening her legs in a firm, medical way, his face finding her crotch and wetly nuzzling there as his soft, almost feminine hands palmed and squeezed her breasts. She gasped with excitement as his mouth fluttered, examined, and worried her sex in a hungry, fervent ravishment, and she said, "Oh, you're so *good* at that." She said, "Oh, that feels so *nice*." And still he continued, with no hint of duty or impatience, and she felt a finger stroking inside her, two, and she felt her heart going like mad, and she thought this freedom, this fun, this letting go was all she'd ever wanted from Albert, was just what

Albert could not give, and it was right to have this intimacy, this tenderness, this sharing of sheer pleasure—it would have been cold, inhuman, and wrong to deny it—and she wanted to thank Isabel or whoever it was for teaching him so well, this Judd who was so self-less and generous and as talented with his tongue as a fantasy lover, and she could feel his fascination, his awe for her, his gratitude for the gift of this, and she couldn't hold back, she cried out and bucked up from the bed again and again, shuddering in orgasm, and then inviting him up from the floor and guiding his erection inside her and joining him so tightly in the clench of her thighs and the hug of her arms that he could not possibly have seen she was crying.

Afterward Judd phoned room service and ordered ginger ale for them and Waldorf salads. "And pretzels," Ruth added.

"And pretzels," he said. Earlier he'd raised all the windows but it was still hot, so they stayed naked atop the fresh-smelling sheets, propped up against a six-foot-high Victorian headboard. Judd reclined on his elbow and admired her body for a while, softly grazing a scar near her navel as he inquired, "What caused that?"

"I had an appendectomy when I was eleven."

He petted near it another scar from an incision. "And that?"

"Surgery so I could get pregnant. Some female things were knotted up. Al blew his stack when he found out. He hates kids."

"I hope we never meet."

"You won't."

Judd gently cupped the underside of Ruth's right breast as though weighing it.

She smiled. "C cup."

"I just can't get over seeing such a gorgeous woman in the alto-gether like this. With *me*."

"I'm guessing Isabel's a prude."

"Oh yes. She manages to be clothed at all times. She even wears these hideous, mannish pajamas that she must find in some sort of *neuter* shop. She's afraid a glimpse of her flesh will get me, as she puts it, 'riled up.'"

She waggled him. "So that's what he was earlier? Riled up?"

"But you soothed the savage beast," Judd said.

Ruth rolled over onto him and softly laid her head on his hairless, alabaster chest. "Tell me about Isabel so I won't be like her."

"I frankly don't know a lot. And I have been connected to Isabel in one way or another for sixteen years. Yet I can't honestly say what Isabel's ambitions are, or her hopes, her fears, her ideals. We seldom talk about heady things. We're raising Jane, we go to the occasional party, play contract bridge with our friends, dance. Always ostensibly together. Married. But not."

A finger abstractly doodled on his skin as she said, "Albert is stingy and I'm generous. He has a horrible temper. He criticizes and accuses. He hates movies or dancing. And he has a slew of hobbies so he's always puttering in the basement or garage when he's home, or haunting the attic with his books, like some old fogy." She gazed up at Judd's face. "I despise him."

"Don't say that!"

She seemed bewildered. "But why not if it's true?"

"Say you're ill matched, Ruth. Say you disagree and your marriage is stagnant. But hating eats away at you."

She stared hard, as if he'd oddly launched into Russian and consigned his opinions to strange irrelevance. And then she slid into another emotion and girlishly asked, "Oh please, can we come here again, Bud?"

He smiled. "Anytime."

"And Henry's. That will be our place, too."

☙ ❧

I faced Isabel with dread. I wanted to tell her, throw myself on her mercy, ask her aid before it was too late. I had not the courage. I kept insisting to myself: "This cannot go on. It would mean a breach in my family, disgrace, unhappiness for us all." I told myself Ruth did not really love me, could not. Our affair would have to end.

But it did not. She called their meetings "trysts," Judd thought of them as "sinning," and weekly stays in the Waldorf-Astoria became so regular that Judd purchased a red leather suitcase to have available for Mr. and Mrs. Gray in the hotel's storage room. Ruth filled it with essentials they bought together: a gentleman's silk pajamas and bathrobe and a matching set for her, white satin slippers, hairbrushes, a hair-curling iron, a blue eye pencil, a pearl-handled nail file, five shades of nail enamel, three toothbrushes, bicarbonate of soda, a box of needles and thread, three shades of Helena Rubinstein lipsticks, Richard Hudnut rouge, perfumed soaps from Erasmic of London, Kotex sanitary napkins, a box of Midas tablets, Amolin deodorant powder, a box containing Day Dream powder and Day Dream cream, Mavis talcum powder, a powder puff, a Gillette safety razor and a tube of Colgate's Rapid Shaving Cream, and the novel *Gentlemen Prefer Blondes* by Anita Loos, with the inscription *As if you didn't know! Your Bud.* But also included in what Judd referred to as their "honeymoon bag" were items that would heighten the scandal of their relationship when newspapers published the inventory: Trojan condoms, K-Y Lubricating Jelly, vaginal suppositories, and a green rubber douche. Each item could be found in many American households but was invariably concealed, and to find them all listed so graphically on a front page made the couple, not the press, seem outrageous.

Elaborate efforts were in fact made by Ruth and Judd to hide what they were doing. To protect their frequent, even compulsive, correspondence, Ruth arranged for Judd to send mail to her care of Spindler's drugstore in Queens, and she instructed her regular postman, George Marks, to hand-deliver solely to her both their telephone bills and letters to "Mrs. Jane Gray."

Judd sought to disguise his identity by altering his handwriting from the Palmer Method, which was gaining currency in business practice, to the loopier Zaner-Bloser style he'd learned as a boy. He had supplied Ruth with his fall sales travel schedule and the address of each hotel on his eastern Pennsylvania and upstate New York routes. Often when he checked in at a front desk there was already a handful of letters waiting for him. "Looks like someone's in love," a girl once said.

And he needlessly lied, "We're just good friends."

But he would write: *It is but this morning that I knelt by my hotel bed and swore my allegiance to my wife while promising I would never contact you again. Reciting the Lord's Prayer for the sake of its closing plea of not being led into temptation, I felt in mastery of our situation. But having got so near you through your last perfumed letter, I feel drawn into a vortex of emotions that upsets all rationality, all quests for honor and moral integrity. Let others name it shameful and scandalous, but a love as glorious as ours cannot be wrong. You have become as essential as breath to me.*

Ruth was generally in a chirrupy mood in her letters, filling them not just with passion and endearments but with short reviews of the movies she'd seen and flighty particulars of her days rendered in the latest slang or in parodies of immigrant accents. But in one letter she was more practical, objecting that Albert carried only a one-thousand-dollar policy on his life. Was that enough?

Judd wrote, "Life insurance is a good investment for a family man." And with the dullness of Sinclair Lewis's *Babbitt,* Judd detailed the estate Isabel would inherit if "something perchance happened to me." She'd be the beneficiary of around six thousand dollars in stocks and bonds, whatever real estate equity there was in

37 Wayne Avenue, and a twenty-five-thousand-dollar policy from the Union Life Insurance Company of Cincinnati. She and Jane would be well set. Ruth should demand the same.

Consequently, in the second week of November 1925, Ruth invited to the Snyder home Mr. Leroy Ashfield, a salesman employed by the Prudential Life Insurance Company. He was a fat, round-faced man in his twenties. His trousers were too short for him and hinted at the union suit he wore underneath. His cheeks were redly patched with the sudden cold.

Albert was sitting on a stool at his easel in the northern sun-room, drinking Pilsener from his stein and executing a rather good oil painting of salmon-pink skies and a spew of zinc-white wave rising high into mist as it crashed onto a shoreline ridge that was mostly raw sienna. Ruth held a hand over her nose because of the turpentine smell and introduced the salesman to him. Albert dabbed his sable brush into linseed oil and mixed three colors on his palette as he ignored Ashfield's offer of a handshake and said, "But you are interrupting me."

"He hates that," Ruth said. She crossed her eyes and Ashfield snorted a laugh as he sneakily glanced at the fullness of her chest.

Albert let his hands fall in his lap and glared frostily at the salesman. *"What?"*

Speeding up his sales pitch, Ashfield nervously said, "You have a thousand-dollar policy on your life that's up for renewal, and yet you make over five thousand dollars a year."

Albert shifted his glare to Ruth. "She told you that?"

Ashfield continued, "Were you to die, and I hope you never do, your family would be penniless in a few months." Reaching into his valise, he said, "I have some graphs here from the company—"

Albert sighed. "What are you proposing?"

"We recommend at a minimum a twenty-five-thousand-dollar policy. Five times your yearly income. Even better would be fifty thousand."

"Yes. Even better for you." Albert resumed painting. "And next thing you'll tell me I need earthquake insurance and lightning insurance and hail insurance."

"We could just concentrate on the one."

"But then I'd be gambling against myself, wouldn't I? I'd be betting I'm going to die soon, and you'd be betting I'm going to live."

Ashfield had heard that frequently and was about to give the company line when Ruth placatingly offered, "With old Winslow Homer here so busy, could you just leave the forms for us to fill out?"

Ashfield seemed deflated. "But you won't know what the premiums would be. I haven't the basis—"

Albert clacked his paintbrush against his palette and sighed again. "What *is* it you require, chum?"

Ashfield hurried to sit on the plump arm of the sunroom's easy chair, got a pencil from his jacket, and placed a fresh insurance form on his knee. "Your full name?"

"Albert Edward Snyder," he said.

"Spelled the easy way," said Ruth. "Like 'snide.'"

Ashfield printed as quickly as he could. "And your birth date?"

Albert said, "Exactly three hundred ninety years after Christopher Columbus arrived in the Americas."

Ruth said with scorn, "Oh, you are so stuck-up!"

"And you are stupid," Albert said. "Evidently, so is he."

Ashfield said, "No, I'm getting it." Ruth could see concentration in his forehead and his lips humming through the children's nursery rhyme until he said with achievement, "October twelfth! Eighteen eighty-two!"

Ruth helped out by saying, "He just turned forty-three."

Ashfield wrote down the birthday.

"Congratulations on your arithmetic," Albert said. "And now I'm finished with you for the evening." And he was squinting at his painting as he said, "Would you leave me a form to renew the thousand-dollar policy in case I decide to do just that?"

Ruth took the insurance forms and gave the Prudential salesman one of those *It'll be okay, honey* looks.

She found her husband in the sunroom the next morning, fully dressed and ready to leave for the *Motor Boating* office but examining the problems and successes in his seascape as he finished a cup of coffee. She called upstairs, "Lora! Breakfast!" and then she said, "I agree."

Albert grinned. "You could stop right there."

"No, I gave it some thought last night and you're so healthy we'd just be throwing premium money away on some gargantuan policy. Let's just renew the cheapest one."

"Exactly what I wanted to do."

"Will you sign?" She put the Prudential one-thousand-dollar insurance policy on the front lid of the Aeolian player piano and handed him a fountain pen. Albert bent over to precisely execute his fine signature and was about to give the fountain pen back to Ruth when she lifted the form to another signature block. "You have to sign a duplicate copy for the agent's files."

Albert shook his head. "Duplicates. Triplicates." But he signed.

"Thanks, sweetie," she said, and kissed his cheek. She said, "Your painting's the berries."

"Which means?"

"It's slang. Like 'the bee's knees.' Like 'nifty.'"

Albert studied his seascape and said, "I agree."

She found Ashfield in his Queens office that afternoon and said, "We're going to renew that thousand-dollar policy we have." She handed it to him and he found Albert's signature there. "And my husband has decided on the fifty-thousand-dollar policy, too." She gave him the form the salesman had started in their house and he saw Albert's fountain pen signature on it.

"Well, great!"

"We were confused about the double-indemnity part."

Ashfield rocked back in his oak chair, glorying in the superiority of an instructor. "An indemnity is just a fancy way of saying 'compensation for a loss.' Since the vast majority of people pass away through natural causes rather than accidents, it's a good deal for the insurance company to entice buyers by making a policy seem like it's worth twice as much. Is what I'm saying over your head?"

She smiled indulgently but said nothing.

With self-importance, Ashfield got out a slide rule for some calculations and then groaned. "We got a problem with the disability clause. Because of your husband's income, my company cannot pay more than five hundred dollars a month, and the fifty-thousand-dollar policy works out to pay five hundred twenty."

She moped. "Oh."

"But if you'll indulge me," Ashfield said, "we could fill out a policy for forty-five thousand that would include the clauses for disability and double indemnity, and another policy for five thousand, without those clauses, and everything's hunky-dory."

Mrs. Snyder seemed to him either confused or conflicted. "Would I need to get Albert's signature again?"

"We have established that he wants fifty thousand dollars in coverage, have we not?"

She nodded.

"With your permission, then, I'll just trace his signature on this five-thousand-dollar policy and we'll change the one for fifty to forty-five."

Ruth smiled. "You're a very handsome man, do you know that?"

He was not, but he blushed and got busy with his forms.

She said, "My husband worries about money and hates handling our bills. Would it be possible for you to personally contact me about the premiums?"

Ashfield leered as he said, "It would be my pleasure." Within ten minutes the forms were finished, and with his commissions Ashfield was five hundred dollars richer. She collected the policies and immediately walked to the Queens-Bellaire Bank, where she locked them in a safe-deposit box that she registered under her maiden name of Ruth M. Brown.

The first accident occurred that weekend.

Lorraine Snyder celebrated her eighth birthday on Sunday, November 15th. After the noon meal, Josephine and Ruth were in the kitchen, lighting eight candles on the birthday cake, when they heard Albert yell in the dining room, "Don't eat with your elbows on the table, Lora! This is not a cafeteria!"

She was still crying when her mother walked out with the cake. Ruth said, "I'll take you to lunch in the city tomorrow, Lora. Wouldn't that be nice?"

She nodded. Ruth gifted her with an "I Say Ma-Ma" doll, a nainsook "princess" slip, and tap-dancing shoes; she got a dollar bill and A. A. Milne's *Winnie-the-Pooh* from Mrs. Brown; and Albert, who still grieved that she was not a boy, gave Lora a jackknife and an Erector Set. Even as her father excitedly got down on all fours in the living room to help her bolt together the struts for an imaginary railway trestle, Lora lost interest and sat cross-legged on the floor in order to chatter with the doll about the state of its pretty rompers and bonnet. Albert knelt upright and frowned at his child, then at Ruth. "Well, that went over like a lead balloon," he said.

"Don't blame me. It wasn't my idea."

Hurt, Albert went outside to the garage to tinker with his Buick.

Half an hour later, Ruth got into old gutta-percha overboots and her favorite leopard-skin coat, then filled a milk glass with Canadian whisky that she carried out through the first fall of snow. She was surprised at how warm it was inside the garage and saw that Albert had installed a natural-gas space heater and a stovepipe that vented through a chiseled-out windowpane. The Buick Eight was jacked up and the left front wheel was off, and Albert was lying on a trolley underneath the car so she could see only his grease-stained khaki trousers and his high-button shoes.

She tapped his left foot with her right as she said, "Al?"

"What?"

"I have some whisky for you with it so cold."

The skate wheels on the trolley screeched on the concrete as he rolled himself out and frowned at the generosity she held in both hands. Sitting up, he took the whisky from his wife, swallowed an inch of it, and coughed. "Thank you."

"What are you doing?"

Albert allotted that smile that was not a smile, that was like the blade of a fishing knife. "I could tell you in detail, Root, but you still wouldn't understand."

"I was just making conversation."

Albert looked at the snow that the garage heat was easing down her gutta-percha overboots and the new water trickling onto the concrete. "You're making a mess of my floor. You should stamp your feet before coming in."

"I'll stamp them going out," she said, and did so.

Albert shook his head in annoyance, then seated the milk glass of whisky on a hubcap, reclined on his trolley, and skidded underneath the Buick again. He fixed the beam of his Eveready flashlight on the master cylinder and slowly followed the hydraulic oil tubing across to the left wheel's drum brakes. He thought he saw the problem and delicately skimmed a fingertip back along the brake line until he felt a fracture in the copper and also felt a cold draft, as if his wife hadn't fully shut the door. And then for some reason the car jack whanged to the floor and the Buick crashed down, slanting forward onto the left wheel drum so that his feet and ankles were free outside the car, but his shins were hurt and his chest was being squashed underneath the Buick's full weight.

"Root!" he shouted. "Root, help me! I'm pinned! Root, help get me out!" Albert thought she could have heard him if she were in the kitchen, but she could have been anywhere in the house. Squeezing his torso out a few inches from under the transmission, he caught his breath and screamed for her until he was exhausted with screaming. And then he managed to turn his head and found those gutta-percha overboots standing near the fallen jack, as if she'd been watching for a while. And this time he took care with her name: "Ruth?"

She hesitated before walking forward. "Are you okay?" she asked.

"I'm just stuck," he said. "Jack up the car."

She got down to her hands and knees and grinned when she saw his fury. "Say 'please.'"

She and Lorraine shopped in the morning at the giant Macy's in Herald Square and Ruth spent seventeen dollars on a girl's red wool overcoat and matching hat for the winter. She confided, "Your daddy's gonna have a cow. But what else is new?"

And then she telephoned the office of Benjamin & Johnes and invited Judd to join them for lunch at Henry's.

Cold eddied from his camel's-hair overcoat as he took off his tweed hat and enthusiastically sat with them, Lorraine on his right and Ruth on his left. He handed the girl a box he hadn't had time to giftwrap, and she lifted the lid to find a pink pinafore inside.

"It's so pretty!" she exclaimed. And she was so impressed that she wiped a tear from her cheek.

Ruth smiled. "She really likes it."

Lora said, "I do! Thank you, Mr. Gray!"

"My pleasure." And then he turned to Ruth. "It's November sixteenth."

She puzzled over it and said, "Oh. Your wedding anniversary."

"Our tenth."

Because Lora was there, they communicated in silence. Then Ruth asked, "So what are you doing tonight?"

"I have reservations at Claridge's for dinner. And then we're going to *Dearest Enemy* at the Knickerbocker. Rodgers and Hart. Their follow-up to *The Garrick Gaieties*." Judd felt Lora watching him, so he turned back to her. "Have you heard why the broom was late?"

She was so confused she didn't answer.

"Because it over-swept," he said.

She snickered.

"What kind of hair does the ocean have?"

She was amused but said, "I don't know."

"Wavy."

She giggled. "Like *yours*."

"Where does the general keep his armies?" Judd asked. She smiled with puzzled expectation, and Judd answered, "Up his slee-vies!"

Lorraine laughed wildly and Ruth felt Judd's hand feel for hers under the checkered tablecloth. She held it and just relaxed in the calm of a luncheon as the man she loved won Lora over with zaniness.

"What has a bottom at the top?"

"Oh brother," she said, and awaited him with a grin.

"Your legs."

She guffawed.

"And why did the burglar take a bath?"

"I have it," Ruth said. "To make a clean getaway?"

Judd smiled as she squeezed his hand. "Your Momsie's very clever, isn't she?"

⚍ FOUR ⚎

LOVESICK

She confessed to Judd that she saw other men. But he was on the road so often and so long, and she'd get stir-crazy at home with the Old Crab hanging around and grousing, and handsome saps were always noticing her, and she just liked to have a good time.

She'd gotten into a navy blue silk kimono after their afternoon sex, and Judd was sitting up in the Waldorf-Astoria hotel bed with the *New York Times* crossword puzzle. With more wonder than jealousy, Judd let the newspaper fall and asked, "Who?"

"Oh, lots of fellas." She grinned. "I've been on more laps than a dinner napkin." Seeing his vexation, she said, "Don't worry, Loverboy." And she smiled as she used his language. "There's no one besides you that I have *congress* with."

She told him she and Kitty Kaufman still lunched with Harry Folsom at Henry's when Judd was on the road. And some of Harry's friends would insist the gals join them at the "21" Club or Club de Vingt. Her cousin's ex was a patrolman in the 23rd Precinct in the Bronx and she met lots of policemen through him. She'd even cruised all the way to West Point in the roadster convertible of a portly detective. She couldn't remember his name—Peter something—but he was a hoot. She flirted with the fountain boys at Spindler's Drugstore and the fresh new pharmacist there flushed with desire whenever she noticed him. And she was strolling by Creedmoor Psychiatric Hospital one sultry afternoon and ended up chatting through the jail bars outdoors with a white-uniformed guard. She'd told him how fascinated she was by crazy people, and he'd gazed back at this girl on a bench whose hands waved in front of her face as if she were food for flies, and he'd said yes, they were very honest about their feelings. And Ruth just had to let him kiss her. Johnny. Johnny would do anything for her. "Each of them is so *hungry*. It's like they can't get enough."

"Well, they can't help it, really. It's biological. You're incredibly beautiful."

"But I feel so sorry for men. *Wanting* all the time."

Judd found it strangely exciting and a source of vanity to imagine those many wolves and jackals lurking around his lover, fawning over her, desiring her, slavishly doing her bidding, as she preserved herself solely for him. But it was in January 1926 that he gradually began to recognize that she was controlling him. At first it was just that Ruth's letters became irregular. There could be four waiting for him when he got to his Buffalo hotel, but there could be no communication at all during his stays in Rochester or Scranton, and he would find himself in a panic of fear and loss and heartache as he finally telephoned her in the morning when the husband he called "The Governor" was certain to be out of the house. She'd soothe him then, the soft velvet of her voice giving him assurances or scolding him for being such a silly pup—she'd simply been busy; in fact she'd written him that morning.

Ecstatic or at least serene whenever he was with Ruth, there were ever more snarling feelings of hopelessness and despondency when she was away and his thoughts could rage, his insecurities grow fangs. She'd gone two days without writing when he got a brutally expensive toll call from her in his Binghamton hotel room. She'd whispered, "Don't go home tonight. Zari's. Eight o'clock." And hung up.

Racing through his downtown sales calls, he managed to telephone his wife to say he wouldn't get home until Saturday, then caught an afternoon train into Grand Central Station and hauled his luggage and trunk of samples with him into Zari's. The hatcheck girl gave him an indignant glare, as though he were a country goober hawking Fuller brushes, and scraped the floor as she tugged his things out of sight.

Ruth waved to him from a rectangular table for four under the mezzanine gallery, and he was introduced to her cousin, Mrs. Ethel Anderson Pierson, and to a heavyset physician in his forties who would give only his first name: Sydney. His tuxedo and white spats hinted at wealth. A fat finger was indented where his wedding ring ought to have been. Ethel was a zesty, fun-loving, pretty housewife of twenty-seven. She had greenish eyes and flaming red hair, but she had a famished look that was the first sign of the still undiagnosed tuberculosis that would kill her in September 1927.

"We aren't eating," Ruth said. "We have to go."

Dr. Syd filled his own highball glass of ginger ale and ice with bourbon from his flask and slid the hooch across to Judd as Ethel instructed him on their scheme for the night. She said she was in love with Syd and was separated from her husband, Eddie. She had no grounds for divorce yet because New York courts required proof of either extreme physical brutality or sexual infidelity. Eddie was not a smack-a-woman kind of guy, but Ethel guessed he was like a lot of bimbos on the force, extracting sex from whores instead of cuffing them, only she'd never caught him at it. She wanted to nail Eddie for alimony, so she needed a camera shot of her ex as he was entangled with some doll.

Dr. Syd translated, "In the very act of committing the offense."

"And that's where you come in," Ruth said.

Ethel reached under her chair and hauled up a rectangular leather holster containing an Autographic Kodak camera that she handed across to Judd. "We'll get in Syd's car, you'll hire a prostitute—"

"I beg your pardon?"

Syd inserted, "I can't risk losing my medical license."

"But what about *my* reputation?"

Ethel screamed, "You're a corset salesman!"

Ruth laid a hand of solace atop his. "We get some hotsy-totsy girl and take her to Eddie's apartment. She'll knock on his door and say she got stood up or something and it's freezing outside."

Judd felt offended but oddly excited. "Have you any idea how *insane* this is?" And yet he stayed there with Syd's bourbon.

Ethel said, "Eddie will let her in, maybe give her a highball, and we'll have her say how grateful she is, how can she ever repay him? Eddie's easily tempted. And when things get hot and heavy, you'll burst in and snap a picture."

"Et voilà," Syd said.

"Easy as pie," Ethel said.

Six drinks later and Judd was drunk enough to do it, strolling up to a chilly girl in a raccoon coat in what was called "the Circus" around 42nd Street. Weaving a little, he too loudly inquired, "Say there, are you a harlot?"

She gave him a *You have got to be kidding me—harlot?* look, but flashed open her raccoon coat to show she wore nothing underneath it. Judd escorted her to Syd's Packard and the five of them headed across the East River to Eddie's apartment in the Bronx.

But Eddie wasn't there. Syd and Ethel and the girl waited in the heated Packard as Ruth and Judd hung out inside the building and were so publicly affectionate in the hallway that renters were able to identify them a full year later. And when Ethel went inside again she threatened to take a Kodak picture of Judd's "hands on the prowl." They were still all over each other when Ethel kidded her older cousin, "Have you heard the saying that a man's kiss is his signature?"

Ruth unclenched and shifted her dress as she answered, "Mae West, right?"

"How's Judd sign his name?"

She smiled at him. "Legibly."

At ten Eddie still hadn't shown and the harlot reminded them that her meter was still running, so Syd ferried them back to 42nd Street and paid the girl for her time. Judd found a tailor shop with a backroom speakeasy where they sold him a 1911 quart bottle of Old Overholt Straight Rye Whiskey, and he swallowed a third of it as Ethel snuggled into Syd in the front seat and Syd drove Ruth and Judd to the Waldorf-Astoria. Looking into the rearview mirror at Judd, the physician said, "Every man has his own code of sexual morality, his own instincts of right and wrong toward womanhood. I happened to meet Ethel at the right psychological moment and our souls and beings were thrown into a turmoil of love. Those passions demand reciprocation. And so, like you, we have lavished affections upon each other despite commitments elsewhere. There is no possible weighing of responsibility to others in such a thrall as ours, and no way for me to justify termination."

Ruth joked, "Don't he talk good?"

Judd leaned forward to tell Syd in a slurred way, "It's not just lust or passion for me."

"I haven't made that accusation."

But Judd would not be overruled. "Ruth, she's my ideal of womanhood. She's a *goddess*."

After that he blacked out. Waking up fully dressed in a corner of the hotel room the next morning, he saw he'd vomited on his shirt and shoes. Ruth was in her silk kimono and sunshine filled the room. Room service had delivered coffee and cinnamon toast that morning. Holding his aching neck, he said, "I feel awful."

She glanced fleetingly at him, then sourly added cream to her coffee.

He got out of his jacket and began unbuttoning his foul shirt. "Why did you let me stay like this?"

"We argued."

"About?"

Ruth told him they'd discussed heading down to Elkton, Maryland, where lax marriage regulations meant they could have gotten hitched.

"And what did I say?"

"Well, actually you couldn't get the words right, but I think you thought that would be bigamy."

Judd was untying his shoes. "Even drunk I'm law-abiding," he said.

"Oh yeah. To a fault."

"Meaning?"

Ruth told him she'd confessed she wanted Albert out of her life, gone, buried, dead, and Judd had yelled that she was insane. Raged that she could go to jail for that. Asked if she had any idea what a homicide meant in the eyes of God.

Stripping off his stockings, Judd asked, "And what did you say?"

Ruth focused her stunning blue eyes on him and said, "I don't believe in a heaven or hell and anything like that."

"Well, that makes all this easy for you then."

"And 'all this' makes you a hypocrite."

"That's true," he said, and he went to the bathroom in his skivvies.

"Oh, let's not fight," she said.

But he was sulking. "I have to get to the office."

That evening Judd journeyed home to East Orange by trolley instead of the train, not because it was cheaper, but because he felt he needed the extra hour to find his role and rehearse his lines. He recalled his freshman year in high school when he first looked up the word: "adultery," from the Latin *adulterare,* to defile. The generality of the definition had called up a host of fantasies, and Ruth was doing the same: calling out his vices, torturing him with affection, exhausting him with liquor and schemes and secrecy and shocking sexual practices until he felt dirtied and defiled. She'd seduced and dominated him, he thought, held his yearning heart in her hands, fondly and expertly played his frailties and hankerings as if he were her pet, her toy.

And yet he found it impossible to stop desiring her, and if there was any infidelity, he thought, it was in his grim and loveless marriage to Isabel, a wedding of unequals that was now not just defiled but dead. All he could offer his wife in the future were the leftover scraps of an old friendship. And all she could offer him was his daughter. But that was enough. Jane was the glue.

Walking up Wayne Avenue to his house, he was still inventing a night in which he told Isabel all about his affair and of his plans to end it, acknowledging that he would have to endure his wife's wretched tears and full-throated screaming, Mrs. K's interference and scorn, little Jane's worries and pain.

But when he got to number 37, he found the front sidewalk and driveway had not been shoveled, just shuffled through by overboots during the week, and he went back to the garage with his heavy luggage, his shoes crunching in the snow, his ears and nose smarting in the near-zero cold as he hauled down the snow shovel from its nail on a wall. And then he saw all three females skeptically watching him through the kitchen window, without gratitude or even welcome, as if whatever slavish job he carried out was a job long overdue. Judd demonstrated his insolence by hanging the wide shovel back on its nail and trudging through snow to the kitchen and the scandal of his Scotch whisky.

There were, finally, some pleasantries after that, some journalism at dinner about the past week's doings, Jane's joyless acceptance of the gift of a jeweled barrette, and Isabel's quiet accommodation of his imaginary lust that night. It all seemed unreal, like the alliances of hotel guests sharing a restaurant table or some radio voice in the club room. Waking in the middle of the night, Judd saw his luggage on the floor, the hinged jaws opened, his blue canvas laundry bag now gone to the basement but his toiletries still there and much of his clothing still neatly folded, as if this were just another stay-over and he'd soon be ready to journey onward.

In the morning, Judd took Jane to Sunday school but let Isabel and Mrs. Kallenbach go to the church service without him, as shame caused him to lie that his mother wanted him sooner than noon.

Mrs. Margaret Gray was surprised by his earliness and not yet fully dressed, but she gave him fresh coffee and a slice of hot apple pie that she'd made from a jar of preserves. And then, as always, she just watched him eat. She said she didn't know if she'd be putting up fruits and vegetables next summer. It was so hard on her hands and arms. She wondered if he was getting enough sleep. Was he losing weight? Bud seemed kind of mopey to her; he seemed to have something on his mind. She didn't see the point of his visiting if he wasn't going to chat. Oh no, she didn't have errands for him or anything else that needed doing. "You go have a nice afternoon with that little girl of yours," Margaret Gray said. "She's been missing her daddy, I'll bet."

As a state senator, Jimmy Walker got legislation passed that allowed attendance at movies, plays, and public sporting events on Sunday afternoons. So Judd could take his daughter to the Orpheum theater and a matinee showing of *The Lost World*. He asked her as he bought the nickel tickets, "Have you heard of the famous English sleuth Sherlock Holmes?"

Jane nodded uncertainly.

"Well, this movie we're going to see is based on an original novel by Sir Arthur Conan Doyle."

She seemed mystified.

"Sir Arthur Conan Doyle created Sherlock Holmes."

"Oh." Jane seemed downcast. "Is this a mystery?"

"No, it's science fiction."

"I hate science."

"Don't say 'hate.'" Judd guided his daughter inside the theater and found she disliked the seats he chose, so they moved. Seeking to get her to smile, he asked, "Where does the general keep his armies?"

She sighed.

"Have I told you that one?"

Improbably bored, Jane asked, "Up his *sleevies*?"

She's been poisoned, he thought, and ran out of things to say to her. But for more than half an hour he just watched her watch the movie, loving how flashes of on-screen light flared in her widened eyes and how the raging dinosaurs scared Jane enough that she once clutched his hand and cowered into him so that half her face hid in his overcoat sleeve. But the scene ended too soon and she sat up again and she coolly extricated her hand from his, just as Isabel would have.

ᔦ ᔦ

Ruth finished the Sunday-night dishes thinking of Judd, and she was thinking of Judd as she wiped the kitchen stove's white enamel, the humming Frigidaire, the soft suede of the kitchen's maple countertops, then tossed the damp dish towel down the laundry chute. She felt addicted to Judd and desperate for him, and when she heard Albert whistling in his basement workshop she hated the noise so much she held her hands to her ears as she hurried to the foyer. She failed in the effort to calm herself as she called in Swedish, *"Moder?"*

Josephine Brown was upstairs helping Lora with her multiplication tables. She walked out to the hallway and quizzically looked down.

"How about a luncheon here tomorrow?"

"You mean with a guest?"

Ruth was queasy with urgency, but she fashioned a smile. "Winter's gotten so dreary."

With solemnity, her mother said, "But, May, it's wash day!"

Ruth felt herself getting faint and held on to the staircase banister. She was lovesick and afraid she'd either scream or whine. She shook as she said, "We can finish that in the morning. There's not much. I'll cook."

Josephine fell into Swedish. *"Vilken?"* Who?

"My friend, Mr. Gray? The Bien Jolie salesman? The baby's met him."

Lorraine heard her mother and called out, "Yes. He's nice."

"Another one of your men?" Josephine asked.

Hinting broadly, Ruth said, "Mama, he sells *lingerie.*"

Josephine shrugged and said, *"Fint."* Okay.

Worried about seeming impatient, Ruth slowed her walk as she went to the kitchen telephone.

Mrs. Kallenbach answered. Judd was reading *The Saturday*

Evening Post and heard his mother-in-law say, "Hello," and "Yes, he is." And he was getting up from his purple mohair armchair when his mother-in-law called, "Bud? Your secretary?"

He hesitated with the intimation that it was Ruth. She'd never called him at home. Rarely did so at work. Judd took the earpiece from Mrs. K with a "Thank you" that he hoped would dismiss her, but she stayed in the kitchen, busying herself with tidying up in order to overhear. Tilting into the wall phone's mouthpiece, he said, "Hello, Rachel. What's up?"

Ruth asked, "Will you come to lunch at my house tomorrow?"

Judd framed his answer with Mrs. K in mind. "Who's going to be there?"

"Just my mother and me. Oh please, won't you?"

Watchful of his tone, he said, "I could."

"Oh, I'm so excited! One o'clock. Was that Isabel who answered?"

"No. My mother-in-law."

"Is she listening now?"

"Yes."

"Because I wanted you to say how much you love me."

Without inflection he said, "I do."

"Shall I give you instructions on how to get here?"

"I'll handle it. See you tomorrow."

She softly whispered, "I'm so horny for you."

Judd blushed as he hung up the earpiece. Mrs. K was scowling. "We have buyers in town now because of the spring line," he said. "I have to see some clients for lunch."

"She sounds pretty." She knew Rachel was not.

"Oh, that wasn't Rachel. She has someone filling in for her."

"But you called her that."

"She corrected me." And then he sneered. "Women do that."

On Monday, Josephine Brown lifted the lid on the basement washing machine, and Ruth plunged a broomstick into the hot water to heave out a heavy weight of towels that her mother fed into the electric wringer so that sheets of soapy water slid back into the drum for the next load. They did not speak. It was far too cold to hang things in the yard, so Ruth collected the wringings and hung them on the white rope clotheslines that Albert had strung from the ceiling joists. She'd already clothespinned on the lines his dress shirts and what Mrs. Brown called his "unmentionables." Albert's whites were always the first wash. Then Josephine's and Lora's colors. And new piping-hot water and Fels-Naptha soap for the household sheets and towels. Ruth took her own clothing to the Chinese dry cleaners on Springfield Boulevard or laundered them by hand in the upstairs bathroom sink and rinsed them with vinegar and boiling water from a kettle.

With the hamper things drying, she went upstairs and waxed the furniture, vacuumed, and put out Tiffany ashtrays for Judd's cigarettes wherever he was likely to sit. She was as persnickety a housekeeper as Isabel was, she took pride in her cooking, she even put up preserves each summer, but she knew Judd had never seen her that way. She was just a flapper he partied with, his sex partner in the Waldorf. And he was born to be a husband.

She hadn't yet learned how to drive, so although Albert's Buick was still in his garage she phoned for a Yellow Cab that took her to Jamaica Avenue and waited as she bought a pound of lump crabmeat at the Fishmongery. She had the taxi idle in front of Paper & Pens while she hunted through the bootlegged wines in the storeroom and found a pricey bottle of Sauvignon Blanc from Bordeaux. She then got cash from the secret "Ruth M. Brown" account at the Queens-Bellaire bank and hand-delivered to Leroy Ashfield the weekly payment for the Prudential insurance policies on Albert's life.

At home, she pinched shell fragments from the crabmeat and

mixed it with an egg white, flour, chives, cayenne pepper, and kosher salt, and formed it into eight patties that she chilled with the wine in the Frigidaire. She went up to the bedroom to change as Mrs. Brown set the dining room table.

Judd took the Long Island Rail Road from Pennsylvania Station to Jamaica and a taxi to a cream-yellow house with green trim on the corner of 222nd Street and 93rd Road. And he was just getting out when he saw Ruth dashing from the front door to him in just her shoes and navy blue housedress, though it was stingingly cold. She grinned as she called out, "Oh, I'm so happy!" She hugged him, saying she regretted she could do no more because of the neighbors. She linked a forearm inside his as they headed toward the white Colonial front door. She pointed to the one-car garage to the right. "We used to have a bigger side yard," she said, "but Albert wanted a hospital for his automobile, so he built that one from a Sears, Roebuck kit. He likes to use his hands, and not just for hitting me."

Was she joking? Judd was going to ask when the front door opened and a dour but friendly Mrs. Josephine Brown called in greeting, *"Välkommen!"* Welcome.

Judd took off his gray buckskin gloves to shake her hand and she said formally, "I have heard May speak so much about you and your fine dancing." She took his overcoat and hat to the foyer closet as generalities about his job and the January weather were exchanged. She frankly said, "You are not very tall, are you?"

"Oh, I can reach just about anything I need."

She listened longer than necessary and asked, "Are you the reaching sort?"

Judd felt like a thief in their house. Was she calling him that? "Well, no," he said. "Things just generally fall to me."

She evaluated him for a moment, and then she privately confided, "May must be careful not to get the Mister jealous with you."

Judd sought to change the subject so he asked how old she was when she first learned English.

"Sixteen."

She still spoke in the metronomic cadence of Swedish, and with a certain daintiness to the *t* sound, but he said, "Well, you're very easy to understand."

"Tack," she said regally. Thanks. She asked his own nationality and he told her English, that his forebears landed in Connecticut on the *Mary and John* in 1630. She took that in and said, "So your folk, they are aristocrats?"

"We're just established, is all."

She said he could call her "Granny," just as Lora and Albert did.

Judd didn't; he called her Josephine. She wore severe round spectacles and was his own mother's age, sixty, though she would claim to be four years younger when the lot of them became famous. She went off and Judd plinked a child's tune on the Aeolian, then lit a cigarette as he sat alone on a floral chintz armchair. Reading the jacket upside down, he noted a booklet on the coffee table entitled *The Modern Home: How to Take Advantage of Mechanical Servants.* A newly purchased Bible, Emily Post's *Etiquette,* and *The Outline of History* by H. G. Wells were the odd family of books on a shelf. And Josephine seemed to have been reading a *McCall's* magazine when he got there. Looking at the contents, he saw an article about the incompatibility of "the stay-at-home husband and the delicatessen wife," and he was paging to it when Ruth called him to the kitchen.

It had the hospital-clean, impeccable look he associated with Scandinavia, with a polished linoleum floor, brilliant snow-white tile, and a new refrigerator and gas range in newly fashionable white enamel, with some pretty accents of Delft blue in the curtains and accessories. Judd said, "This must require no end of work to keep in such spotless condition."

"Oh, it's not work," Ruth said. "We love to scrub and scour and make everything shine, don't we, Mama?"

She agreed by quoting, "Idle hands are the devil's tools." Josephine put the crab cakes in a skillet and said, "I'll finish the cooking, Maisie. You let your friend see the house."

Ruth took him down to the basement to proudly display rack after rack of widemouthed mason jars filled with the fruit preserves and garden vegetables she'd put up in August. She said, "You may not have noticed, but in this part of the tour we see what a good wife I am."

But vying for Judd's attention were Albert's dress shirts and boxers, hanging on the clothesline like flags of ownership. And then to the left there was Albert's workshop and its organized tools, his glass tank of fermenting wort, his poster of a naked Josephine Baker dancing in Paris's *Folies Bergère*. Resisting her husband's ghostly presence, Judd fitted himself behind Ruth and kissed her neck, and she grabbed his hands to her breasts and felt him hardening before she moaned, "We'd better not get started."

She took his right hand and urged him upstairs and through the kitchen to the gleaming dining room, where she held up a glinting silver spoon. She vainly stated, "Chambly, from France." She then gently touched a crystal wineglass and said, "Baccarat."

"Lovely things," Judd said.

"And that vase on the sideboard is a Lalique."

Josephine heard and called from the kitchen, "But she's thrifty, too! May sewed all the drapes and curtains her own self!"

Judd winked and called back, "I just knew she'd have to be good with her hands!"

Ruth smiled but swatted his forearm to hush him. She took him into the foyer and held up a photograph of a simpering, sweet-faced woman in the full covering of a white Victorian gown, her great length of black hair piled up on her head in a fashion from before the Great War. She was sitting beside a tweed-suited, bow-tied, ruminative man in his twenties with wavy, receding, sand-colored hair, his hands knitted as he reclined on his left forearm on a rough altar of flat stone, seemingly near the ocean.

"I presume that's The Governor," Judd said.

"And his first love, Jessie Guischard. A public-school teacher and, as he puts it, 'the finest woman' he's ever met. Which means finer than me. She died of pneumonia in nineteen-twelve, just before he could marry her. The dead are difficult rivals." Ruth put the photograph back. "Al's got a scrapbook filled with his captioned pictures of her: 'Jessie relaxing in the Catskills,' 'Jessie blowing a kiss in the Adirondacks.' Albert used to own a motor yacht with the name 'Jessie' painted on its transom. After we married, I forced him to rename it 'Ruth' and he did, but then he lost interest and sold it. Each day when he gets into his suit jacket, his finishing touch is a stickpin with the initials 'J.G.' so he can hold her next to his heart."

"The Governor's a piece of work, isn't he?"

"You ain't kiddin'." Ruth looked toward the Aeolian player piano and chintz furniture, a sunroom beyond them. She found nothing to say but, "Those are his paintings on the walls." And she crossed her ice-blue eyes in a funny estimation of the artistry. She whistled sharply once and a yellow canary instantly sailed from its golden cage in the sunroom and roosted on her right shoulder, where it furtively sidled over to nuzzle its beak below her ear.

"You trained it to do that?"

She smiled. "I have a way with animals." She kissed the air and the canary tapped its beak against her pursed lips. "This is Pip," she said. "Pip's the canary in *Little Women*. Have you read it?"

"No."

"At last. I have found a hole in your education." She then took him by the hand again. "Upstairs."

There were two photographs of Albert laughing with dogs in the hallway: one with a stocky boxer held next to his face, and another with a hound between his shins. And yet Ruth oddly told Judd in passing, "Albert hates pets."

At the south end was a bathroom that seemed to have been cleansed with the same 20 Mule Team Borax that Isabel used. Across from that was Lorraine's room, which looked so much like Jane's that he felt a pang. But Ruth pulled him to Josephine's room, just above the front-door vestibule and foyer, with white, nineteenth-century furniture from the Old Country and a pink velour chair. And finally she opened the door to the northern master bedroom. She grinned. "And this is where you'll be sleeping."

"Don't know that I like the twin beds," he said.

"We can change that. Right now the gulf between those beds is just what the doctor ordered."

Hanging high up on the wall and between the twin beds was an oval picture frame with a sculpted mahogany bow and inside it a studio photograph of what seemed to be a raven-haired Jessie Guischard as a girl.

"You have *got* to be kidding me," Judd said.

"Albert says it's not her, it's just a picture he happens to like. But he stares at it as he's having at me."

Judd shook his head. "What a thoroughgoing cad he is."

"*Cad?* Wha'ja do, walk out of some Dickens novel?"

Josephine called, "Luncheon, you two!"

Ruth asked the canary, "Wanna go night-night?" and Pip flew down to his first-floor cage.

Judd whispered, "This is sheer happiness, just being with you." She took the fleeting opportunity to kiss him, and Judd's palm cherished his lover's sensuous hip as they went down to the dining room.

There Mrs. Brown served Ruth's crab cakes with Ruth's

coleslaw and roasted potatoes and the Sauvignon Blanc that only Judd drank, and finally finished off. Josephine seemed untroubled by that, and Ruth abetted it.

Judd was generally a hit with older women, and Josephine, too, seemed prejudiced in his favor, noticing his good manners, his suave flattery, his handsomeness and fine tailoring. Josephine would much later claim she knew he was no gentleman from the first time she met him, that "he seemed like a slick fellow" to her, but that afternoon she enjoyed the way he focused his full attention on her when she spoke, how his hand touched hers whenever he teased, how he could make her laugh with his funny anecdotes about selling lingerie in farm villages or meeting the likes of Romney Brent, Sterling Holloway, and Libby Holman backstage at the Garrick Theatre.

Retiring to the music room so he could smoke, Josephine flirtingly sat on the sofa with him as Ruth went to the dining room to collect the glassware and dishes. But as she did so she called for him to tell Mama a Swedish joke.

Judd was drunk enough that he was forced to think hard, and then he told her, "A Swedish immigrant not in the least like you was hired to paint the white center stripes on a highway. His foreman carried over a bucket of white paint and put it on the ground and handed him a paintbrush and said, 'Go to it!' And he was very happy to note that the hardworking Swede completed a full mile of road on the first day! But the foreman was disappointed that the hired man only painted a hundred yards' worth of stripes the next day, and he was fit to be tied when the Swede finished a mere thirty feet on the third. Catching up to him that afternoon, the foreman asked what the heck the problem was. Well, the Swede was panting as he straightened up and pointed his paintbrush backward to the horizon and said, 'It just be dat da paint bucket ist getting so far a-vay.'"

Josephine hooted and slapped both hands on her thighs. She said, "Oh, that's rich!" She noticed that his wineglass was empty and she took it with her to the kitchen. Judd felt forsaken. And then she returned with a square glass filled with Scotch for him. "I have to say I was leery at first, but you are *such* a delight, Mr. Gray. And it's so nice to have a gentleman here instead of—" She left the sentence hanging as she glanced to the dining room to see that her daughter was out of earshot. "May's *so* unhappy, and Albert don't care. It just ain't right."

"Which reminds me," Judd said. "Do you know how to keep a German sailor from drowning?"

Josephine wrinkled a smile as she warily answered, "No."

And Judd said, "Good!"

Ruth heard that and found it hilarious.

And then the front door opened and it was Lorraine returning from grammar school. Seeing him, the affectionate eight-year-old grinned and without getting out of her cold overcoat ran into his hug, yelling, "Mr. Gray!" She kissed him on the mouth just as she'd seen her mother kiss him. "You'll stay and play with me, won't you?"

Judd said, "Just for a little bit, sweetie." And he gazed over her pretty blonde pageboy haircut to Ruth, who was glorying over their happy, happy family and the grand future that was just in front of them.

The following Saturday in February, Albert hauled a sixteen-foot ladder to the front sidewalk and banged it up against the huge elm tree that was older than their house and taller than its roof beam. Jamming the ladder feet into frozen sod, he ascended with a ripsaw to get rid of some dead, shedding limbs that threatened to tear loose and crash on his car whenever flustered by the wind. Shifting his weight as he fought the binding of saw teeth and wood grain, he felt the ladder teeter and then fall from his foothold so that he had to lunge for a limb and hang there some twenty feet from the ground. Looking down he saw Ruth just below, holding a grocery bag and staring up with fascination.

"Don't just stand there! Help me!"

She rested the groceries on the frosted sidewalk before gloomily heaving up the ladder again. "Lucky I chanced by," she said.

She was soon recognized as Mrs. Gray by the staff at the Waldorf-Astoria and would be given their lockered honeymoon bag and their regular room, number 832, even before Judd could get there and register. The first time the concierge told him, "Mrs. Gray is waiting for you upstairs," Judd felt a jolt of panic that his wife or mother had found out about his infidelity. But "Mrs. Gray" was gloriously naked on the hotel bed, like a glamorous concubine in a Turkish harem, and all thoughts of his wife or mother flew.

Ruth's thirty-first birthday, on March 27th, 1926, fell on a Saturday and she'd made arrangements with her stodgy husband to celebrate it with an all-too-uncommon party at their house, to which, of course, Judd could not be invited. So she met him at Henry's Restaurant on that Friday. But Lorraine's school was out, and Josephine Brown was nursing someone in Brooklyn, so the little girl accompanied her mother. Judd had already registered for a room at the Waldorf but hid his disappointment with friendly affection and jokes. Lorraine ate a grilled cheese sandwich. The lovers ordered lobster Newburg on points of toast and Judd gave Ruth a birthday gift of Parfum Madame by the house of D'Orsay. And then, on the walk to Penn Station, Ruth sweetly asked, "Baby, could you stay in the Waldorf lobby while Mr. Gray and I go upstairs?"

Judd was shocked, as was the jury later, but up to their room he went, with Ruth waving gaily to her daughter as the elevator doors closed. Lorraine slumped in an overlarge chair under the lobby's golden chandeliers, watching the hands on the huge bronze clock until it was one fifteen and the Westminster chimes rang. She'd have been frightened or bored but it was afternoon and the guests around her seemed so jubilant. A bellhop bent down to say, "Hi, little girl. You like that clock?"

"Uh-huh."

"It was created for the Chicago World's Fair."

"Oh."

"Don't kick your shoes against the chair," he said.

She got up and wandered down the glamorous, mirrored hallway called Peacock Alley that connected the old Waldorf mansion to the Astoria. Lorraine took after her mother in the joy of liberty and movement. She twirled underneath the grand chandelier in the Empire Room, where the Waldorf-Astoria Orchestra was rehearsing for its Saturday-night radio program. She touched all the floral greens in a Palm Garden that was being arranged for a dinner, and she stepped into the gray cloud of cigarette smoke in the North Café, where it seemed a hundred loud businessmen stood at the four-sided bar and a waiter finally shooed her away.

Upstairs in the overheated room, Judd fell back against the headboard, still naked and wheezing with exhaustion. "Oh, Momsie!" he said. "That was wonderful!"

"Uh-huh," she said. "*You* were." She grazed her large breasts against his stomach as she tenderly tugged his condom off him and tossed it into a tin trash can. And then she groused, "It's so *hot*!" She got up to lift the sash on a double-hung window.

Judd watched. "What a gorgeous derrière you've got. It's like an upside-down heart on a valentine." He put his thumbs and forefingers together to imitate the shape and held them out to spy her buttocks within them. "So sexy. So perfect."

Cold air gave her gooseflesh and she crawled onto him, resting her chin on his chest. She watched as he reached for his cigarettes, lit a Sweet Caporal, then coughed as he exhaled it. She said, "I'm fascinated by whatever you do. Each action, each word you use. Like 'derrière.' It's all so different and odd—in a good way."

"Oh, I'm a wowser of an entertainer. That's how I make my sales."

She laid her head to the side and skimmed her fingertip along a bulging vein in his wrist. "I have these wild dreams. We find a little bamboo hut in Tahiti, right on the South Pacific. White sand and soft breezes. We're like this. Without clothes. Like Adam and Eve. And we find our food hanging on trees." She got up to her forearms. "And I have this other one. Wisconsin. I haven't ever been there, but I imagine this pretty little farm. We raise peaches and grapes and apples and take them to market in these great big baskets. Would it be a dairy farm, too? We'd have cows you and Lora could milk and there'd be white and blue pans in the kitchen and willow trees overhanging this sweet little brook. We'd have chickens and eggs and homemade bread . . ."

"Wisconsin seems rather grueling."

"Don't you see, Bud? We could be happy there, or Burma, or Timbuktu." She got distracted as she twisted his forelock with a finger. She tucked a tuft of hair behind his ear.

"Are you grooming me?"

She petted his head. "We just need to be together. With Albert gone so he won't get in the way. Really, Judd, whatever you do, wherever you want to go, I'll go with you."

Judd smiled. "Have you read The Book of Ruth?"

She felt accused. "I don't think so."

Judd slid open the drawer in the side table to seek a Gideon Bible. "It's in the Old Testament."

"Then definitely not."

Riffling through the pages, he said, "It's right after The Book of Judges." He turned a few more. "Here. Chapter one, verses sixteen and seventeen. 'And Ruth said, Intreat me not to leave thee, or to return from following after thee: for whither thou goest, I will go; and where thou lodgest, I will lodge: thy people shall be my people, and thy God my God. Where thou diest, will I die, and there will I be buried: the Lord do so to me, and more also, if ought but death part thee and me.'"

"Oh, that's so beautiful," she said, as if it wasn't. She angrily got up from him and curtsied to get her clothing from the floor. "Lorraine will be waiting for us."

"Is there something wrong?"

She skewered him with a fierce glare as she said, "*Intreat* me not."

"I have no idea what I've done, Ruth."

She was seething as she got into her underwear. "You don't take me seriously, that's what. 'Where thou diest, will I die'? Well, I *am* dying, *Loverboy*. And you're watching it happen. Because you're lazy and weak and it's easier that way. All you can think of is how oh-so-pleased you are to get your piece of 'upside-down heart' on a regular basis."

Judd stabbed out his cigarette and stood to get his own clothing on. "But, really, what am I supposed to do?"

She raged, "Albert! Gone! Get it?"

Riding in the elevator, Lorraine watched the hand on the floor indicator halt at eight and the old, blue-jacketed operator slid the doors open. The little girl was surprised and pleased to find her mother and Mr. Gray standing there, though Mr. Gray seemed unhappy. "Hi!" she said.

Ruth smiled. "Were you having fun, baby?"

"She was my company," the old operator said. "We've been riding up and down."

"We've been doing that, too," Judd said.

Ruth's health was affected that spring. She went to Dr. Harry Hansen, a family physician in the neighborhood, and complained of fainting spells, occasional loud and rapid heartbeats followed by a lingering soreness, occasional swellings in the throat that made her feel she was being strangled, increasingly scarce monthly periods, and a horrible depression or melancholy that could cause her to become hot-tempered or disintegrate into a flood of tears. Dr. Hansen's workup found her heart weakened, her thyroid enlarged, and her system anemic, but he failed to diagnose that Ruth was in fact describing the first stage of Graves' disease. He gave her iron and iodine tablets and a box of Midol. He turned away as she got into her clothing and he heard her say, "I also have these queer feelings of doom, like something tragic is going to happen."

"Oh, it will," the doctor said. "We all die."

Office work on Saturdays was standard for even high-level jobs then, and Ruth and her daughter frequently met Judd at Henry's at one o'clock and joined him for the *Ziegfeld Follies*, children's theater, or motion picture matinees afterward. But on one afternoon when the baby stayed home with her father, Ruth insisted on riding the trolley to East Orange with Judd, squeezing his hand with giggling excitement that she might be recognized as "the other woman" if Judd's friends or neighbors got on board, and then just kissing Judd good-bye at his stop and riding an eastbound trolley back to the city.

And one night in April when it was still light at seven, he got to his front door and felt watched, and he saw Ruth in the grim black clothing of a widow, far down Wayne Avenue, just observing his nightly routine. Judd initiated a move toward her, but Ruth turned away and walked off.

Because of his Elks club membership in Orange, Judd was permitted entrance to the Elks lodge in downtown Syracuse and he invited a Barringer High School classmate, Haddon Jones, to join him for a luncheon after Judd made his morning sales calls. Haddon was a tall, rail-thin man with slicked-back hair, horsey ears, and a pen-line mustache. He sold insurance and real estate for Hills and Company and was, as he said, "doing quite well, thank you. The business, she booms."

Sitting at the Elks club bar, Judd ordered, "Medicinal whiskeys for both of us, Doctor."

The Elks bartender disdainfully said, "I'm no doctor."

"I tell a lie," Judd said. "You are a *pharmacist* with a limited inventory!"

Haddon grinned and said, "I seem to have some catching up to do."

"Emptied my flask by eleven."

"Burying your sorrows?"

"Exactly the otherwise, my good man. I'm belated. Excuse me, *elated*. I have a paramour of great beauty who is not my wife and to whom I am now affianced. Without sanctification of God or state, mind you." Judd tapped his forehead. "But *mentally*. Have I showed you her picture?"

"This is the first we talked about it."

Judd struggled with his trousers as he got out his wallet and flattened its wings on the bar with both hands. Then he meticulously pinched a photograph of Ruth out and put it next to Haddon's rye whiskey. "I shall not tell you her name for she is legally spoken for. But I would like your frankest evolution—evaluation, excuse me—and we shall determine if you need your eyeses examined."

Haddon held up the photograph and turned on his bar stool to find better light. "She's beautiful."

"Beautiful, yes. Entirely just assessment. But you are too moderate in your opinion because you have not drunken enough the alchemy of the poet. And, I must be frank, the picture does not do her justice. She is a *goddess*."

"You guys on the road. You got 'em coming and going, don't you?"

Judd shook his head and wagged a finger. "But there you are wrong, sir. She has *me*."

Ruth preheated the kitchen oven and simmered a cup of pitted prunes in a saucepan until they were soft. Mrs. Brown was in her nurse's whites, heading out to a five-dollar job night-watching an old woman who'd broken her hip. Scowling at the ingredients on the counter, she asked Ruth, "Are you making a *prune whip*?"

"Yes."

"But you don't like prunes. Lora won't eat them."

"Albert does."

Josephine linked shut the neck of her brown cape as she said, "Well, don't hold your breath waiting for his thank-you." She went out the kitchen door.

Ruth pureed the prunes in the saucepan and used a hand egg beater to stir in and dissolve one-third of a cup of sugar. She added a teaspoon of lemon juice, a teaspoon of vanilla, then hand-mixed six egg whites in a separate bowl and dripped some cream of tartar into the froth and hand-mixed again until the froth stiffened. She found her purse on the kitchen table and got out a packet of gray powder. Her hand circled the froth of egg whites as she poisoned it with the powder, and then she folded in the prune puree and poured the mixture into a buttered and sugared baking dish. She baked the dessert for forty minutes, chilled it, and after that night's dinner served it to Albert with whipped cream.

She confessed what she'd done the next afternoon at Henry's. She told Judd she and The Governor fell into a gruesome argument and she'd become so incensed that she'd poisoned him.

Judd exclaimed in a hushed way, "You *didn't*!"

She nodded, and hot tears fluently ran down her face.

"And Albert?"

She carelessly said, "Oh, he just vomited all night."

"But why would you do such a thing?"

She shrugged and sobbed, "I wanted to see what effect it had on him."

"How'd you get the poison?"

She caught her breath and said, "Actually, it was only an overdose of medicine I got at Spindler's."

"Still, it would have been murder!"

She couldn't stanch her tears even with the linen table napkin. Restaurant staff were frowning and confiding about them. Harry Folsom was dining alone and filling out a hosiery order but heard Judd's raised voice and scowled from across the room.

"Don't *yell* at me," Ruth said. "I wasn't trying to *kill* him. I was just angry and irritated. And it was like an experiment."

Judd fell back in the booth and stared at Ruth, fully appalled. "I find your experiment loathsome. Wild, thoughtless actions like that—it's really beyond the pale."

"I hate him so much, though. There's no love, no friendship, no interest in me. He either treats me like his servant or his whore."

And then she halted and her face changed, and it was as if he'd turned a page in a book, or rather, as if he'd been reading one book and then gone to another, for she glared at him with a ferocity he'd never seen before, stood up from the table, gripped her muskrat coat at her neck, and said with so much venom she seemed to hiss, "But I guess I had you figured wrong. I guess you're a coward and a sissy. You won't help or defend me because Albert's a he-man, and you're just a low, cringing sneak who's out to get his jollies with me, nothing more."

Judd was so hurt and astonished he could only gape as she spun away and hurried to the entrance. He was getting up to rush after her when she stopped with a hand reaching out to the door and then seemed to crumple. She fell to her knees in a faint before Judd could get to her. With jostling emotions, Judd crouched over Ruth as she lay unconscious on the floor and he saw a face that wore the innocence of a sleeping child.

Waiters and onlookers crowded around as Judd gently patted her cheek and said, "Ruth. Ruth, wake up."

Harry Folsom scooped crushed ice from the smorgasbord and folded it inside a wet hand towel that he stooped to put on Ruth's forehead.

She seemed to gradually feel it and fluttered her eyelids and then focused on Judd and smiled. "Hi," she said.

"You fainted. You said hurtful things."

She ignored that to say, "Hi, Harry."

"Hiya, Tommy. You feel okay?"

She gazed up at all the strangers surrounding her. "I feel like a celebrity."

Harry Folsom smiled. "Well, maybe that's your destiny, toots."

⌒ ⌒

Judd later wrote in his memoir:

> *As to conditions in my home, we had reached the stage that so many couples reach in their married life. We were just floating with the tide. The overpowering consciousness of guilt caused me to lie awake night after night, trying to work out my problem until I exhaustedly fell asleep. And vowing that the thing could go on no longer. I did not know that I was so steeped in this poisonous infatuation that it ultimately would hold me in the grip of death.*

Ruth knew he idolized her and she loved his infatuation. But she loved even more the exercise of power over Judd, an intoxicating authority and governance she'd never felt in school, on a job, with Albert, or even with Lorraine. She'd softly tease Judd's naked torso with a pheasant feather until he was giggling and excited, and then she'd shock him with a hard slap to the face. She'd kiss him with great tenderness and then abruptly spit into his mouth. She called him cruel names during intercourse so he'd ram her in a hot rage. She made him grovel and feel off balance and then she'd coo and caress him as he rounded into a fetal position at her feet.

Eventually, she brought two quarts of ersatz Scotch whisky up to their room in the Waldorf-Astoria and affectionately watched him as he finished a water glass of it.

She asked, "How is it?"

Judd coughed. "That's the strongest, queerest stuff I ever tasted."

"This will help," she said. She got her green alligator handbag and took out two small vials of powder. She dumped one vial into the water glass and filled it with more whisky. "Bottoms up," she said.

Judd hesitated. "What is it?"

"Remember that Johnny at Creedmoor Psychiatric? The orderly? He stole it for me. We know what it does to his patients. I want to see what effect it has on you."

He held up the glass, inspecting its contents. Some fine grains of powder still swirled and clouded the whisky and descended in it like flakes of snow. "And I do that for what reason?"

She was all sweetness as she said, "Because I asked you to."

Judd drank it down.

She asked, "Aftertaste?"

He winced. "Yes, it's bitter."

"Here," she said, and repeated the earlier process with the other powder. "Sample it first," she said.

Judd just dipped his tongue to it.

"Can you detect it?"

"Yes. Like that sweet syrup in Chinese food."

"Okay, maybe that's better. Drink it down."

"But what will it do to me?"

Her face was innocent, even daft. "I'm not sure."

"I could be poisoned."

She fiercely told him, "Oh, just *do* it, Judd!"

Judd obeyed. And soon he was affected. At first he couldn't stop pacing the room, but he felt he was on stilts and he finally had to lie down. Wherever he looked, the hotel room seemed acres wide and as high as a cathedral. Air molecules struck his eyes like cold raindrops. His hearing changed so that Ruth's sentences seemed to find him from a great distance. She was telling him she had to get home to Queens Village that night. Judd gallantly walked her to the hotel room's door but then fell onto the bed, and he was sitting by the telephone and staring at the intriguing topography of his fingertips when Ruth called up from the lobby to find out how he was.

Hearing his slurred sentences and senselessness, she said,

"Don't leave the room! Stay there! Sleep! I'll be back for you in the morning."

But Judd must have gone out because he had a faint memory of a funny little lunchroom and a Reuben sandwich, and around four in the morning he found himself back in the room offering the Waldorf-Astoria's night porter all his dollar bills.

Ruth called him at nine on Saturday morning. "And now how do you feel?"

"Terrible. Everything's veiled. I can hardly navigate."

"Well, you need to snap out of it. Don't go to work. Call in sick. I'll be there in a jiffy."

An hour later she found him sleeping in a filled bathtub, its hot water now cold and his head just inches away from drowning. She woke and washed and toweled him. Judd got his Gillette safety razor and insisted on shaving himself, but she felt his face and informed him he already had. She ordered room service coffee and Bayer aspirin for his headache as he dressed. And then she smiled. "Well, I nearly finished you, didn't I?" And to his silence she said, "Oh, don't pout!"

Judd was a wreck, but he could totter forward if his hand braced him against the wall. Ruth hugged his waist as if he were an invalid and gave him instructions about each shift and forward movement. She paid a cashier eight dollars for the room and the chipper girl said, "Please join us again, Mrs. Gray."

Walking fraily down to Pennsylvania Station with her, Judd said, "You have achieved supremacy, you know. I have relinquished my will and judgment. Because I'm so helplessly in love."

She disdainfully said, "You're mewling."

"And you're demeaning!"

She deflected that by noticing a fierce orange chow chow that was leashed to a fire hydrant and was snarling and leaping at shying passersby, his jaws and fangs chomping at the air near their bodies until the taut leash hauled him by the neck to the sidewalk and he got up even angrier. "Oh, look at the doggie!" Ruth said. "Want to pet him?"

Hearing her, a shocked man said, "That chow's vicious, lady!"

"Oh, applesauce!" she said. And she called in that soothing, silken stroke of a voice, "Hi, sweetie! Hi, baby!" as she crouched toward the bulky dog that now cocked his head with curiosity. She got on her knees and face-to-face with him, and he sniffed her hair and then licked her. She giggled to Judd, "Don't you love dog kisses?"

But Judd was thinking, *My God. That's me.*

FIVE

SOMEONE TO WATCH OVER ME

In June 1926, Albert Snyder rented a gray vacation cottage on Shore Road just off Setauket Harbor on Long Island Sound. Around that time, Judd Gray matched him by renting a waterfront house on the Atlantic Ocean that was less than an hour's drive southeast at Shinnecock Bay. Each husband took the train to the hot streets of Manhattan on Monday mornings, stayed alone at home for three nights, then journeyed back to his wife, daughter, and mother-in-law on Thursday evenings for salt air and sunshine on three-day weekends.

Each morning as Judd went into the city, and each evening when he went out to the cedar-shingled waterfront house, he realized there was a good chance The Governor would be a passenger with him for at least half the jostling ride, and Judd would find himself strolling through each of the railroad cars like a conductor, scanning the faces for some glimpse of Ruth's offensive husband.

But there were so many gruff, haggard, and indignant men in nearly identical suits and hats that it was impossible to interpret who could have been the tweed-jacketed Albert in that prewar photograph Judd had seen. Had he encountered him, Judd thought he would say, *You are hateful and unjust* or *She deserves so much better*. But in rehearsal each sentence embarrassed him with its melodrama, was like those gaudy, white-lettered snatches of dialogue in heart-wrenching motion pictures.

Selling for Bien Jolie in the city, Judd once found himself in front of 119 West 40th Street and recalled that the Hearst offices for *Cosmopolitan* and *Motor Boating* were there. Looking ridiculous, he knew, with his corset sample cases weighting down his hands, he took the elevator up and found the temerity to inquire of the *Motor Boating* receptionist if the art director was there. She glanced to the far end of the room, where a muscular, wide-shouldered man was hunched over a slanted drafting table, his Oxford-shirted back to the office entrance and his left hand raking his sandy hair as his right sketched the dummy of a page layout. "Looks like he is," the girl said, and she turned back to the salesman, saying, "Shall I—?" But she halted midsentence when she saw that he was already hurrying out.

The Grays hosted a clambake on July 4th on Shinnecock Bay, but as their friends and Isabel retired for the night, Judd stayed out under the silver pepper of the stars, facing not seaward but northwest toward Port Jefferson and the Sound, imagining the glorious evening that would have been his had Ruth been there, an evening that now was forever lost.

Ruth seemed to pine for him, too, and each day sent his office at Benjamin & Johnes hasty notes or sepia postcards that were without inscriptions but featured shy, grinning beauties in clinging wet bathing suits that were intended to conjure pictures of her. And there was one she sent of a blond, brawny, Albert-like lifeguard, scanning the horizon, and on the back she'd written, *What if he drowned?*

And Judd found himself thinking, *All our problems would be solved.*

In July, Ruth's friend and hairdresser Kitty Kaufman and her husband, Bill, lifted Ruth's spirits by renting a saltbox just next door to the Snyders. Because of Bill, Albert was happily joined on his full-day fishing runs for cod, fluke, ling, and striped bass, and the wives, Lorraine, and Josephine swam and suntanned and read *Woman's Home Companion* and *Photoplay* magazines in the shade. Ruth and Josephine spoke Swedish to heap comical abuse on the bodies and beach attire they saw. And through Albert's motorboating connections at the Setauket Marina, the Snyders also found new friends in Milton Fidgeon and his wife, Serena, whose permanent address was not far from theirs on Hollis Court in Queens Village. The Fidgeons were party-loving extroverts addicted to contract bridge and martinis, and each night they invited the Snyders and Kaufmans over so Serena could instruct them in the intricacies of the card game as Milton served enough gin and vermouth from his cocktail shaker that all but Ruth stumbled with intoxication.

In August, when Albert and Bill were hunting skimmer clams for bait, Ruth went to Port Jefferson to mail a letter that she'd written on a page she'd ripped out of Lorraine's *The Adventures of Old Mr. Toad.* But she could say little more than *We are having so much fun! I hope summer never ends!* She forgot to say she loved or missed Judd, and she failed to consider that in his forlorn mooning he would infer hints of mockery in a children's book page about Old Mr. Toad.

Rather than heading out to Shinnecock that August evening, Judd worriedly took the train to Port Jefferson and then a taxi to Shore

Road, wandering up to strangers in his straw boater and seersucker suit and inquiring about the whereabouts of the Snyder family until a fisherman told him, "Heard there's a go-to-hell dinner party at the Setauket Marina."

Walking to it after ten, Judd saw a half-dozen automobiles heading away and stirring up dust from the parking lot, couples in evening gowns and tuxedos drunkenly singing as they exited a huge circus tent, and others getting onto their motor yachts to continue the party at sea.

Judd went inside the circus tent and found waiters collecting leftover food and dishware and rolling the round folding tables out to idling vans. But an orchestra was still playing and there was a gang of loud, hulking college-age men vying for the chance to get closer to Ruth. She'd shockingly cut her hair in the boyish fashion that was newly popular and she seemed to Judd to be flirting outrageously, heckling one lad for his shyness and twirling so wildly away from some kidding hands that her organdy gown slunk off her right shoulder and her full white breast was exposed. Ruth just laughed at the howls and cheers as she readjusted her gown, and Judd heard a woman insist, "Albert's not here. You rescue her."

Judd turned and recognized Kitty Kaufman being tugged from the dinner party by a man who was probably her husband. Judd hurried through a work crew onto the planks of the dance floor as a lovely girl in a shimmering gown tilted toward an orchestra microphone to credit Irving Berlin for the next song, and then she sang the introduction to "Always."

Judd firmly caught hold of Ruth's right shoulder and she spun with surprise that changed to glee as Judd asked, "May I have this dance, madam?"

She grinned and said, "Of course," and she fell into the rhythm of his graceful waltz.

"Have you been drinking?" Judd asked.

"Just a little. Was I being noisy? Albert says I'm noisy when I drink. Because that's one reason I don't drink. Noisiness. And I get sick."

"You've cut your hair," he said.

"*Vogue* calls it 'the Eton Crop.' The Old Crab says it's too mannish. Kitty and I were bored."

"And you're very brown."

"You too."

"Tennis, golf." He scowled at the college boys scowling at them. Liking the pun, he said, "I haven't ever seen you as *boisterous* as that."

"Oh, they're nothing to me. You know that, don't you?"

"I frankly needed reassurance."

Ruth listened to the singer and tipsily smiled. "Let's make this our song. 'Always.' Okay?"

And then Judd sang in his baritone that he'd be loving Ruth forever, that his love would be true forever, and when the things she planned needed a helping hand, he would understand. Always.

She didn't want to go back to Himself with it not yet midnight, so they strolled to West Meadow Beach, where they necked like kids and she tipped into Judd as they sat on fish-scented slabs of rock. She watched high tide flow over a sloping shelf below them and slide along it like a hand along an ebony table, wiping off silver dust. Judd drank from his flask and Ruth said, "I nearly became a widow this week." Judd's face was without reaction. She told him Albert had the Buick's engine running in their Setauket garage as he adjusted the tappets and timing, and he felt himself weakening and getting faint, when he saw that the garage doors he'd flung open had somehow shut. Reeling, he got into fresh air. "The jerk has nine lives," she said.

"Eight now," Judd said, and tilted his flask again.

She grinned. "That's it. Albert's just a problem in subtraction, right?"

Judd said nothing. Alcohol had stolen his vocabulary.

There were flashes of light and the mutter of thunder far off on the Sound. There was a tang of rain on the breeze.

"You'd better hurry," she said.

Judd got on all fours and then hesitantly managed to get upright. "I fine," he said.

She stood and hugged him. "I'm so glad you got jealous and found me."

But Judd just turned away and lopsidedly tottered toward Port Jefferson in search of a taxicab.

In September 1926, Judd and Isabel spent Labor Day weekend visiting automobile dealerships in Newark and East Orange and purchased, for $595, a new, cream-colored, four-door Chevrolet Series V Touring convertible with whitewall tires, black fenders and running boards, and a black canvas top. Isabel finally consented to its extravagance when Judd mentioned how much fun Jane and her friends would have on jaunts with the roof down—"It would be like a hay ride," he said—but he was in fact fantasizing about Ruth snuggling into him in the crisp autumn air, the front brim of his hat blown upright, and both of their woolen scarves sailing behind them.

Hearing about the convertible, Ruth pleaded girlishly over the phone, "Oh, I want to go with you on your next trip! Oh, can I, please—pretty please with sugar on it?" And in order that she could join Judd on his ten-day sales route through upstate New York in October, she convinced her husband she was going to Canada with friends, Mr. and Mrs. Kehoe. It was just a name she'd seen on a mailbox, but the lie scarcely mattered, for Albert took so little notice of what she did by then that he failed to cross-examine her; in fact, except for his worries about handling school days with Lorraine, he seemed relieved she'd be gone.

She was late, but on Monday, October 11th, she exited the subway in Newark in a green cloche hat and a knee-length coat of soft muskrat fur dyed to resemble mink. And she saw Judd smugly relaxing against his jazzy convertible in a raccoon coat and Yankees baseball cap. She asked, "What fraternity you pledging, college boy?"

He took the Hartmann suitcase from her and grinned as he swung it into the back seat. "Which one has the hosted bar?"

Riding north through the Hudson River Valley with Judd, she grimly told him The Governor and she had been arguing without letup since they returned from Setauket, and then she shifted to another mood, gladly reacting to the fall foliage as if she were seeing it for the first time, laughing as she called out the leaf colors as "carrot orange," "saffron yellow," "harlot red," or "horse pee." She was gay, hectic, joshing, tender, and so sexually insatiable that the judge at their Queens County trial threatened to forbid ladies to be seated in the courtroom when Judd gave his testimony about that jaunt through upstate New York.

Early on Ruth gave him fellatio as he drove, and after their luncheon in a village above Newburgh, she went with him into the wet moss and crackling leaves of the woods. Judd joked, "To err is human, but it feels divine." And when they got in the car again, Judd was charmed to see her fling off her hat and lie down in the front seat, hugging her knees. She tranquilly slept just as Jane would on long trips, waking up, as Judd later wrote, *pink and refreshed and happy as a baby.*

At four thirty, Judd checked them into the Stuyvesant Hotel in historic Kingston, introducing Ruth as "Mrs. Gray," and then sitting as formally upright as a bailiff as he used the hotel room's telephone to arrange the next morning's sales calls. They strolled along Rondout Creek after dinner, Judd found a speakeasy that sold Taittinger champagne, and she wore him out with lovemaking until two in the morning.

She woke him in the middle of the night by saying, "Albert's birthday!"

"Hmm?"

"It's October twelfth, isn't it?"

"I guess so."

"He's forty-four today. I forgot to leave him a gift. Even a card."

"Don't feel guilty, darling."

"Actually, I feel just the opposite. Ain't that somethin'?"

Wanting sleep, Judd lit a cigarette instead, and Ruth held him in the night of the room, liking the softness of his English skin, the traffic of his breathing, the male scent that was not Albert's. She said, "We married in my mother and father's place in front of some minister I'd never met. Walking from the kitchen in my grandmother's ugly old bridal gown and Al's sister banging Wagner's 'Wedding March' on the piano. And me thinking, *Aren't you supposed to love the groom?* But I didn't at all. I mean, Al was handsome and smart and talented, and I was full of admiration for him, but there was nothing else. And even as the minister was having us repeat the wedding vows, I was thinking, *This doesn't have to be permanent. I can divorce him.* And then I got violently ill. Mama told Albert I had the flu so his feelings wouldn't be hurt, and he went home alone that night. And I realized how *jubilant* that made me. After a few days I had to admit I was well again, and I found out the old grouch gave up on the idea of our Poconos vacation after canceling our hotel reservations, so we never had a honeymoon." She kissed Judd's cool shoulder. "This is my first. And I'm overjoyed."

Judd exhaled smoke. "And that makes me happy."

"I have never felt sexual pleasure with Albert, just disgust and . . . what's that word for making you feel lousy about yourself?"

"Degradation?"

She snuggled into him. "Whenever he gets into bed with me, I feel like killing him."

Judd was silent.

"Are you listening?"

"Yes."

She felt the shift in the mattress as he rotated to stub out his cigarette. "I feel like killing him," she repeated. Judd's thoughts hung like his cigarette smoke. She could feel his sentences forming but in his hesitation they soon deteriorated, and he finally offered only, "I have to get to sleep."

She woke with him kissing her forehead, fully dressed and shaved and scented with Eau de Cologne. "I'm off," he said.

"Oh, please, won't you stay here and play?"

Rather sternly, he said, "This is a business trip, Ruth. I owe it to my employers."

She noticed then that he held a tumbler that was half-filled with whisky. "Are you *drinking*?"

"Hair of the dog that bit me," he said, and swallowed all of it before he left the hotel room.

With Judd for full days now, she realized just how much liquor he consumed. Something to get over his hangover the first thing in the morning, then something in his breakfast cup to "give his coffee legs," a hit from his flask and Sen-Sen licorice breath fresheners before he carried his sample cases into a shop, gin and ginger ale with his lunch, more hits from his flask through the afternoon, and then a full-on job of drinking after five.

She worried so much about his intake that after sleeping through their first days in Kingston, Albany, and Troy, she decided to accompany him on his Thursday sales calls in Schenectady, just waiting outside in the Chevrolet at the first shop, but getting so bored—the car radio had not yet been invented—that she described her mouth with Kissproof Lipstick and strolled into the other shops with him. She was introduced as his wife, which excited her, but then Judd added other lies that she found less delightful: that she graduated from Smith College, that she was a high-paid fashion model, that "You'll see that hourglass figure of Mrs. Gray's in our next Bien Jolie catalogue." It was like she wasn't good enough as is.

She considered Judd's spiel too formal: "Your choicest gowns," he'd say. "Don't they deserve a foundation no less perfect than that afforded by this exquisite one-piece corsette?" And he could be overly teacherly: "Excuse me, miss, but our line is pronounced Be-Ann Jo-Lee." But he flirted with even the not-pretty clerks and shopkeepers, and he could seem so intrigued and compassionate, frowning as if he were listening hard and feeling each of their joys and sorrows. Judd congratulated them on their changed hairstyles, flattered them for their shaped and painted fingernails, their choice of perfume, and those jujus and fashion accessories that other men failed to notice. And even though Ruth was watching, the women were so affectionate, each joyfully hugging Judd in greeting, kissing his handsome face, their hands fondly finding his forearms and chest as he conversed in his sane and soothing baritone.

She fidgeted. She felt she was suffocating, even that her throat was shutting. And her heart was hammering so loudly that she felt sure people even a few feet away must have wondered at its noise. And then Ruth fainted.

She woke on the floor some minutes later and found Judd kneeling over her, fanning her face with his fedora. Oh so concerned. "You son of a bitch," she said.

"Ruth, please, darling. Don't say that. You're hysterical."

All his adoring women were glaring down at her. Ugly sluts, the lot of them.

Ruth got some rest that afternoon, but she was still plagued with the certainty that he would not have resisted the solace and reward of sex given so many opportunities on his route. After all, Henry Judd Gray had established himself as a man who cheats on his wife. And Ruth was jealous enough that after he'd registered them into the Montgomery Hotel in Amsterdam, she sought to get even with his presumed infidelities by insisting she expensively call home on the Benjamin & Johnes account. As she heard the Queens phone ringing, she asked, "Where would I be by now?"

"Oh, Quebec somewhere, I suppose."

Judd relaxed on the hotel bed and finished what was left in his flask as Ruth shouted over the long-distance line, "Hello, Mama? I'm in Quebec! Montreal! Yes, it's very beautiful! In fact it's *bien jolie*! And everyone here is so intelligent! Even the little children speak French!" Ruth's palm covered the mouthpiece as she told Judd, "She didn't get the joke." And then she shouted, "But, Mama, how are things there? How's the baby?"

Judd shot up from the bed and got back into his jacket and hat. "I'll be right back," he said, and walked a few blocks in Amsterdam's downtown before he found the still-open hardware store where he knew he could purchase whisky in the basement. A hijacked quart of Johnnie Walker Scotch cost him a full day's commissions, but he thought high-end whisky would give him gentler hangovers.

She was getting off the telephone when he got back. "Albert's ill," she said.

"Very?"

"Josephine says so."

Judd filled a water glass with Scotch as he asked as a formality, "Would you like to go back?"

"Nah. Let the Old Crab die." She was afraid she'd shocked him, but she found he was smiling.

"Wow," he said, reflecting on it. "We could have a real celebration then."

She walked to him and held him close as she whispered into his ear. "Oh, I love you so much right now. Shall we have sex all night long? Wouldn't that be swell? Would you like that?"

"Would it be manly to object?"

She stared into his flannel-blue eyes with grave sincerity. "Are there wild fantasies you've had? Anything at all you'd like to try out?"

With a hint of shame, he said, "Yes."

She grinned. "Then let's."

Each night on Judd's sales route they stayed up later until Judd was waking at noon, still exhausted and in a whisky haze. After Amsterdam there was a sales call in Gloversville, followed by a jaunt through the gaudy woods alongside the Black River to a ladies' everything shop in Boonville and three lingerie stores in Watertown. And on Saturday evening it was Syracuse, where Joseph Grogan, the front-desk manager of the Onondaga Hotel, was familiar with Judd and so pleased at finally meeting Mrs. Gray that he rewarded them with a palatial room that seemed fit for a Spanish grandee. Judd woke the next morning to the chiding of church bells but found jazz on the radio and ordered up coffee and apple pie for them both. Lounging in their matching silk pajamas, he confessed to Ruth that he would have liked to take her on a Sunday drive south to Cortland, where he was born, but he still had relatives there who might see them. And he told Ruth that when he was in Syracuse he generally looked up a high school classmate named Haddon Jones who sold insurance there, but though Judd's old friend had been told she was in a gruesome marriage and he even had seen Ruth's photograph, Haddon had not yet been given her name, and Judd felt it was not the right time to introduce them.

She fetched his cheek with the tenderness of her hand. "Oh, don't worry about that," she said. "We'll have time for greetings when we're married. We're just a golden world of two now. That's paradise enough."

She liked chop suey so they went to a Chinese restaurant Sunday night. She gifted Judd with all her cash—thirty-four dollars—because he'd exhausted his. Waiting for the food, she asked, "Remember telling me about Audrey Munson when we first met? She's from around here, isn't she?"

"Close. Up north, near Lake Ontario." Judd bent over a match to light a cigarette.

"And how was it she tried to commit suicide?"

Exhaling smoke, he said, "Bichloride of mercury tablets."

"Well, I was reading about them, and there are so many household uses! You can swish it in your mouth for gum diseases. You can swallow tiny amounts for chronic diarrhea and dysentery. It's a skin lotion, a gargle—"

"And it's poison," Judd said. His face was a sheriff's.

She smiled. "Oh. You caught on."

"With jars on my hands, I could catch on."

"But just think of all the accidents you could have with it if you weren't careful."

"Oh, Albert," he said. "You poor bastard."

"Won't you take me seriously?"

Judd looked off to the kitchen. "Ah," he said. "Our food."

She watched him pour whisky into his water glass, then wedge his cigarette into the notch of an ashtray. She ate in silence, fuming, and Judd fumed over that. A five-member band was there, playing hits like "Linger a While," "Rhapsody in Blue," and "There's a Yes! Yes! In Your Eyes." And suddenly Ruth grinned, with sparks in her own flashing, yes-yes eyes, as if her mood had been chemically altered. She said, "Hasn't this week been heavenly? Please say this is how happy we'll be from now on."

Surprised, he said, "Yes. Always."

She noticed that the dance floor was still empty, and when the band started "Somebody Loves Me," Ruth stood and yanked at Judd's hand, saying, "Okay, Bud. You're up. We haven't danced since we left."

Judd joined her in a fox-trot, but the Chinese manager hurried over and told Judd, "There no dancing allow Sundays."

Reddening with fury, Ruth screamed, "Why are you getting in the way, you *Chink*? Why can't you let us alone for one night? Why are people always *interfering*?" She scurried over to their table, collected her muskrat coat and purse, and ran off, jaggedly crying, as Judd worriedly paid the bill.

But she was waiting for him just outside the front door. Ha-ha-ing. "Wasn't that *funny*?" she said. "See his face?" She squinted and formed buck teeth and skewed her face grotesquely.

"The fellow was just following rules," Judd said.

She frowned in another kind of infuriation and said, "You can be so dull and disappointing, Mr. *Gray*." She quickly stalked ahead of him on her clacking high heels toward the Onondaga and Judd did not want to tag along, so he found the Elks club, where he calmed himself with four rounds of liquor. An hour later, he let himself into the hotel room and found Ruth tilting into the telephone on the dresser. She genially wiggled her fingers at him in hello as she said, "Oh, that's so nice, Lora! I'm so glad you had a good time. Mommy has, too. But I'll be back home very soon."

Albert was reading *Field & Stream* magazine in his attic roost when she concluded ten days with Judd on Wednesday evening. Although he noticed his wife's ascent on the stairs, he just smoked his cigar and flipped the page on a freshwater fishing article. There was gray in his hair, and hours of squinting on the sea had caused wrinkles to flare out from those steel-blue eyes, but Albert seemed more handsome now than when he first halted in front of Ruth's typewriter at *Cosmopolitan* and invited the pretty nineteen-year-old to dinner. She'd said yes and he'd swiftly left, and she grinned at the hoots and envy of the other office girls. All of them so ignorant of Galahads like him.

Albert finally seemed to notice her and inquired, "Was *Canada* all you dreamed it would be?"

She caught an insinuation in the question but airily answered, "It was lovely."

"You'll have to tell me all about it," he said, still reading.

"Are you feeling okay now?" Ruth asked.

"It was just a bad cold."

"I'm glad." She'd prepared for an inquisition but it seemed there would be none. "I hope you got my birthday card."

"Yes," Albert said, and as he took the cigar from his mouth he seemed to try to slay his wife with a scowl. "And you sent it Special Delivery? You seem to think I'm made out of money."

"I felt so embarrassed about forgetting."

He importantly tapped cigar ash into his chrome pedestal ashtray. "Well, you should be embarrassed, but not for that."

"And what's that supposed to mean?"

There were mathematics in his smile. "Oh, whatever you like."

After letting Ruth off on Wednesday evening, Judd headed to East Orange, feeling gloomier and more lost with each minute she was gone. And he was surprised when he saw parked in front of his house the Cadillac V-63 that belonged to his sister's husband, Harold Logan. Worrying that Isabel or Mrs. Kallenbach had died, Judd rushed into the house but found nothing wrong. And he hated himself for feeling let down.

Although Harold Logan was the general manager of the jewelry firm Judd's father founded, he still fancied himself a handyman, and Isabel had called him over to fix a double-hung window that was seizing when she tried to lift it. Harold was now just reassembling the window sash. Judd watched him hammer the trim and lifted a five-pound, foot-and-a-half-long bar of pig iron with a broken eyelet on one end.

"What's this, Harold?"

Harold glanced to Judd's hands. "Old sash weight. You got one hiding on each side, hanging on pulley rope. Helps raise it up once you get it started." Harold banged a nail into the trim, indenting the wood with his hammerhead. "There you go. Looks like hell, but it'll work."

Judd got out his wallet. "How much do I owe you?"

"Oh, just for the hardware. Eighty cents oughta do it."

"We'll say a dollar," Judd said, but in retrieving the bill, Ruth Snyder's wedding snapshot fluttered to the floor.

And Isabel was there to lift it up. She studied the face. "Who's the girl?"

Judd pretended surprise that it was even there, and said, "Oh, that's Maisie. She's a clerk at a shop in Binghamton. She just got married and gave that to me as a memento."

Isabel accepted that lie with the languid disinterest she'd adopted for all his job-related explanations. And yet as she went to the food that was steaming in the kitchen, Judd found himself wondering how it would have been had he told Isabel the truth. Would he have felt freedom and relief? But then he was fairly certain of the outcome: a financially ruinous divorce, ill fame in his job, his faithful little mother devastated.

Judd saw his brother-in-law grimly interpreting the situation. But Harold loftily quoted Jesus: "'He that is without sin among you, let him cast the first stone.'"

Albert went out on his regular bowling night on Thursday, October 28th, and when he got home excited Ruth by saying Harry Folsom invited them to join the Halloween festivities at his New Canaan address the next night. But Albert decided they weren't going.

"Why not?"

Walking past her into the kitchen, he said, "Have you any idea how far New Canaan is from here? Thirty-three miles. Wearing humiliating costumes. Seeing people I despise."

"Well, can *I* go?"

Albert shot a cold look. "With whom?"

"Kitty?"

Albert poured some of his homemade Pilsener into a porcelain Zimmerman stein. "Kitty wasn't invited. Harry's wife rightly distrusts her."

"We're just staying home then?"

Albert leaned back against the kitchen counter and swallowed some beer. "Try it," he said. "You might like it."

"You are so *frustrating*!"

"Yes," he said. "Well . . ." But he found a new interest in his stein and failed to continue his thought.

She and Judd still regularly met at Henry's or the Waldorf-Astoria lounge, Ruth rehearsing The Governor's latest infamy and Judd criticizing the vileness she was forced to endure. And she was increasingly concerned about her cousin Ethel's ill health and Ethel's continuing failure to find grounds for divorce from her

Bronx policeman. "Eddie always had a thing for me. You know—
I'd catch him catching a peek of the goods. So I told Ethel I'd get
alone with him. Work him up for a telltale photograph."

Judd fell back against a Waldorf sofa. "But that's *insane,* Ruth!
Ethel would gain an adultery charge against her husband, but
Albert would also have photographic evidence of the same charge
against you. You could get divorced but lose Lorraine."

She looked at him solemnly. "Are you telling me not to do it?
Because if you insist, I won't do it."

"I insist."

"And you'd do likewise for me, right?"

"What?"

"Like if I insisted you do or not do something."

"Certainly," he said.

In mid-November Josephine was hired for a weekend job nursing
an old woman, and Lorraine went off to a Saturday-afternoon
birthday party with third-grade friends. Ruth found Albert lying
on the sofa in the music room and announced she was going
grocery shopping, but when he failed to reply she realized he
was drunkenly asleep. She noticed, too, the floor pipe that fueled
the zone heaters with natural gas. She went from room to room,
fastening the windows shut, then hustled down into his shop and
chose a monkey wrench. She got into her overcoat and hat and then
crouched to quietly joggle and jam the joint of the floor pipe until it
fell apart and she could smell the foul odor of rotten eggs streaming
underneath the sofa. She held her nose as she walked out the front
door, locked it behind her, and laid the monkey wrench on Albert's
garage workbench. She then went grocery shopping.

She was gone an hour. She didn't worry that the natural gas
would be ignited by a pilot light. She could fix that ruin. But she

realized that she'd forgotten Pip in his golden cage in the sunroom, and she began to worry that the canary would die. She'd heard that canaries fell out of the air, dead, hours before humans in coal mines sniffed a problem.

She hailed a taxicab and was sitting in the back seat with two sacks of groceries when the cab turned onto 222nd Street. And there she was stricken at seeing Albert tottering on their front sidewalk, his hands on his hips and gasping for air. "Oh shoot," she said.

She telephoned Judd in his office and confessed that homicide attempt as if it were funny. But he stiffly asked in his snooty way, "Are you aware they electrocute people for murder in New York?"

"Not if they don't get caught." And before he could say anything more, she shifted the conversation by inviting him to the house for a Wednesday luncheon. She'd be alone. She asked him to bring along twenty or so of the little one-shot bottles of various liquors that Benjamin & Johnes gave as treats to their lingerie buyers. She would be having family for Thanksgiving.

And so Judd walked over from the Jamaica Avenue bus stop in Queens, his filled briefcase clinking with liquors, and went up to the kitchen stoop, where he whistled the waltz tune to "Always."

The kitchen door opened and Ruth happily greeted him by yanking wide her muskrat overcoat. She was naked underneath. Like the harlot he'd hired on 42nd Street. Judd worriedly glanced behind him, but she said, "Oh, don't be such a scaredy-cat."

She kissed him in the kitchen but removed his avid hands, then took his fedora and coat. Hanging them up in the foyer closet, she indicated the joint to the gas piping that she'd wrenched apart.

Judd found himself laughing at the outrageousness. "What a dolt!"

"Who?"

"The Governor. Could he really be that clueless?"

"Oh, he was so schnockered that morning he didn't know what he did." She hung up her fur overcoat and presented her gorgeous body to him, then took him up to Lorraine's room.

Judd could later recall no precise time when he told Ruth he would help kill her husband. And if only for that reason he felt she'd hypnotized him. But he could recall mentioning sedatives that Wednesday afternoon with his feet hanging off Lora's too-short bed, the hot breath of the furnace on their love-flushed skin, and Ruth cuddling into his chest, her right hand gently arranging his sleeping penis, then fondly holding his scrotum as he talked. "You could try to get a barbital," he said. "The only brand name I'm familiar with is Veronal. Highly addictive and calms a person by quieting the respiratory system. Chloral hydrate works on the central nervous system. You could expect deep sleep in a half an hour. Whiskey exaggerates its effect. Chloral hydrate and whiskey is called a 'Mickey Finn.' I guess Mickey was a Chicago bartender who used the concoction to rob his customers."

"Nice lesson. What else?"

His high school hankering to be a doctor was excited. "Well, there's a variety of salts available from a pharmacist. Sodium bromide, potassium, ammonium—"

"Who'd need them?"

"Well, I believe bromides are used as anticonvulsants for those with epilepsy."

"My father was epileptic. I could be, too."

"But you'd need a doctor's say-so. That's the hitch with any sedative."

She rolled onto him, her round breasts saucering at his waist.

She folded her hands on his chest and rested her chin on them as she gazed up at him with dazzling, magnetic eyes. "Anything you don't need a prescription for?"

"Well, chloroform. It's an anesthetic."

"Which means?"

"'Without feeling.' 'Senseless.' You can render a man unconscious with it. Even kill him with too much."

"And it's available?"

"Strangely, yes."

She flicked his left nipple with her tongue and grinned. "Would you get some for me?"

Judd heard himself saying he would. And when he was in his office after Thanksgiving, he urgently telephoned Ruth to say he definitely would not.

"Oh, that's fine," she said, as if he'd simply refused a second helping of succotash. And she patiently moved on to a wholesome conversation about housecleaning, making it seem his ethical dilemma was insignificant.

She knows me so well, Judd thought.

At first he pretended that his plotting was just an entertainment on sleepless nights. Ignoring the fact that murder was their intention, Judd concentrated on getting to the house and getting away, on establishing an alibi, not accomplishing the act. *The act* was his term for it, just as it was for intercourse. And his reveries about it were just as erotic.

Everything seemed to feed into their plans. She and Judd went to the movies and saw *Flesh and the Devil* with Greta Garbo, in which John Gilbert is an Army officer and illicit lover who kills Garbo's husband in a duel over the vamp. Onstage, they saw Alan Dinehart and Claiborne Foster in *Sinner,* Judd's view of himself, and just before the show was shut down for being lewd and obscene, they saw Mae West in *Sex,* the hottest farce on Broadway. Theodore Dreiser's controversial novel *An American Tragedy* was adapted for the stage and Judd took Ruth to a hit performance at the Longacre on West 40th Street. Afterward, in the Ritz, they discussed Clyde's murder of Roberta, the pregnant mother of his child. Clyde left too much to chance, Ruth thought; if he needed to do it he ought to have thoroughly prepared rather than act instinctively. Ruth said, "Hitting her with a camera and letting her drown? What a goof! That's not a murder, it's a flip of the coin."

Because there was a cat burglar in Queens who'd been getting into houses through upstairs windows, Albert had purchased a .32-caliber handgun and Ruth said he flourished it whenever she crossed him, shouting once, "Any day I choose, I can blow your brains out!"

Judd never wondered if she was lying to incite a reaction from him. Rather, he worried that Ruth would be dead the next time he called.

Lorraine was discovered to have the condition called "lazy eye," and every other Saturday Ruth brought her into the city for examinations and exercises. Judd would meet them at Henry's and always give Lorraine a dime and some candy. Ruth coached Lorraine to sneak her hand into his and affectionately say how much she loved him. Lorraine once smiled as she asked, "Are you sure you're not my father?"

Albert, Judd thought, *is as bad as that.*

"Tell him about this morning," Ruth said.

The girl was puzzled. She cocked her head. "What?"

"Daddy grabbed your English muffin from you and . . ."

"Oh, and he scraped off some of the peanut butter. Because I was wasteful, he said."

Ruth prodded, "And what happened next?"

She smiled. "I cried and said I wanted *lots* of peanut butter."

"And he got angry . . . ," Ruth said.

"Yes, then he got angry and slapped me. I hid behind the dining room chair because I was afraid of him and then Mommy stood right up to him and yelled things." The nine-year-old seemed to have trouble recalling the morning, and then she recited, "But then Daddy rushed upstairs and ran back down a few minutes later with a gun in his hand, yelling, 'I'll kill the both of you!' Only he used some swearwords. And he shoved the gun into Mommy's chest."

Judd petted the pretty girl's head. "Oh, sweetie. I'm so sorry," he said. And he was dismayed that she would be just as direly affected if he did what Ruth was hounding him to do.

But Ruth winked at him and said, "All's well that ends well."

On Christmas Eve 1926, the three met at the Waldorf-Astoria to exchange presents, and Judd widened Lorraine's eyes with a girl's very adult-seeming pink silk lingerie that she was thrilled by. Ruth, too, was in high spirits as he gave her a jeweled blue purse that she liked enough to carry into the courtroom four months later. Lorraine presented him with a silk Brooks Brothers tie of the sort he favored, and Ruth handed him a gleaming silver grooming set for the road. And next to the hairbrush he found a check for two hundred dollars, or two weeks' wages, written against the account of Mr. and Mrs. A. E. Snyder.

Because Lorraine was there, Ruth could only say, "You've been so generous to us. We need you to stay out of hock."

"But how can *you* afford it?"

With the seriousness of a tutor, she said, "I have great expectations."

Judd cashed it, and the canceled check with his signature on it would be found by detectives on March 20th.

⌒ ⌒

In January 1927, in Buffalo, Judd dreamed that a faceless Albert was crouching toward him in a corridor, seething with hatred. Huddled behind a curtain beside Judd were Ruth and Lorraine, Isabel and Jane. Judd was teasing Albert forward, hoping his rage would let him bypass the mothers and daughters, but the curtain was fluttering out and tangling and Ruth's fair calves and thighs were exposed. Albert turned in vengeance and lifted an ax and Judd woke in a scream.

But he knew it was not just a nightmare that scared him. Albert represented everything wrong in his life: Judd's negligence of his job, his worry over conditions at home, his failing physical stamina, and the ever greater excess of alcohol that was wrecking his health and his future. Judd did not fall asleep, he passed out; he did not wake up, he came to. Even the fine memory of which he was proud was becoming so faulty that he was forced to scribble notes about whatever he'd done or had to do.

And Albert's health, too, seemed ever more precarious. In January, Ruth wrote Judd that The Governor couldn't stop hiccupping and Judd replied in his letter that a customer in Geneva, New York, recommended pineapple juice. Ruth laced the juice with bichloride of mercury tablets, and instead of dying Albert just vomited all day and was cured. With a mixture of dashed hopes and renewed admiration, Ruth wrote her lover that she'd never seen anyone so deathly ill pull through.

Judd primly wrote back that he felt she was behaving in a monstrous manner. But when they dined at Zari's the next weekend he confidentially said, "I find it so mysterious. Had you said you wanted to kill a dog or cat, I would have broken all connections with you. And yet I have to confess to an excitement I don't understand. I'm entranced by your bravery. Your outlawry." Judd unscrewed the silver cap to his flask, filled his glass with juniper-flavored grain alcohol, and finished half of it. "I have two beings inhabiting my skin, Ruth. One strives to act normally but is wildly incompetent, while the other seeks the outlandish and forbidden and is gaining influence over me. I'm becoming a mess. I hunt hither and yon for my jacket and find I'm wearing it. I twist on the bath's faucet handles and forget them and flood the floor. I feel like I'm in a coma. Yesterday Isabel and Jane were there to meet my train, and I was in such a haze that I failed to recognize them and walked right by."

Ruth laughed.

"But it feels so *unfunny,* Ruth! We have known each other for only a year and a half, and by whatever measure you choose, my life is in what the biplane pilots call a 'death spiral.' And yet I wouldn't change a thing. You are an enormity—"

"Well, thanks a lot."

"Oh, I don't mean it that way, darling. I mean you have become the object of everything I do. The source of all that I am. Am I making any sense?"

She held his hands in hers. "Only if you meant to compliment me."

"Really, it's not flattery. It's practically theology."

The orchestra started "Someone to Watch Over Me" and Ruth requested the dance even in his drunkenness. She took him out to Zari's dance floor and clung to him. Alcohol's depressant effect caused Judd to jealously notice other men watching Ruth's body as she moved, but she just joked, "Hey, it's better to be looked over than it is to be overlooked."

The skillful dancer he was could do nothing more than a box step, but that only caused Ruth to cling to Judd more tightly. After a while she shifted against his erection and slyly whispered, "I can feel Henry getting interested in me."

But Judd was in a wretched and romantic mood. "I have no idea how this story ends, do you? Are we just going to continue like this?"

Seeming to ignore him, she sang along with the orchestra about a man who was not handsome but who carried the key to her heart. She sang that she wished the guy would get up to speed, because she was in need of his help.

And then Judd fell off balance.

Ruth caught him and said, "We need to plan."

They stayed overnight at the Waldorf-Astoria. Judd called Isabel and said he was too drunk to get home. She found it easy to believe him. Ruth failed to inform her husband of her whereabouts and Albert's sisters would later claim that was a sign of his great love for his wife, that he so often gave her such freedom.

Judd struggled out of his jacket but could do no more, so Ruth undressed him and asked what his plan for getting rid of The Governor was.

Tilting off balance, Judd said, "I'll confront him and we'll get into a fight. Have it out."

"Well, no offense," she said, "but you're not strong enough."

"Prolly not." Concentrating hard, Judd finally decided on, "Remember that one movie we saw?"

"No."

"Sure you remember. That movie? The guy gets hit over the head?"

She unbuckled and unzipped his trousers and yanked them down. "Lift up your right leg. And now your left."

"A bur-la-gry."

"Burglary."

"Right," Judd said. "I hit him over the head. And we make it look like . . . that word."

"A burglary."

"Uh-huh."

Alcohol poisoning finally felled him where he stood and Judd woke up in his underwear and gartered stockings six hours later. He found Ruth kneeling in the half-filled hotel bathtub and rounding forward to rinse an avalanche of white foam from her hair. An amber bottle of Blondex shampoo was on the floor. She rose, twisting a tawny hank, and gasped with shock when she glimpsed Judd slouched against the doorway. "Oh! You scared me."

"I scare myself sometimes." He raked his hand through his hair and excused his exit to unconsciousness by saying, "The drink took a drink."

She sat back on her heels, water gleaming on her breasts, and she grinned at his attention as she soaped a washrag. "Are you going to keep your promise?"

Judd knelt beside her and stole the washrag. "Which was?"

She allowed him to bathe her right arm, hand, and fingers. She smiled. "Like they say, give a man a free hand and he'll run it all over you."

Judd stayed with his question. "*What* did I promise?"

"You vowed your passion for me was so immense that you would go to infinite depths for me, even if it meant giving up your own life or erasing another's. At least, that was the gist of it."

"I'm guessing I was less coherent."

"But you *are* going to keep your promise?"

Judd meekly said he would. And the plot developed.

At home, no one spoke to him. Even Jane left the front room at his entrance. Judd heard whispers of conspiracy being hissed behind closed doors. And so in a late February snow, and earlier than he'd planned, he left for upstate New York to sell the Bien Jolie fashions for spring.

Ruth secretly went to the Queens-Bellaire Bank and got out the safety deposit box registered to Ruth M. Brown. She'd told no one, not even Judd, about the Prudential insurance policies on Albert's life. She scoured the fine print again, jotting on a scratch pad *$1,000 + $5,000 + $45,000 x 2 = $96,000.* She could do the arithmetic without a pencil, but reading the numbers was more thrilling.

She then went home and called Judd in his office. When she was told he was on the road, she said she was a lingerie buyer calling from Batavia. Would he be there this week? The office secretary said she knew only that Judd was first heading to Albany. Ruth consulted the hotel list he'd given her and she wrote Judd at the Morgan State House Inn, saying she was so miserable she was going into Manhattan to find its highest building and end it all, and by the time he received this letter she would be dead. She gave the stamped envelope to the postman, George Marks, just as he was walking next door. The postman smiled at seeing the sender's name was Mrs. Jane Gray. "I'll see he gets it, Tommy."

"You think tomorrow morning?"

"Oh yeah."

Judd frantically called Queens Village the following night, and she answered in the foyer. "Are you free to talk?" he asked.

She whispered, "They're all upstairs right now."

"Your last letter frightened me."

"Which was that?"

"About suicide."

"Oh," she said. "That was just a mood I was in."

"Well, I don't want you to give way to such moods."

"There's only one thing you need to do."

"Look, I'm going to rescue you from your dire straits very soon."

Ruth loudly called to no one, "Just a salesman!" And then she softly said, "I have to hang up."

Albert Snyder and his wife were invited to a Saturday-night card party at Milton and Serena Fidgeon's home on Hollis Court in

Queens Village on February 26th, 1927. Joining them were Serena's brothers, George and Cecil Hough, and Dr. Arthur W. Stanford and his wife—Ruth forgot her name. A folding table was placed in the front room and the dining room table was used for the second bridge game. Water pitchers filled with Gilbey's gin and ginger ale were within hand's reach, and jazz, *Live from the Empire Room,* played on the radio.

The Snyders played north and south at the dining room table, with Milton and Serena in the east and west seats. Serena touched Ruth's forearm as she said, "Won't it be delightful being together on Shore Road again next summer?"

"Oh. You're going back?"

"So are we," Albert smugly said. "Same cottage. I just put the deposit down."

Ruth restrained a scream as she asked in a tight voice, "Weren't you going to consult me, honey?"

Albert seemed flummoxed. "When have I ever? And *why?*"

"Careful, friend," Milton said. "Thin ice."

Serena frowned at Albert as she dealt out the cards.

Within an hour Albert became so vexed by Ruth's unpredictable bidding that Milton invented a rule that some players needed to rotate, which sent Albert to the folding table as Milton invited George Hough to team with Ruth.

Albert was loudly saying, "I open with one heart and she says one spade. I haven't the cards to help out in that suit so I bid two clubs. And what does she do but follow that with three no-trump!"

George Hough was a hale, farmerish sort of man in his twenties. Hearing Albert, he winked across the dining room table at Ruth and loudly said, "My gosh! What husbands have to put up with! And she's so ugly, too!"

"You play a few hands, you'll see," Albert said. And he glared at him over his highball glass.

Radiators were overheating the house and around eleven o'clock George helped Milton collect and hang the men's jackets.

Albert grinned and patted his thigh as he temptingly called to his wife in German, *"Na Kleiner, komm doch mal rüber."* In English: Hey, sweetie, come over here. Ruth vaguely understood what the sentence meant, but she did not understand that in Germany it was the street invitation of a prostitute.

She went over to the folding table and fell girlishly into Albert's lap. She hugged him tight and asked, "How's it going, honey?"

He finished his highball. "I'm losing."

"Look at the lovebirds!" Serena called.

Ruth kissed his head. "It's so true. Cantankerous is just an act with him. Albert's my sweet little lamb."

"Who's *she* describing?" Dr. Stanford asked, to general laughter.

"Are we going to play bridge or what?" Albert said.

"Okay, okay," George Hough said, sitting down again. "Don't get your kidneys in an uproar."

"Kidneys? My kidneys are fine. Are you a wiseacre, George?"

"Oh, calm down," Ruth said, and walked back to the dining room.

Albert filled his highball glass, failed at distinguishing clubs from spades in the next hand, then forgot what happened to his jacket.

"I hung it up," George reminded him.

"Oh? Well, we'll see about that," Albert said. He swerved when he walked to the foyer closet.

"Snyder!" Ruth called.

But he was already rooting around, swatting overcoats aside. And then he was hunting through his jacket pockets and yelled, "Where's my wallet?"

"Look on the floor," Milton called.

Albert bent low inside the closet. "It's gone! Who stole my wallet?"

Milton stood. "I'm sure we'll find it somewhere."

"But I had seventy-five dollars in it! And it's gone! What kind of friends you got, Milt?"

"Hey, watch it!" called Cecil Hough.

And now his brother stood. "Are you talking about me?"

"I don't know," Albert yelled. "Are you a thief?"

Ruth just looked down at the dining room table and in exasperation called again, "Snyder!"

"Would you like to mix it up?" George asked. "*I'll* oblige."

Albert smiled as he unbuttoned his shirt cuffs. "Oh, fella, you are barking up the wrong tree."

But Milton Fidgeon intervened, and Serena put on a platter of Paul Whiteman hits, and within the hour Albert was laughing heartily at Dr. Stanford's jokes.

Walking to the railway station from his final sales call in Albany, Judd noticed his haggard, gloomy reflection in the front window of an old-fashioned apothecary. *Your face says it all,* he thought. *You are being destroyed by all this.* And yet he went in and purchased a half-pint of Duncan's Pure Chloroform that had been imported from Scotland and a pair of green rubber chemist's gloves that would conceal his fingerprints.

And then, checking into the Stuyvesant Hotel in Kingston on March 3rd, he was given a short letter from Ruth. She began: *My Own Loverboy, Gee, but I'm happy. Oh, ain't I happy. I'm so very happy, dear, I can't sit still enough to write what I'm thinking of.* She mentioned that she'd seen the movie *Johnny Get Your Hair Cut* and thought Jackie Coogan was *a sweet kid and a marvelous actor.* She continued: *All I keep thinking of is handling A.—and you, you darn loveable little cuss. I could eatcha all up.* She ended with

Hurry home, darling. I'll be waiting for you. All my love, Your Gal.
Judd studied it, then carried the letter over to the fireplace and
watched the writing paper brown and warp and convulse into
flame.

Upstairs in his room he made a long-distance telephone call to
Queens Village. Ruth answered. Judd asked, "Can you talk?"

In a hushed voice, she said, "Carefully."

"We can't use a hammer. Cops know that a burglar wouldn't
carry one. We need something that'll do the trick but is hard to
identify."

"Like what?" But before Judd could answer, she said, "I hear
footsteps," and hung up.

The next afternoon, Judd walked into the L. S. Winne hardware store on Wall Street in Kingston and purchased a sash weight.
The owner would remember Judd because his fine tailoring in a
hardware store was like a flare that said *Notice me,* and because the
owner could recall saying, "Don't know as I've ever sold only the
one. You sure you don't want a pair?"

Judd said, "I have just what I need."

When Judd returned to Manhattan from upstate, he hid his
purchases with his golf clubs in his office. Arranging to meet Ruth
for lunch at Henry's on Monday, March 7th, he got a few yards of
butcher paper from the mail room and wrapped the murder items
as if each were fragile, including with them a socket and electric
cord, an empty Pinch bottle of Scotch whisky, and a piece of green
felt because she'd read instructions in *McCall's* on how to make a
cute lamp. Judd carried the paper-wrapped bundle into Henry's at
noon and waited thirty minutes for Ruth to arrive. When she did,
she was joined by Lorraine. Judd was vexed that the nine-year-old
was being involved.

Ruth forgot to apologize for her tardiness as she shoved his package into a soft-sided tapestry bag. But she did say, "You look terrible, Judd."

"I *feel* terrible."

Ruth glanced at Lorraine beside her and penned on a paper napkin that she passed across to him: *But you'll do it tonight?*

Judd nodded.

Lorraine lifted to watch as Ruth took the napkin back and penned: *Still trying to get chloral hydrate.*

Judd asked, "What's it say, Lora?"

She told him, "I can't read cursive."

Judd penned: *We don't need that stuff now.*

She wrote: *Just you hit A. + chloroform?*

In a frenzy, Judd looked around the restaurant as if the hand-writing could be heard. There was a squat red candle on their dining table and Judd set the writing on their napkin aflame. Lorraine was solemnly considering him. Judd squeezed a hand inside his trouser pocket and exclaimed, "But I'm forgetting! There's a dime in here for New York's prettiest girl. And that's you."

She fisted the coin and said, "You're so nice, Uncle Judd." But now it sounded scripted. As did he, Judd admitted.

A bovine old waiter with a handlebar mustache ambled to their table and leaned on his knuckles to inquire if they were ready to order.

Judd said, "I'm sorry but I won't be eating. I have to get back to work."

Ruth scanned his face with panic. "But you'll be there?"

Lorraine scowled in confusion.

"Don't forget your bag," Judd said, and left them.

If I had possessed any mind at all, I certainly would have acknowledged the wrong that was being evidenced in my very

*soul and would have come out like a man and told her so. But
I never recall it coming to my mind, that this is the wrong or
right thing to do. It was simply a question of whether I could
go through with it, or hoping something would happen to pre-
vent it.*

*If I had not lost all consciousness of God and drifted away,
I could have stepped from the abyss and deterred her, too. Certainly, God was prompting my spiritual self to do right. But
if that self has been quelled to the extent mine was, it is a hail
from a friend unrecognized.*

That night, March 7th, Judd took the bus up Jamaica Avenue to
222nd Street and soldiered north, intending to finally get it done.
She'd told him that if he saw a lamplight at her mother's window
just above the front door, Judd was to go around to the kitchen
stoop and she'd meet him there. But there was no light on and Judd
couldn't recall another contingency plan. He took some hits from
his flask and just watched the house for a while.

Crouching forward, Judd looked through a cellar window and
watched Albert filling a fifty-gallon steel drum with water from
a garden hose, then hefting his Johnson outboard motor into his
shipshape workshop. Albert spun the motor's propeller, seemingly
hearing faint problems; softly ran his hand along the keel-like
skeg; then hauled up the Johnson and dunked it into the drum
water as he tightened the transom bracket on the drum rim. Albert
tested the tiller, unscrewed the gas tank lid and looked in, then
exchanged an old spark plug for a new one. He yanked on the
starter rope just once and the motor throbbed alive, churning up
blisters on the water's surface and puffing smoke into the workshop until Albert jammed off the choke. Each of his motions was
confident, efficient, perfectly mechanical. And he smiled through it

all, with complete serenity and purposefulness. Such a man could pass hours in this way, could glance at his wristwatch, be nicely unprepared for midnight, and trudge with happy weariness up the stairs.

Judd walked around the block, working up his courage, feeling the nettles of conscience. The collisions of sport were familiar to him until his right eye was harmed when a friend flung a handful of seaside sand at his face and almost blinded him. And since then he could not recall even the hint of injury from anyone, let alone recall himself rousing a fanatical aggression for an ordinary man. The Henry Judd Gray he hoped to present to the world was affable and ingratiating; he ignored slights, forgave wrongs, sought always to make friends even of strangers; and he felt Ruth had misjudged him if she thought he was the type to lash out in fury, let alone kill.

Judd was not aware of how many times he walked the perimeter of the block the Snyders lived in, but others were, and a woman telephoned the police to say there was a burglar or Peeping Tom in the neighborhood and he'd just strolled by her house for the third time. But before a patrol car could get there, Judd had finally determined, *I cannot,* and at eleven o'clock when he passed 9327 a fourth time, he heard from inside the Snyder house a rapping on the kitchen window.

Ruth was at the kitchen stoop when he got there, holding a full glass of whisky. Judd took it and she asked with irritation, "Are you going to go through with it or not?"

"I'll miss my train to New Jersey," Judd said.

She glared at him for a half minute. But then she relented. "Shall I hold on to the things?" she asked.

"No. Just the sash weight. Hide it."

"And then what?"

Judd shrugged. "I have sales calls upstate for the next two weeks."

She frowned at him but heard a sound from the basement and hurried inside. Judd slunk into the darkness of Albert's garage until she returned with the items in a grocery sack. She caustically asked, "Are you *ever* going to go through with it?" But she shut the kitchen door before he could answer.

THE MURDER OF ALBERT EDWARD SNYDER

Waking just before sunrise on March 19th, she gazed through a northern window at the yellow halo of the arc light across the street. Even as she watched, the glow was strangled and then snuffed. She softly rolled right and stared across the chasm between their beds that was not wide enough. Albert was sleeping on his side in his flannel nightshirt, too unfairly strong for her to handle by herself. She hated the gargled sighs as he inhaled and exhaled, hated the stink of his breathing, hated the hoarse shouts he'd use when he called her name to fetch or cook something.

She felt the ache of menstruation and went into the bathroom. But she was ending her period. She found just a spot of blood on the Kotex, and she took that as an affirming sign that she'd be rid of Albert soon. She wakened Lorraine to say they'd be shopping for Easter clothes in Manhattan, and then she hurried over to Kitty Kaufman's house to have her hair bleached as blonde as Mae West's.

Judd woke at eight in Syracuse and took a hot bath with Epsom salts. Soaked until his fingertips pruned. Shaved with a new razor blade. Each item of clothing he wore would have to last a full day and night, so he chose fresh skivvies, a new pair of knee-high black stockings, a starched white shirt, the gray wool suit and vest that were faintly threaded with blue, and a navy blue foulard necktie. Lacing up his shoes, he caught himself thinking, *The killer wore black, high-grade Oxfords.*

Carefully establishing himself in Syracuse, he went down to the Onondaga Hotel's basement coffee shop and ordered waffles with whipped cream and cherries for breakfast. "After all, it's Saturday," he told the waitress. She regarded him strangely. *Was he too loud?* Each sentence, each gesture and glance, was thrilling to him. He signed for the bill in a florid hand and included a quarter tip.

Kitty drizzled hydrogen peroxide into a saucepan of bleaching powder with great seriousness and stirred until she'd concocted a perfect mixture. Ruth wrapped an old towel around her neck and stooped over the kitchen sink as Kitty tugged on rubber chemist's gloves and then dabbed on the stinking mixture with a paintbrush.

"What's the special occasion?" she asked.

Ruth was thinking there would soon be a candid rotogravure portrait of the grieving widow in the papers, but she instead said they were going to the Fidgeons' house to play contract bridge.

"Oh," Kitty said. "Them."

"Albert seeks out friends who drink like he does."

"He could always spit out the window. There's plenty like him since Prohibition."

And Ruth thought, *Judd.*

Kitty painted the wet hair forward, then back, and then handed Ruth a rubber bathing cap. "This stuff's poison and nasty, so we can't let it stay on your skin too long." She glanced at a wall clock to get the time as Ruth put on the bathing cap and tucked her cooking hair inside.

Kitty snapped off the chemist's gloves and they sat at the kitchen table with mugs of coffee. She flipped open the New York *Daily Mirror* and hunted a middle page. "Have you read Betty Clift today?" Seeing Ruth shake her head, Kitty scanned Clift's column and then went back some sentences to read aloud: "'Heed this advice, men. It is born in woman to long for your praise, for your attentions, for your demonstrations. When you withhold them she suffers an actual starvation. If she is a strong character, she worries along without them. If she is of lighter caliber, you suddenly find yourself without a sweetheart, or even a wife, for some other more accomplished adorer has circumvented you.'"

Ruth smiled. "When she says 'lighter caliber' she means bleached blonde, right?"

"Yep," Kitty said. "Betty's got you pegged." She sipped from her mug and slyly grinned as she asked, "And speaking of adorers, how's Judd?"

She'd hoped Kitty would mention him. "I haven't seen him in a while. Upstate on his sales route, I guess."

"Any action on that front?"

Seeking to lay out an alternate version of the night's events in case things went awry, Ruth said, "Nah. I'm slowing it down. I have to make sure Judd stays far away from Al—he's threatening to kill him."

"Oh, guys are always saying stuff like that," Kitty said.

"Well, I'm scared he'll do something rash."

Kitty checked the clock and looked underneath the bathing cap. "We've got to rinse off the bleach and shampoo you," she said. "Bleach too long and you'll burn off your hair."

Ruth stooped over the kitchen sink again and Kitty noticed the excess mixture in the saucepan as she ran water from the tap. "Darn it," she said. "I made too much again."

Ruth said to the hairdresser, "Just bottle it up and I'll serve it to my husband."

Kitty laughed.

The Syracuse *Post-Standard* predicted the Saturday temperature could get as high as sixty degrees, so Judd left his herringbone overcoat and gray buckskin gloves behind in the hotel room as he strolled the few blocks to Haddon's insurance office in the Guerney Building, his face finding the sun and holding itself in that heat. A horse team and hay wagon stood between an old Ford Model T and a Hudson Essex parked at a slant on the street.

In the first-floor offices of Hills and Company, "Real Estate & Insurance," Haddon Jones was selling a fire insurance policy to a skeptical farmer and his wife, his slick black hair parted in the middle, his jaunty mustache glistening with beeswax, his hands widening over the array of brochures on his oaken desk in a gesture that seemed to say the universe had been laid out beneath their frowns. And then he noticed his friend and excused himself to shake Judd's hand.

Haddon seemed even taller, reedier, and more looming than he'd been at William Barringer High School when the unmatched friends were nicknamed, after the newly popular comic strip, Mutt and Jeff. "Have a seat out here," he said. "I have a feeling this could be a while. But good to see you, Bud."

"You too."

Judd lingered for a half hour more in the office parlor, paging through a *Saturday Evening Post,* his gray fedora on his knee. His mind was an aviary, his thoughts flitting and screaming. He could not recall one item he'd read. He heard Haddon's voice coaxing a

choice that the farmer seemed unwilling to make, and Judd finally
stood up.

"Lunch?" he called to the next room.

Haddon nodded.

It was ten thirty.

Judd strolled by shops and in a five-and-dime purchased a
sixty-cent navy blue bandanna that he felt sure was like the one
Tom Mix had worn in *Riders of the Purple Sage*. The shopgirl at
the cash register failed to lift her gaze to him as he mentioned that
impression and offered his dollar bill. She said she hadn't seen that
movie as she gave him his change.

Walking into an alley, he finished his flask and hunted a gin
mill where he could refill it.

The Snyder house's three females left through the front door
just after eleven and found Albert outside in a cardigan sweater,
vigorously raking life into a tan yard flattened by winter. Some
Jewish children in Halloween costumes who'd hesitated over
interrupting the father in his angry work scurried forward on
the sidewalk when they saw the pretty mother and child and they
recited in chorus: "Today is Purim! There can't be any doubt! Give
us a penny and throw us out!"

"Aren't you cute," Ruth said, and found a penny in her purse
for each.

Albert watched the transaction with a mixture of inquisitive-
ness and Scrooge-like disdain. Curdling clouds were on the eastern
horizon and the evening would be cold and wet, but there were still
zephyrs that seemed almost sultry and the hints of spring lightened
his mood. When the children had raced away, he asked, "Where to
now, you three?"

Mrs. Josephine Brown said, "Oh, that nursing job for Mr. Code
in Kew Gardens."

"All night then?"

"Noon to noon."

Albert frowned at his wife with confusion. "Lora will be joining us?"

Ruth sighed. "We *discussed* it last week. Remember?"

Albert didn't. "And now I suppose you're going shopping?"

"The baby needs Easter clothes."

"Clothes, clothes, clothes!" he said, but tilted the rake against the house. "In the car, the all of you. I'll give you a lift."

"Thank you, Daddy," Lorraine said.

Albert hatted her blonde head with his hand. "*There's* a good girl."

Josephine and Ruth got into the back seat and Lorraine into the front. Ruth stared at his sandy hair and hawkish profile and realized she hated his head, too, the fine wrinkles in his neck, the gray whiskers on his shaveless weekends, the steel in his eyes when he concentrated, the way he occupied so much space. After he stepped on the floor starter and shifted gears to reverse onto the street, Albert forced Lorraine to reach her hands out to the glove box and tiringly hold them there as a brace against potential accidents. Looking into the rearview mirror, Albert said, "I'm thinking of putting in a flower bed out front this April. Assorted colors of peonies."

"What a good idea," Ruth said, as if it were idiotic. "So festive."

Josephine slapped her wrist. "Don't take that tone with your husband."

"What tone?"

Josephine settled more deeply in the seat. "You know very well, May."

Albert ignored his wife, shifted into third gear, and smiled as he hummed the tune from Puccini's *Gianni Schicchi,* his cue for his daughter to sing the aria he'd taught her.

She thought a little and sang in Italian the opening verses of "*O mio babbino caro.*"

Ruth interrupted. "Is that a lullaby, baby?"

Lorraine said, "A girl is telling her papa she's in love with a handsome boy and she wants to get a wedding ring."

Albert said in his teacherly way, "*Mio babbino caro* means 'my dear papa.' Lovely melody, isn't it? And if she can't have him, she'll throw herself into the river Arno." Albert jumped to the end of the aria and Lorraine laughed as she joined her father in singing the Italian.

Ruth said, "Well, *I* feel left out. How about you, Ma?"

"The lyrics mean 'Oh God, I want to die,'" Albert said, and grinned into the rearview mirror. "Remember when Florence Easton first sang it at the Metropolitan Opera? In 1918? Were you with me?"

"I hate opera," Ruth said.

"Oh, that's right," he said, and then he was stonily silent the rest of the way to Jamaica Station. And he continued to say nothing, as if he were hurt, when Ruth and Lorraine slid out of the Buick Eight and he headed west with Josephine to Kew Gardens.

The nine-year-old watched as the family car growled away. She asked, "Was Daddy mad at us?"

"Oh, he's just moody," Ruth said. "Daddy's fine."

Ambling into the downtown Elks lodge, Judd offered a fraternal hello to Chester, the porter, and was cheered that he was remembered from earlier visits to Syracuse. Straddling a bar stool, Judd ordered a gin martini with two green olives, then held the folded blue handkerchief to his nose, a hint of sweet chloroform in its newness. He avoided his face in the wide and distorting mirror that doubled the liquor array. Within a minute he was ordering another martini. He heard the clack of billiard balls in the adjoining room and when he'd gotten the martini, he heard some

men protesting a card play. Judd tipsily twirled on his stool like
Jane or Lorraine would have and saw at the far end of the lounge
four men in their shirtsleeves and ties at a green felt table, earnestly
listening as one of them announced the scores thus far in a gin
rummy game. Each of them seemed so normal, the salt of the earth.
But bored and boring, old before his time, and vaguely irritated
with his lot in life. Like he was before Ruth May.

Judd turned back to the bar to order a third martini and
announced his intention by saying, "You know, sometimes too
much to drink isn't enough." But the bartender was avoiding him
as he inventoried his cityscape of liquor, his pencil tinking each
bottle as he counted it.

So there was nothing for Judd to do but chain-smoke Sweet
Caporals in the gentlemen's club room at the Onondaga. An RCA
radio with a gooseneck loudspeaker was tuned to New York City's
WRNY and a soprano named Nita Nadine was singing. A few
other commercial salesmen he'd noticed in weeks past were loudly
there, but he feared he might give something away if he joined
in their conversation. At twelve thirty he requested permission to
tune the radio to WEAF for the Waldorf-Astoria Orchestra and
forced himself to ignore the night's scheme by recalling the luxury
of so many glorious nights at the Waldorf-Astoria with his lover.
And then he thought of their first time. July, was it? In the offices
of Benjamin & Johnes. She'd had a sunburn; he took her upstairs.
She'd said, *I feel like a child on an escapade.* And he'd said, *We're not
doing anything wrong.*

At one, he went upstairs to room 743, and he nestled inside his
tan leather briefcase the half-pint of Duncan's Pure Chloroform
and the green rubber chemist's gloves he'd bought in Kingston,
the navy blue farmer's handkerchief he'd gotten that morning, and

a wreath of circled picture wire he'd stolen from the New York office. And he was just snapping the briefcase shut when Haddon Jones rapped on the door with his familiar shave-and-a-haircut, six-bits.

The hotel's basement coffee shop seemed just fine to him.

Each ordered black coffee and a sandwich of fried ham on rye. Initially, Judd talked about the Benjamin & Johnes Company and his new financial interest in it. Judd called it fractional ownership and he loaned Haddon his gold Cross mechanical pencil so his high school friend could jot arithmetic on a paper napkin to guess Judd's probable increase in earnings and his need for wider insurance coverage. But Haddon heard himself selling, lost interest in his estimates, and handed the Cross pencil back, and the shop was silent except for the waitress sawing a fresh loaf of bread.

Although tempted to confide his night's plans, Judd presumed nothing could alter his path and he'd only make his friend a co-conspirator, so he sought instead just an alibi. "Say, Had," Judd finally said. "I need you to do me a favor."

His friend sighed and said, "Ho boy," but he was smiling.

"Nothing strenuous, just a little manly deception. A fib."

Haddon's hazel eyes were wolfish. "You going to get yourself some nookie?"

"Remains to be seen. Remember that photograph I showed you once? The blonde?"

"Oh yeah. Her? She's a doll!"

"We're meeting in Albany tonight."

"You rascal."

Judd fetched a hotel key from his pocket and slid it next to Haddon's plate. Aware of the usefulness of seeming a dunce at adultery, Judd said, "Don't want the firm or Isabel to suspect, so I'm hoping you'll mail some letters for me. So I'll have the night postmarks on them. And would you phone the front desk to say

I'm sick? And hang out the 'Do Not Disturb' sign? Also, toss the room a little before the hotel maid shows up Sunday morning. I'm afraid you'll have to make two trips just in case housekeeping gets too helpful."

Haddon grinned and wagged his finger in a schoolmarmish way. "'Oh what a tangled web we weave when first we practice to deceive.'"

"You've been there, too, pal o' mine."

Haddon became stern. "Hey, one out of every three husbands do it. Scientific fact."

Judd watched for the waitress to head into the kitchen and he got his flask of brandy from his suit-coat pocket, tipping an inch into each of their cups. He smiled as he whispered, "Let's see if we can't make that coffee stand up on its hind legs."

Haddon lifted his cup in salute and sipped it and pleasurably exhaled. He frowned some and said, "I'm trying to remember your nickname for her."

"Momsie," Judd Gray said.

Walking from Pennsylvania Station to Macy's on Herald Square, Ruth decided she would soon be rich and hailed a taxi to instead convey her and Lorraine up to Joseph and Lyman Bloomingdale's luxurious store at 59th and Lexington. With wide-eyed surprise, Lorraine watched her mother overspend on a girl's white sateen middy dress with Bulgarian embroidery, a girl's felt hat with side tassel, and a girl's size-ten lamé coat, its collar and cuffs trimmed in dyed Viatka coney.

Ruth helped her daughter carry the paper-bundled Easter clothes to Women's Apparel, where Lorraine overheard her mother whisper to a saleslady, "I have to attend a funeral." Lorraine then watched, evaluated, and voted as her mother purchased patent-leather pumps, a black silk dress designed by Jeanne Lanvin, and a silk coat with a collar of dyed ermine.

And then they went to the Palm Court of the Plaza Hotel for an extravagant lunch. Looking at the steep menu prices, Lorraine asked, "What can I have?"

And Ruth smiled. "Anything you want, baby. From now on. Anything your heart desires."

Haddon returned to his office at one forty-five and Judd went upstairs to write a letter to Ruth on Onondaga Hotel stationery, penning *Syracuse, N.Y. Sat. 6 p.m.* in the upper right corner because the last train to Manhattan left at four. He wrote: *How the dickens are you this bright beautiful day anyway? Gee, it makes you feel like living again after all that rain yesterday if we only have a nice day tomorrow now we will be all set—as we have had so many miserable Sundays they are lonesome enough as a rule without adding rain.* He mentioned Haddon stopping by for *a little smile* and that he might run out for a movie or vaudeville at the Strand after supper, *but this warm weather doesn't give one a heap of pep. I feel tired when the day is done.* Inquiring if tonight wasn't the occasion for another bridge party with Mr. and Mrs. Fidgeon, he innocently hoped *you have a lovely time and have one for me—but see you behave yourselves.* He added that he planned on visiting his aunt Julie in Cortland on Sunday since he hadn't *seen her since Xmas time.*

Sealing and stamping the letter, he addressed it to Mrs. Jane Gray in Queens Village and then composed a similar letter to his wife, signing it *All my love, Bud,* and addressing it to 37 Wayne Avenue, East Orange, New Jersey. After that Judd filled out his weekly sales report for Benjamin & Johnes. Angling the three letters on the pillows of the hotel bed so Haddon couldn't fail to find them, he washed up and brushed his wavy, chestnut-brown hair; changed into a fresh starched shirt with French cuffs since the morning's was soaked through with anxious sweat; got into his gray herringbone overcoat, gray buckskin gloves, and fedora; and sauntered down to the Elks lodge for a toot and a chance to fill his flask with whisky.

The Syracuse-to–New York City run was so familiar to him he had the railway timetable memorized and he would normally be so casual that he got to the station just minutes before the four o'clock Empire State Express pulled out. But on March 19th he was earlier and was forced to loiter in a men's room stall so no one would recognize him. Crude penciled drawings of bosoms and vulvas defaced the stall walls, and as if he were preserving Ruth's honor, he wetted his handkerchief at the sink to scour them away. *Loverboy,* he thought.

Haddon fulfilled Judd's request. Around three forty-five, he left his insurance office to see the newsreels at the Strand Theater and ache his sides through Buster Keaton's *The General*. Walking back to the office at five thirty, Haddon scanned his mail and telephone messages, locked up his desk and file case, then waited for ten minutes on the sidewalk in front of the Guerney Building for his wife and the old Studebaker, the flivver he would be getting painted on Sunday. The sky was cobblestoned with clouds. He whistled "Ain't We Got Fun?"

His wife stayed in the driver's seat as he got in and instructed her to go to the Warren Street side of the Onondaga. "I have to do something for Judd," was all he said. Haddon took the elevator up to the seventh floor, tipping the operator a penny, and found three addressed envelopes propped up by the pillows, one to Judd's employers, one to Isabel, and another to a Jane in Queens Village whom Judd addressed by his own last name. *The guy gets around,* Haddon thought. He lifted up the telephone and held the hearing piece to his ear as he flicked the cradle. The night manager at the front desk answered. Like a functional character onstage, Haddon stated, "This is Mr. Gray in seven forty-three. I'm feeling ill and I'm going straight to bed. Please hold all calls for me until at least midmorning."

"Very good, sir," the night manager said.

Haddon hung the blue "Do Not Disturb" sign on the door-knob, locked the door, and fitted the stamped envelopes in the mail chute so they would be postmarked at the eight o'clock collection.

His wife failed to ask what he'd been doing as she drove them home.

The invitation to the card party at the home of Mr. and Mrs. M. C. Fidgeon on Hollis Court Boulevard had instructed the guests to arrive at eight, but stout, wealthy Milton, a formal sort of man who still wore spats, heard the doorbell at seven and was astonished to see Albert on the front porch in a navy blue, doubled-breasted suit and a regimental tie with that gold stickpin in it. Water from his hair-combing still trickled down his neck and was blotted by his stiff shirt collar. Ruth stood behind him, chagrined, and their pretty daughter found harbor under the mother's arm.

Milton stabbed at a joke. "Have you come for dinner?"

Walking past him inside, Albert said, "We were just cooling our heels at home. You go ahead with what you were doing and don't mind us. We'll just sit in the front room and wait."

Ruth offered Milton a woe-filled look, like *This is what I have to deal with every day.*

~ ~

Riding most of the way to Manhattan with just three others in the smoking car, Judd noticed an Italian newspaper front-page section on the floor under the sole of his shoe. *L'Arena* from Venice. Tilting forward with drunken effort, he fetched it up and found the language was gobbledygook to him. But Italians were dangerous, were Sacco and Vanzetti or the wild and violent immigrants on Mulberry Street and Staten Island, so he thought he could put the pages to use, fling them somewhere in the house as a false clue, a red herring. With the elaborate movements of alcohol impairment, Judd wrapped the chloroform bottle within the pages, snapped the lid of his briefcase shut, and congratulated himself by finishing his flask of whisky.

And then he found himself in Grand Central Station at 10:20 p.m. Walking across the upper level, he halted at a Pullman window to purchase his return ticket to Syracuse. Reginald Rose, a dark young ticket seller who would be described in the Queens trial as "sheikish," would remember Henry Judd Gray because of the peculiarity of requesting a Pullman sleeper for a midmorning journey to Albany, as if the harried passenger in fine clothes had figured he would be up all night.

Judd hadn't eaten, but the odors from the diner at Grand Central Station were so off-putting that he exited the terminal at 42nd Street. Although it was raining, he headed by foot down Fifth Avenue to Pennsylvania Station. *Why I walked to Penn Station I do not know, unless it was to kill time.* There seemed to be no sound to his footsteps so he threw pennies in front of him just to hear them ring on the sidewalk. Walkers dodged aside when he staggered.

At Penn Station, he bought a hot dog with sauerkraut and tried to read the newest scandals in a *New York Evening Graphic* but the overhead lighting hurt his eyes, so he just stared at the erotic sculptures of Audrey Munson, imagining Ruth as even lovelier, then walked out into the night and caught a bus for Queens Village, claiming later that he was still undecided about what he would do when there.

Serena Fidgeon sought to entertain Lorraine with *Favorite Fairy Tales,* the only children's book in the house, but the girl discovered a stack of *Motion Picture* magazines and filled the night hunched over articles about Colleen Moore, Ramón Novarro, and Norma Shearer. At the folding table, Cecil Hough and his wife, from Far Rockaway, were joined by Howard Eldridge and his wife, from just down the street, while Albert, Milton, Serena, and Serena's kid brother, George Hough, played contract bridge in the dining room. Dr. George Stanford, of St. Mark's Hospital, switched between tables when players wanted a break while Ruth just kibitzed, genially chatted, or flipped the pages of *Motion Picture* with her daughter. All through the evening, Milton served his famous martinis to the card players, but Ruth had found the host in the kitchen with the chrome shaker and requested of Milton, "Will you give my share to Al?"

George Hough and Albert both could be hot-tempered when intoxicated, and by midnight George could no longer let the sleeping dog lie, loudly recollecting for Howard Eldridge the altercation with Albert three weeks earlier when he'd been accused of stealing Albert's wallet.

With a glare, Albert added, "And seventy-five dollars."

A fascinated Ruth was on the sofa with Lorraine, watching the argument restart and wondering if it helped or hindered the night's plot.

Offended once again, George said, "Well, it's pretty small business to accuse a party of friends of such a thing."

"Says you," Albert said.

And George Hough fell back into grammar school. "Darn right, says me," he said. "Would you like to try and stop me?"

Albert sneered. "I could be coaxed." But he was so drunk he had difficulty in getting up from his chair and dropped back into it again.

"Here now!" Milton said. "We don't want any fisticuffs."

"I'm *fine* with it," Albert said.

"Me too," said George. Words were failing him.

Serena cautioned her brother. "We can't have the police here again."

Cecil Hough had gotten up from the folding table and was crouched so he could talk sternly into his brother's ear. George listened and was helped up from his chair by Cecil and Howard and guided over to the sofa, falling down into it and against Ruth. Albert failed to notice because Milton was humoring him with flattery about his musculature and boxing skill.

Woozily, George Hough glanced up at Ruth and managed to say, "Are you treated right at home?"

She shook her head just a little, as if she were afraid to say more.

"Somebody oughta kill that Old Crab," he said.

She smiled.

Judd wakened to a hand shaking his shoulder and heard the bus driver instruct him that this was the Queens Village stop he'd wanted. And then he found himself with rain hitting his face on the sidewalk of Jamaica Avenue at the corner of 222nd Street. Still tipsy, he tilted off balance but caught himself on the arc-light pole before he could fall. His briefcase surprised him by being firmly gripped in his left hand. He patted his overcoat pockets and found his buckskin gloves tucked inside them. The pair had cost him eleven dollars. Couples were hurrying by him in the rain, but he was, he knew, the sort of insignificant fellow that people failed to notice, and so he felt safe in strolling the few blocks north to the Snyder residence.

And then he just stood in front of the cream-yellow corner home for a while, seeing lights on in the kitchen, the music room, and the second-floor hallway, and watching for movement. She'd said Josephine would be nursing in Kew Gardens. The large white Colonial door that faced west would be locked, Ruth had said, and he drunkenly remembered he was to go to the kitchen door on the south, next to Albert's one-car garage. Albert's Buick wasn't inside it.

On the kitchen porch, his shin banged the hinged wooden milkman's box and he ouched, then checked the neighborhood to see if he'd been heard. The households were sleeping.

Judd tried the side door and found it unlocked, just as Ruth had promised. On the kitchen table she'd placed a fresh pack of Lucky Strike cigarettes—she'd forgotten his favorite brand—which was to have been a signal to him that the family was not at home. Or did it mean just the opposite? He listened and found that the house was silent but for the faint whisper of the furnace consuming coal just below him. Still he hushed himself when a kitchen chair shrieked as he yanked it out to heavily sit on. His head ached. He hunched forward with his elbows on his widened knees and held his face in his hands. Sleep would have been so nice.

But the canary Pip cheeped from his cage in the front of the house, waking Judd enough that he stood and stared at the cigarette pack: *Lucky Strike: "It's toasted." And I'm toasted,* he thought as he swayed there. Remembering that Albert smoked only cigars and would notice it, Judd pocketed the cigarette pack, then trudged up the oaken stairway between the dining and music rooms, teetering on some steps, and at the upstairs hallway went down it into the bathroom to urgently urinate. His face in the medicine cabinet mirror was so shaded, sickly, and gruesome that he felt pity for its owner and smiled at his joke. He tilted back down the hallway for Ruth's mother's room above the foyer and front door, his right shoulder banging and sliding along the floral wallpaper. Heat was breathing through the vents and the house was hot as blood. Remembering not to switch on Josephine's ceiling light fixture, he struggled out of his fedora, overcoat, and gray woolen suit coat, threw them with aggravation into Josephine's closet, and fell down on the soft velour chair beside the white Swedish bed. With effort he checked the Ingersoll clock on Josephine's vanity table, twisting the clock's face to catch some of the hallway light and guessing that the hands illustrated that it was about one o'clock on Sunday morning.

But he finally did recall the functional plot in Ruth's letter to him of a week earlier. Which he'd burned. He lifted Josephine's pillow with interest and found underneath it, as promised, electrician's pliers, the five-pound window sash weight, and a half-pint bottle of rye whiskey that Judd unscrewed and sniffed. She'd meant it for Albert, just in case, and she'd spiked it with bichloride of mercury. The chemical scent put him off and he instead discovered that Ruth, sweet lady, had left on the floor by the pink velour chair a new bottle of Tom Dawson whisky, one of five quarts she'd purchased for next Saturday's party on the eve of her thirty-second birthday. Judd cracked it open and took some swills of that, tasting the Scotch flavors of iodine and seaweed, his throat burning in just the right way. Although he was instructed to use the electrician's pliers to cut the telephone wires, when he tried to stand up from the chair he flopped against the wall in his drunkenness and slid to the floor like a rag doll, losing the pliers under Josephine's bed.

Judd tilted the bottle and the whisky had some more of him. Soon his shirt was soaking with sweat. Waiting made him think of fishing with his father and sister, the *glub* of water under the boat as he bobbed and watched his line bleed across Lake Skaneateles.

A nibble, a yank, and then nothing. Everything was fuzzy now but for the fact that he was there to murder a man he'd never even met, whose first name he could not then remember. The Governor; that was all. His willingness to kill for Ruth mystified and scared him, just as it had earlier in the month. The Ingersoll clock read two o'clock. Soon the family would be home and he would have to go through with it or Ruth would give up on him and find a stronger man. And then he had a wild impulse to run away and he tried to, fighting hard to scrabble upright and forgetting his things as he fled downstairs. But he'd gotten only onto the landing when he heard a rare automobile on 222nd Street and saw its high beams sling yellowish light across the dining room windows. Judd clawed and stumbled back up the stairs in a panic.

The coroner would find that Albert Snyder's blood-alcohol level was .3 percent, almost four times the police department's measure for intoxication. Had Ruth and Judd done nothing at all, Albert may have died in his sleep. But still he insisted on driving his wife and daughter home, gloomily silent as he wove his big Buick down the streets, just missing other cars and overcorrecting on his turns as Ruth quietly offered him needed directions like the most forgiving of wives. At their house he swerved a hard right toward the one-car garage and banged into the curb. Albert gave Ruth a vengeful stare, as if daring her to criticize him.

"We'll get out here," was all she said, and Albert said nothing as she got a sleeping Lorraine out of the back seat. The girl was, at nine, too heavy to carry, but Ruth let her huddle under her arm as she helped the girl to the front door. Ruth unlocked it and hesitated in the foyer, listening for Judd, but there was no sound but the tick-tocking grandfather clock and Pip chirping his hello.

Ruth took off her black satin turban and lynx-trimmed polo

coat and hung them in the foyer closet. She said, "Let me get you some water, Lora," and went into the lighted kitchen without her. She saw the cigarette pack was gone, a kitchen chair turned out. She filled a water glass from the faucet and carried it back to the foyer with her. Lorraine's school shoes were off and her new lamé and fur-trimmed coat was pooled at her feet. She was wobbling there with her eyes shut, close to fainting with exhaustion. She'd sleep through anything now. "Will you climb the stairs for me, baby? I can't lift you."

Lorraine held on to the handrail and on to her mother's waist as she trudged upstairs just as Judd had. "Where's Granny?" she asked.

"Working," Ruth said.

"Oh. Right," the girl said. She angled straight into her bedroom without switching on the ceiling light.

Ruth rested the water glass on the vanity. "Will you get into your pajamas, please?"

Lorraine said nothing but started.

Ruth went to Josephine's door and softly whispered, "Are you there?"

She heard Judd hiss, "Yes, go away." And she saw the dark boulder of him squatting in a corner, seemingly hugging his knees. She left him.

Lorraine's pajamas were a girl's version of a sailor's uniform but she hadn't finished buttoning the blouse before she drooped to her side with overdue sleep. Ruth jerked the blankets out from under Lorraine and tucked her in and kissed her forehead just as she would on any night. She gently shut the girl's door behind her, locked Lorraine inside with a skeleton key, and went to Josephine's doorway to say only, "I'll be in shortly."

Even in his acute drunkenness, Albert was cautious enough to inch his beloved automobile inside the garage until the windshield tapped the warning tennis ball that was hanging on string from a joist. Albert turned off the ignition and just sat there for a while as he generated the energy to get out. At last he forced himself to yank the handle and fell forward from the car, lurching into a garage wall before he righted himself and tottered toward the kitchen. Wanting a nightcap, he slammed open kitchen cabinets but found no alcohol and crashed his way upstairs.

Ruth was in their room, unclothed and, presuming there would be bloodshed, choosing a red nainsook nightgown from its satin hanger. She considered its beauty in the floor-length closet mirror and remembered that the embroidery style on its trim was called Lorraine, and she thought that would mean good luck in the night. Squirming into the nightgown, she felt oddly embarrassed that Judd was there, in the nearness and intimacy of their home. She heard her husband's too-heavy, annoying footfalls and was giving her freshly bleached hair a brush when she saw Albert facing her in the floor-length mirror, irate and poisoned with alcohol, all language and intelligence gone, and seemingly with no notion that his lifetime now could be measured in minutes. "Are you okay?" she asked.

Albert said nothing and fell into the wall as he first yanked off his shoes and clothes, then jammed his arms into his pale blue flannel nightshirt. With his home so hot, Albert rammed up a window, its stiles screeching in the wooden casing, and Ruth watched with interest as he then crouched onto his mattress, scooched forward on his elbows and knees like a ridiculous old man, and floundered facedown as he sank into the blackout he called sleep.

Ruth went into the bathroom, brushed her teeth with Ipana, then went into Josephine's room. Judd was still silently squatting there, seeming so Oriental. She stooped forward and kissed him. Her hand pressed the bed pillow as she asked, "Did you find everything?"

"Yes."

"Have you been here long?"

He shrugged. "Hour. Don't know."

Whisky scented his speech. "Have you been drinking?"

"Plenty."

"But you're going through with it, aren't you?"

"Don't think I can."

"Oh no," she said. She stooped again and kissed him. "You *can*." And once she'd felt his drunken pawing of her thigh, she disappeared from Josephine's room.

Judd stood up as if ordered to and felt his sore knees and calves tingle with a fresh rush of blood. He unsnapped the lock on his briefcase, took off his owlish spectacles, and folded them neatly inside their case. He swallowed more whisky, then put on the green rubber chemist's gloves and waited for Ruth, his head hanging like he was her victim, too.

She'd kept the curtains and Venetian blinds open as she got into the twin bed nearest the closet. She lay flat on her back as she watched her husband snore. The street's arc light glared through the northern windows and seemed to cage them in stripes of shadow. Albert was facing her, which meant his left, hearing ear was muffled with the pillow and only his deaf, right ear was available for sound, but she could never recall which was the good ear, the right or the left, so she couldn't be certain that he wasn't listening whenever she shifted, whenever she and Judd talked.

She waited until a quarter to three, just staring at Albert, then felt safe enough to get up from bed and go to Judd. She was pleased to find him gloved, with the five-pound sash weight in his right hand. Judd was just staring at her. Sullen. She got the chloroform and navy blue handkerchief from his open briefcase as she said in a soft voice, "You know what's funny? One of the guys at the party tonight said he would kill the Old Crab if he didn't treat me better."

"Me first," Judd said.

She put on his gray buckskin gloves and winced at the chloroform's sweet smell as she doused the handkerchief and some wads of cotton gauze, and then noticed Judd wrapping the sash weight in the front section of the Italian newspaper. She frowned. "Why are you doing that?"

"So it won't hurt him so much."

"You *do* realize you're going to kill him?"

Judd meekly nodded.

Ruth took him by the hand, like a child. She guided him to the ajar bedroom door and then stood aside at the lintel as Judd entered.

Ruth's husband was so immediately there, just a few feet inside the room, that Judd almost yelped in surprise. Suddenly, murder seemed an actual possibility and he assayed his target. Wide-shouldered. Muscular. Skewed hair receding from a high forehead. There was a chest of drawers, a dresser, a chiffonier. The headboards were not ornate; the linens were probably Sears, Roebuck. Hanging high up and between the twin beds was the oval picture frame with a sculpted mahogany bow and inside it the studio photograph of raven-haired Jessie Guischard as a girl. Seeing that, it was easier for Judd to sidle up and raise the sash weight high with both hands and chop down at the sleeping head with fierce hate.

But his trajectory was wrong and the sash weight glanced off the headboard, only injuring Albert, who jerked up and yelled with fury and flung an arm out as Judd struck down again, gashing the older man's nose. Albert snatched at his assailant and hollered "Ruth!" and one hand caught Judd's foulard necktie, choking him. To quell his yelling, Judd's gloved left hand seized Albert's throat so hard he left five finger gouges, and he flailed at Albert again, his weapon striking the pillow. And then he lost hold of the increasingly heavy sash weight and even as he was strangling the man, he was being strangled himself. Judd was so afraid he could lose the fight that he screamed out, "Momsie, for God's sake, help me!"

Ruth was beside him then, and Albert was shocked and wide-eyed over his pretty wife's betrayal as she squeezed the chloro-formed handkerchief over his mouth and nose. Albert seemed to surrender to the anesthetic and then Ruth lifted up the fallen sash weight and hammered down hard—Judd would later say "she belabored him"—and there was a wild spray of blood that accom-panied the gruesome sound of rain-sodden wood being struck. Albert lost consciousness.

Judd fell off him onto the floor.

"Is he dead?" Ruth asked.

Judd looked at the faint rise of the chest and answered, "I don't think so."

"He's got to be dead," Ruth said. "He saw us both. This has got to go through or I'm ruined."

Judd said, "I'm already ruined."

With cold efficiency, she went to the closet, carried back one of Albert's silk, university-striped neckties, this one red and yellow, and commanded Judd, "His feet."

Snagging off the chemist's gloves and hiking up the white lin-ens, Judd hitched the ankles together with the necktie as Ruth tore off strips of the cotton gauze, shook more chloroform on them, and shoved roots of them inside Albert's nostrils with her little finger. She then stuffed his mouth with chloroformed cotton and flat-tened the chloroformed handkerchief on the pillow before rolling her husband so that his face was smothered by it. Tying his wrists behind his back with a white hand towel, Ruth told Judd, "Look for his handgun."

That jarred him. "There was a *gun*?"

Worried that his rising voice could be heard, Ruth scowled and shut the open window. He could be such a child. She instructed, "Look under his pillow first."

The pillowcase was so soggy and reeking with blood that Judd had to turn his head. A Bien Jolie corset he'd given Ruth was on the floor, which meant she'd been wearing it. Which, in his drunkenness, pleased him. His fingers grazing a leather holster, he pulled it out and hinged open a .32-caliber revolver, pointlessly shook out three, but not all, of its bullets, imperfectly gripped Albert's still-warm right hand around it, and flopped the pistol onto the bed next to Albert's left elbow.

The police could construct no scenario in which that tableau made sense.

Ruth was in Josephine's room, scouring Judd's briefcase for something in the dark.

"I'm frazzled," Judd said. "I need a cigarette."

She gave him a scornful look but said nothing. She carried the coiled picture wire and Judd's gold mechanical pencil into the bedroom. She wasn't surprised that in spite of everything Albert was still very slowly and wheezily breathing. She could even admire him for that: a diehard. Wanting to be thorough, she jabbed an end of the picture wire under the cold skin of his neck, made a noose, snugged it and tied a granny knot, then twisted the noose so tight with Judd's Cross pencil that Albert made a faint gargling sound and blood oozed over the indenting wire. Wife of his dying, she'd waited so long for this moment that she almost wanted it to linger. With her head just above his, she whispered, "How's that, *o mio babbino?*" She turned an ear and listened until she was sure Albert's breathing had ceased. And then she went out, forgetting the mechanical pencil, which the police would find and eventually match with the gold Cross fountain pen still snug in Judd's inside jacket pocket.

Judd had gotten his Sweet Caporals and gone downstairs into the darkened music room. He'd wrenched his knee in the wrestling with Albert and his limp would make him far too noticeable all that Sunday. He sat on the Aeolian player piano's bench, massaging his knee and watching gray smoke untangle from the fiery red ash. When the cigarette was so short it singed his bloodstained fingers, he left it in a tin ashtray on the keyboard, as unsecret as a clue in a children's party hunt.

Ruth heard him heading upstairs as she went into the bathroom and switched on the light. Her hands were red with blood, and her nightgown was aproned with blood, and blood was trickling onto the floor in pennies of shining red. And then Judd was behind her. "My God," she said. "Look at me."

Judd inclined toward the mirror in his nearsightedness and found Albert's blood on the front of his shirt. Sunday-school memories of Cain's murder of Abel floated up: *What hast thou done? The voice of thy brother's blood crieth unto me.*

She asked, "Can we wash out the stains?"

He remembered asking his mother that when he was socked by a bully at age ten, and Mrs. Gray had said, as he now said, "No."

"Give me your shirt," Ruth said.

He unbuttoned his gray vest, took off the shirt, and dully watched her hurry downstairs. He then slouched out of the bathroom toward the whisky, taking some swallows, then flopping down into Josephine's chair with the Tom Dawson bottle cradled against his stomach. His head slackened so that his chin touched his chest and he fell asleep, waking to find Ruth in front of him in a green nightgown now, holding out one of Albert's new blue shirts, which was still squarely pinned and wrapped in tissue paper. He asked her, "What did you just do?"

"I burned our things in the cellar furnace."

Judd got into Albert's shirt, thought it overlarge, and asked,

"Could you cut a new buttonhole? This hangs like a horse collar on me."

She sighed with impatience but got some scissors and soon the collar was fitting and he was tying his necktie in the bathroom mirror as if he were just setting off on his morning calls. Adrenaline or sheer brutality had slightly sobered him. "We still have to make it look like a burglary," he said.

Ruth went into her mother's room and quietly tossed it as she thought a burglar would. In the couple's bedroom, Judd flung their purple armchair's back and seat cushions onto Ruth's twin bed. His forearm swiped across the chiffonnier and a hairbrush, perfumes, cufflinks, and pocket change flew. Judd failed to notice in the scatter Albert's fine gold Bulova watch and his gold necktie stickpin with Jessie Guischard's initials on it. J.G. Recalling that the Italian newspaper was wrapped on the sash weight, Judd found it and flung the pages up, watching them seagull down to the Wilton rug.

The widow returned to the couple's bedroom, scowled at Albert's corpse, and handed Judd some packets of sleeping powder, his sales route list with hotel addresses, her Croton cocktail watch, and a Midol box that she said contained bichloride of mercury tablets.

Judd hunted through The Governor's suit and overcoat pockets and finally found the new wallet. He filched its contents of five twenty-dollar bills and a ten and flipped it onto the floor. Holding up the cash, he said, "You'll need some of this."

She shook her head. "The police will suspect something." She was rooting through a jewelry case, snatching out expensive rings, earrings, and necklaces. She held their winking abundance out to him. "Could you take these with you?"

"Of course not."

"But burglars would steal them, wouldn't they?"

"Hide them then," Judd said, and went out.

Ruth shoved the jewelry between her mattress and box spring, where the Queens police found them on Sunday afternoon. She'd forgotten where she'd put the chloroform container and frantically searched the room in the faint arc light from the street until she found it beneath Albert's sheets, against his right thigh. She then hugged herself as if with cold as she hovered over Albert's head for a final confirmation of his extinction. She felt like hitting him again, just because, but said only, "Good riddance to bad rubbish."

"Shall we go?" Judd asked. He was swaying, but his suit coat and owlish eyeglasses were on; his hat, overcoat, and briefcase were in his hands.

She smiled and slid her left arm around his waist and she quietly helped Judd step downstairs. There, in his drunkenness, Judd yanked the chintz cushions from the sofa but did not steal Ruth's fur coats and scarves in the foyer closet; he tipped over chairs in the dining room but did not steal the Chambly silverware. Crazily, he ransacked the kitchen.

Ruth had gone into the cellar to hide her blood-sprayed pillowcase in a hamper, hopelessly confusing the tale she would tell, and Judd followed her to burn up his sales route list. With exactitude he flicked chunks of coal into the furnace so he would make no noise and then broomed the floor wherever his shoes had been. She'd hidden the sash weight in a box of tools and Judd carried over some furnace ash to pepper it with so that the hardware would seem to have been there for weeks. But in the faint light he did not notice a spot of blood that was still on the sash weight; detectives did.

Upstairs again, Judd got a fresh quart of Tom Dawson whisky from a sideboard, filled a water glass with it, and fell down into a chair in the kitchen, sliding a dollar bill under the quart bottle to pay for what he took. She sat with him, rehearsing the tale she would tell. He half-finished smoking a Sweet Caporal, but the night was graying and she worried that the milkman would soon be on the kitchen porch, so she took Judd upstairs and into Josephine's room.

"You have to slug me," she said.

"I can't do that, Ruth!"

"But I have to say the burglars gave me an awful whack on the head and knocked me out."

"Still, I couldn't ever hurt you."

She smiled and petted his sweet cheek and said, "Oh, you. What a sweet boy." She turned and he tied her wrists behind her back with clothesline rope, then he over-tied her ankles, and he lifted her like a new bride, laid her down on her mother's bed, and softly cupped her right breast through her nightgown as he tenderly kissed her good-bye.

He felt he was in a movie romance as he said, "You won't see me for a month, two months, perhaps ever again."

Ruth took up the same tone. "Oh, no, don't say that!"

Judd straightened, got into his herringbone overcoat, and fixed his fedora at a rightward cant. "Remember, if the police catch up to me before I get back to Syracuse, I have no excuse for being here."

She said she'd die before giving up one word against him. She said she still had a capsule that had enough poison to kill a dozen people and that particular one she was going to keep for herself, just in case. And then, as he was exiting, she told him, "Unlock the baby's door as you go out."

He forgot.

And now thou art cursed from the earth, which hath opened her mouth to receive thy brother's blood from thy hand; when thou tillest the ground it shall not henceforth yield unto thee her strength; a fugitive and a vagabond shalt thou be in the earth.

SEVEN

THE ENDLESS
DESOLATION OF THE SOUL

She heard the milk truck and fell asleep again, and then she heard a creaking of the door. Ruth lifted up from Josephine's bed and saw Albert hunching against the frame, his head hideously swollen and purple, his flannel nightshirt soaked in blood, his handgun dangling from bloody fingers. Wads of cotton spilled from his mouth as he said, "Look what you did to me, Root."

And then she really did wake and Albert was not there. She looked to the Ingersoll clock and saw it was almost half past seven. The hands tied behind her back were tingling. She swung her clotheslined legs to the floor, knelt beside the bed as if childishly praying, and then rocked from knee to knee in an awkward waddle to the hallway and south to her daughter's room. She fell to her side there and felt her green satin nightgown was hiked up but could not arrange it. She caught her breath and softly thudded the oaken door a few times with her head as she called, "Lora. Lora, it's me."

Anyone who saw Henry Judd Gray on Sunday seemed to remember him. At five minutes to six in the morning, an old man named Nathaniel Willis walked up to the bus stop at the major intersection of Springfield Boulevard and Hillside Avenue in Queens Village and saw a man in a gray fedora and herringbone overcoat buttoned up to his chin as if it were below zero. Swaying as he stood on the corner, that man asked, "Any idea when the bus gets here?"

"Seems to be late," Willis said, and then he noticed Officer Charlie Smith, a member of the New York City Police Department, sweeping out his traffic booth. Willis kidded him about cleaning house so early in the morning. The officer ignored him as he collected the night's beer bottles from the sidewalks and streets, stacked them on a curb thirty yards away, crossed to his booth, and took his handgun from its holster. Willis thought he saw Judd flinch. And then, not four feet from Judd, Smith half-turned in an official way, with his left hand on his hip and his right arm and revolver extended, and fired, his right hand jerking up with each of five ear-ringing shots at the beer bottles. He smashed all five. Woke the neighborhood.

Judd Gray remarked to Willis, "I would hate like hell to face him in a firing squad." He meant it in the friendliest way, the innocent jest of an ordinary fellow just waiting for a bus, but his throat was so tight with tension that he squeaked like a juvenile, and so he was stared at by both men and later recalled.

Willis and Judd and a janitor got on the same westbound bus and Willis noticed the limp of the man in the finely tailored clothes as he edged down the aisle. Judd got off near Jamaica Station on Sutphin Boulevard with the intent of riding the Long Island Rail Road west into Manhattan, but three policemen were standing just inside the station entrance, holding coffee mugs and seriously conversing. Judd looked to the street.

A teenage Yellow Cab driver with a face like an altar boy's was waiting outside the Jamaica railway station when a soused man in a herringbone overcoat fell into the taxi's back seat. In an evasive maneuver Judd soon realized was pointless, he told the driver to go to Columbus Circle at 59th and Broadway. Otherwise nothing at all was said, though Paul Mathis remembered that as they crossed over the East River the passenger rolled down the window to feel the cold and sobering air on his face. The final fare was $3.50 and Judd tipped him just a nickel. Mathis scowled at him in the rearview mirror and said, "Thanks a heap, pal."

Judd simply clutched his tan, Italian-leather briefcase to his chest, floundered outside, took a southbound bus to 42nd Street and Fifth Avenue, and walked east to Park Avenue and Grand Central Station. There his hunger overwhelmed him and he went into a railway diner for his first real meal since lunch on Saturday. Waitress Becky Sinclair recalled a hungover man in owlish spectacles confessing, "I'm ravenous," and ordering enough breakfast for three. But he hunched over his food with a fork in his hand and finally did not eat, just swishing coffee in his mouth before he wearily paid and walked out. It was eight o'clock.

About that time on Sunday, Haddon Jones was entering room 743 in the Onondaga Hotel. He fully twisted the white porcelain bath handle labeled *Hot* and let the faucet gush as he jerked the coverlet, blanket, and linens around, swatted the pillows, and yanked a bath towel off its rod. On a hotel envelope, he penciled a note: *Bud: Perfect. Call when you are ready. Had.* He tucked the left edge of the note into the frame of the bathroom mirror so Judd couldn't fail to see it, noticed that bathwater was nicely wetting the floor, and turned off the faucet. Exiting the room, he tossed the blue "Do Not Disturb" sign inside, then locked the door with the hotel key. Haddon left the Onondaga without being seen, got some gas for his Studebaker, and whistled "Blue Skies" as he drove home.

At eight thirty, Judd boarded Pullman car 17 of the New York Central Railroad's train number 3, which was heading for Chicago. Though he was the only passenger in the car, Judd examined his ticket, properly took chair number 1 in the sleeper compartment, and found in his overcoat pocket the pack of Lucky Strike cigarettes that Ruth left for him in the kitchen. *Sash weight + Albert + lucky strike.* He finally caught Ruth's joke but found it not funny. He lit a cigarette.

Colonel Van Voorhees, the New York Central's chief conductor, walked down the main aisle ahead of the Pullman conductor and took Judd's ticket from him. Looking at it, he asked, "Are you going through to Syracuse with us, or do you intend to stop at Albany?"

"I'm going through to Syracuse," Judd said.

"Well, the Pullman won't go there. You'll have to change to a coach."

"Right."

The conductor so seriously stared at him that Judd forced a smile. "I'm memorizing your face," Colonel Van Voorhees said. "That way I can keep your railroad ticket and wherever you are in this car afterward, I'll remember you."

"Nice to know," Judd said.

Twenty minutes after the train left Grand Central Station, he got up to flush the packets of sleeping powders and poison down car 17's toilet, but he found in the lavatory mirror that there was a handprint of Albert's blood on his vest that was just concealed by his overcoat. And he felt so condemned by it that he kept the poisoned rye whiskey just in case suicide seemed the only option later. *An eye for an eye, a tooth for a tooth.* Returning to his seat, he folded a *New York Times* to the section that carried the crossword puzzle and only then noticed that his Cross fountain pen was there but his mechanical pencil was missing. Wondering about that was too tiring for him. And in his fuddle and exhaustion, the puzzle was too hard for him and he discovered he could neither read nor sleep, so he just stared outside at the cool and misty countryside.

In Queens Village then, Assistant District Attorney William Gautier was inviting a gum-chewing teenage stenographer into Lorraine's bedroom to record Mrs. Snyder's initial statement. Ruth smiled in kinship as she told the girl, "I was a stenographer once. At *Cosmopolitan* magazine."

Sitting prissily on a too-small, straight-backed chair, the girl asked, "Where'd you learn?"

"Berg's Business College."

"Me too!"

Attorney Gautier interrupted to say, "Shall we continue?"

The girl flipped open a stenographer's pad and Ruth got more upright on the child's bed, shifting to pillow her spine. "Where do I begin?"

He prompted, "You went out into the hallway . . ."

"Then a giant man with a mustache grabbed me," she stated. "He looked like an Italian. He whispered, 'If you yell, I'll kill you.' Then he hit me a whack over the head and I know nothing more until morning when I came to and called my daughter."

About the time Judd's train was rolling through Ossining, a hearse was taking Albert Snyder's remains to the Harry A. Robbins Morgue at 161st Street, Jamaica. When Judd was outside Poughkeepsie and saw the Hudson River lazing along below the railroad tracks, Ruth's jewelry was being discovered underneath her mattress. Judd frantically yanked down the window and got up to fling the briefcase containing the chemist's gloves, chloroform bottle, and bloodstained Croton wristwatch out into the weather, poking his head outside like a scamp so he could watch the Italian leather briefcase splash into the green water, rock on it awhile, and sink. Ruth's Moroccan leather address book was found in a Windsor desk. And as Judd changed railway cars in Albany, Queens police found a freshly bloodstained pillowcase in the basement hamper and weekly twenty-dollar canceled checks made out to the Prudential Life Insurance Company, seeming to communicate that Mrs. A. E. Snyder would be the beneficiary of a great deal of money.

At five p.m. in Queens Village, police detectives conveyed Albert Snyder's widow to the Jamaica precinct house. She discovered that Milton and Serena Fidgeon and their bridge party guests were gloomily there for questioning. She accepted their sympathy for her great loss. And then Commissioner McLaughlin courteously invited the widow into his office. Agitated but not grieving, she would be there, off and on, for eight hours.

In Syracuse, it was snowing. Judd arrived in his room at the Onondaga Hotel and found Haddon's note on the bathroom mirror. He tore up the note and his Pullman ticket stub and threw them in the wastebasket, which he'd later regret, then telephoned Haddon at home.

Mrs. Jones answered. She said Haddon had spent his day dismantling the two-tone Studebaker's hood, fenders, and doors for painting and was "too pooped to pop," so he was napping. Judd said he envied him. She hoped Judd was still coming over.

"Wouldn't miss it," Judd said. Rooting around in his Bien Jolie sample case, he found a fresh quart of Scotch whisky that he'd forgotten was there and he filled a water glass twice with it as he took a hot bath, and filled the glass once more as he paced room 743 and hatched a plot to hire a car and kill himself in a fatal wreck off the highway to Auburn or Lake Skaneateles. At five forty-five, when he was telephoned in his hotel room, Judd was freshly attired but spent. He hadn't slept in thirty-four hours and was focused on the half-pint flask of rye that she'd poisoned with bichloride of mercury tablets. Hearing the hotel's room phone ringing, he thought of Isabel for the first time that weekend, and he was tentative as he lifted the telephone earpiece. "Hello?"

But it was not his wife. "Would you still like to come over for supper?" Haddon asked.

He had a mental stammer and finally said, "I have forgotten your address."

"Two hundred seven Park Avenue."

The hint had failed. "Will you come and get me?"

"My Studebaker's still laid up," Haddon said, and he heard Judd sigh. "But I'll have a friend drive me down."

The friend was Harry Platt, another insurance salesman and a fat, gray-haired, half-bald man with circular spectacles. He'd joined Haddon in the elevator lift up to Judd's room on the seventh floor and Judd affably invited both of them in for a highball. Harry would testify that Judd was "nervous and excited." After introductions and getting out of their overcoats and hats and slouching down on the sofa with Scotch whisky and seltzers, Judd swiveled a desk chair around and straddled it and said, "I have some 'fessing up to do."

"Ho boy," Haddon said, and turned to Harry. *"Cherchez la femme."*

"What is that? Is that French?" Harry asked.

Judd interrupted. "The fact is I'm in deep trouble. Real deep. And I need your help."

Haddon's face wrinkled with concern as he said, "Count on it, Bud."

"Had, I told you I was going to Albany to meet a lady."

"Oh yeah," Haddon said. "That sweet morsel Momsie."

"Right. But there was a telegram for me, written in code, which advised me to continue on to her house in Queens."

Harry asked, "Am I adult enough to be hearing all this?"

"Please, no jokes," Judd said. "This is very serious. I did as I was told—the kitchen door was open—but while I was in the house, waiting for her, there was a burglary. Seemed like Italian thugs. Didn't know what to do so I hid in the closet for I don't know how long. Hours. Hiding behind the dresses hanging on the hooks as the Italians ransacked the house. But then the family got home from a party and got caught in the middle of it."

"The *family*?" Haddon asked. "Wasn't she intending to see you alone?"

Judd delayed his story as he considered amendments. Haddon and Harry watched him lift his highball and swallow some. Judd finally settled on, "There must have been some miscommunication. I could hear the ruckus from my hiding place. She was assaulted and her husband was slugged and bound. And I couldn't do anything to help them."

"Why not?" Harry asked.

Haddon intervened. "Well, for criminy sakes! Was he supposed to jump out of the closet? Wouldn't the husband figure out Bud's been having a fling with the wife?"

"I guess so," Harry said. "Caught between a rock and a hard place, you were."

"Cowardice was forced on me by the situation. I just hoped they weren't too badly hurt. After things quieted down—golly, it must have been just about sunrise—I hightailed it out of there. Caught a bus to Grand Central Station and then the train to Syracuse."

Haddon frowned. "Were the husband and wife okay?"

Judd had forgotten elements of his tale; he'd have to rehearse it some more. "Oh, sorry. I'm so ashamed to admit it that I left out the worst part. I huddled there in the closet until I heard not a peep in the house, then I screwed up my courage and investigated. The wife had fainted and her wrists and ankles were tied with clothesline, but she seemed otherwise unharmed. I thought it better to let her sleep, to let her think I hadn't gotten there rather than to have to confess my fear and weakness. But I found the husband lying on his bed, unconscious, and maybe I got too close as I listened for a heartbeat because I got his blood on me. And then I ran out. Calling the police was out of the question. The jealous husband versus the philandering salesman caught in his house? I saw no way of defending myself against their accusations." Judd watched their faces with interest as he finished his whisky.

"Was there a heartbeat?" Haddon asked.

"Well, I'm no doctor," Judd said, and filled his own and his friend's glass with more Scotch as he figured out the right thing to say. "A faint heartbeat, I think." Harry finished his highball and held out his glass. Judd poured. "Seltzer?"

"No, thanks," Harry said.

Judd raked his hair with his hand. "But what if the husband winds up dying from his injuries? Then it's murder, and I'll be the principal suspect, won't I? Italian burglars will sound like some thugs I made up from whole cloth. Even if I'm just called in for questioning, my poor mother will be horrified, my wife and child humiliated, if not lost to me. I'll probably be fired from my job. To be frank, I'm in such a fix that I have been entertaining thoughts of suicide." Judd held up the half-pint of rye. "I have poisoned this. And I'm prepared to drink it."

Haddon exclaimed, "Shame on you for even thinking that!"

Harry told him, "Calm down, Judd. You had a rough night, but it's over now and who's going to know you were there?"

Judd put the flask on the desk and sank down on the chair with his head in his hands.

"There's my Bud. That's better," Haddon said. "Don't get overheated. Aren't there steps we can take to protect you?"

Judd lifted his face. "But I hate involving you both."

"We've been in jams, too," Harry said.

Consolingly, Haddon asked, "Really, how can we help?"

Judd smiled with soft pleasure in his high school chum's friendship and with a full measure of disdain for his gullibility. "We need to destroy the evidence."

And so it was that they cooperated in packing a small black suitcase with the gray wool three-piece suit with its handprint of blood on the vest, Albert's patterned blue shirt with its scissored buttonhole, and the bloodstained gray buckskin gloves that Ruth had worn. Then they got into their overcoats and hats and Judd held the black suitcase to his chest as the three rode in Harry Platt's car to the Onondaga County Savings Bank Building on Salina Street. The night watchman took them up to the sixth floor. Harry's insurance office was in room 641. There Harry got on his knees to snatch the clothing out of the suitcase and tightly bundle it inside brown shipping paper, tying it closed with twine. Haddon Jones was the tallest of the three, so it was he who lifted the empty suitcase onto the highest shelf in the office as Judd helped a huffing Harry to his feet.

Early Monday morning, Harry Platt would take the package of bloodstained clothing down to the furnace room, where a janitor heaved it into the fire without inquiry about it. And during her lunch hour, Harry's pregnant secretary would haul the suitcase to the Onondaga Printing Company, her husband's job site, for incineration in that furnace. She later claimed she did not ask Mr. Platt why that was necessary.

On Sunday night, Harry Platt ferried Haddon and Judd to

Haddon's house but floored the car even as Haddon was inviting him inside. Waiting for dinner, Judd entertained Haddon's "two little rascals" by reading the Syracuse *Post-Standard*'s comics page, handling the ballooned dialogue in different voices, and after gin and sandwiches, Judd helped them with their Sunday school homework. Easter would be on April 17th in 1927 and he stunned Haddon and his children with the esoteric information that each year Easter occurred on the first Sunday after the first full moon after the vernal equinox. Judd faintly smiled at Haddon's surprise. "I was a churchgoer once."

"Well," Haddon said, "religion's fine as long as you don't take it too seriously." Haddon couldn't read Judd's face. Was it sneering gloom or regret?

Haddon's wife put the children to bed and Haddon and Judd stayed up, forcing themselves to recall old times in their fraternity at William Barringer High School and finishing off a quart of London dry gin. Each avoided mention of the night in Queens Village. Around eleven, Judd was slurring his words and confessed he was hallucinating, with weird shapes like panthers crouching in the periphery of his vision.

"How long have you been without sleep?"

With sighing effort, Judd did the arithmetic. "Forty hours."

"We'd better get you to the hotel."

At eleven thirty, a taxicab driver collected Judd at 207 Park Avenue and conveyed him to the Onondaga Hotel and later told an investigator that his passenger was snoring soon after he snapped down the metering flag. Judd tore off his clothes as soon as he entered room 743, filled a water glass with whisky that he put within reach on the vanity, folded his tortoiseshell spectacles next to it, and got into bed in his underwear, falling asleep at once.

‿ ‿

Reporters had already filed their newspaper stories about the slain *Motor Boating* art editor, and Albert Snyder's widow was getting ever more confused as forty-year-old police commissioner George V. McLaughlin cross-examined her. Around half past one o'clock in the morning, Detective Lieutenant Michael McDermott walked into the office with a notepad on which he'd written the name "Judd Gray." McDermott crouched to whisper into McLaughlin's ear and the commissioner solemnly nodded, then held the notepad in front of Ruth and concentrated on her sleepy face as she read it. Soothingly, he asked, "Was this the man who killed your husband?"

Ruth finally accepted that she was caught and asked, "Has he confessed?"

The Syracuse Police Department received a cable from the Jamaica precinct house at 1:47 a.m., and acting on Mrs. Snyder's information, three Syracuse detectives arrived at room 743 in the Onondaga Hotel at half past two.

Judd woke to a hard and continuous knocking on his hotel room door and was so disoriented that he presumed he'd overslept and that housekeeping was there to collect his laundry. He switched on a light, hooked his spectacles over his ears, and fell toward the knocking in his drunkenness, finding three sour-looking men in the hallway. Cold eddied off their overcoats.

"Mr. Gray?"

"Yes."

A looming man held up his wallet so Judd could see a Syracuse Police Department badge. "I'm Detective Firth. The New York City Police Department seems to need you for questioning about a homicide."

Weakly trying to buy time for his thoughts, Judd lied, "I don't know what that word means."

"Homicide? It means murder. The City wants to question you about a murder."

The jocular corset salesman took over to say, "Fellas, the only thing I ever killed was a pint of liquor from time to time."

Another detective named Finocchio commented, "We got the joker in the pack, didn't we?"

Firth said, "You'll have to come with us, Mr. Gray."

Entering the hotel room, Finocchio and Firth looked intently at everything, finding a gold Cross fountain pen in his overcoat and a Sunday *New York Times* on his desk, but forgetting to root through the wastepaper basket. A friendly older detective named Kerrigan watched Judd wash up and brush his teeth with Pepsodent in the bathroom, and he leaned into the wall next to the closet as Judd dressed nattily and, because his suitcase was in Harry Platt's office, crammed his hangered suits and shirts into his samples trunk.

"Don't you have luggage?"

"I have to travel light."

Judd found the half-pint of rye that Ruth had contaminated with bichloride of mercury and slipped it into his suit-coat pocket.

"What was that?" Detective Kerrigan asked.

Judd winked. "Cough medicine."

"Well, I'll have to confiscate it for now."

Handing it over, Judd watched as the detective unscrewed the cap and sniffed. Would he taste it next? Judd irritably said, "For God's sake, don't drink it. It's poison."

"Really?"

"Really."

"Huh," Detective Kerrigan said.

At three in the morning on March 21st, a genial Henry Judd Gray was treating the interrogation as either a regrettable mistake or a lark, and he seemed so unlikely a threat to flee or inflict injury that he was not handcuffed as he was escorted outside to a waiting police car. Recalling that he hadn't checked out, Judd gave one of them thirteen dollars for the hotel bill, and as the policeman went inside to pay, Detective Finocchio turned around in his front seat to ask, "You have a lot of friends and associates in New York City?"

"Of course," Judd said.

"Why is it you haven't asked who was murdered?"

All through the night at the Syracuse police headquarters the interrogation continued, and Judd insisted on the fantasy that he'd stayed at the Onondaga all weekend. Around sunrise, Detective Lieutenants Martin Brown and Michael McDermott arrived by train from the Jamaica precinct house, took Judd into an office, and first confirmed that his rather feminine hand size matched the finger gouges on Albert's throat, asked him if he knew Mrs. Snyder—he said he did, and that he loved her—then laid out all the reasons why his fiction didn't fit the facts. But Judd held to it and even added to his lying by convincing them he'd graduated from Cornell University, Detective Brown's alma mater.

Syracuse Police Chief Martin Cadin would say, "I've been in police work for over twenty years, and if he is guilty of this crime, he is the calmest individual I've ever come across."

Around two o'clock in the afternoon, Judd was told that Ruth had confessed and incriminated him, but Judd continued to deny that he'd committed the homicide. Haddon Jones was hauled in to testify about his Sunday evening with Judd, but he just idly worried the Elks club tooth hanging from the gold chain of his pocket watch and in fraternal loyalty offered nothing of value even though he could have been charged with conspiracy.

Acting like a bodyguard, Haddon was grimly on the left of Judd when McDermott and Brown took him into custody for the railway journey to New York City, and it was Haddon's hand that hid Judd's face from the hordes of reporters and photographers that swarmed them when they exited police headquarters.

Was it because it had been almost three in the morning that the detectives overlooked the contents of Judd's hotel wastebasket? A chambermaid named Nellie Barnes heard about the hotel guest's arrest when she got to work on Monday morning. She wisely collected the wastebasket when she cleaned 743, locked it in a closet of cleaning supplies, and then, at lunchtime, contacted police, who found in it cigarette butts and struck matches, a hotel envelope with Haddon's penciled note, a Long Island Rail Road train schedule, an envelope with a Jamaica postmark that was addressed to Judd in Ruth's handwriting, and the 8:45 a.m., Sunday, March 20th, Pullman ticket from New York City to Albany, with a coach connection to Syracuse.

Judd was on the same train to Grand Central Station by four o'clock and had been shown an afternoon Syracuse newspaper with the headline "MRS. SNYDER CONFESSES!" In Albany, Queens assistant district attorney James Conroy and Deputy Inspector Gallagher got on board and Judd heartily shook their hands, genially saying, "This is the first time I've been in the clutches of the law." Judd joined their party in the dining car for supper, gleefully told ladies'-underwear jokes in his nervousness, and even grandly footed the bill for them. He was still treating his predicament as an incongruous misunderstanding and said, "We'll all laugh over this someday."

And then over coffee, Detective McDermott rocked back in his chair and told him, "Oh, by the way, Judd. Did you know we have the contents of your Onondaga Hotel wastepaper basket?"

Judd's face whitened as he thought of what could be in there. "Mac, what did you find in that basket?" Hearing of those findings and realizing how they niftily connected the dots, Judd finally confessed, "Well, gentlemen, I was at that house that night."

And thenceforward, as one journalist put it, "every syllable he uttered was gospel insofar as human fallibility allows."

Alerted to a huge crowd waiting for their arrival at Grand Central Station, the police hustled Henry Judd Gray off the train at 125th Street and took him by car to the Long Island City Courthouse, where he was interviewed by the Queens County district attorney. Though he was just forty-six, Richard S. Newcombe seemed fatherly and old-fashioned, even Victorian, a short, deep-voiced, hand-wringing man who seemed to hurt when he spoke and whose hank of silver hair was woven over his head to give the faint illusion that he wasn't in fact bald. Wincing as he did so, Newcombe went through the details of Ruth's confession that seemed to match the evidence of the crime scene and that implicated Judd in the murder.

"She seems to have turned on you," Newcombe said. "Had she sworn that she'd love you always?"

Judd then felt, he later wrote, *the endless desolation of the soul,* but all he could say was, "How did you know?"

With sadness, Newcombe said, "Well, it happens."

Judd told his story as well as he could in his daze, signed the confession at four in the morning, and was hurried downstairs to be photographed and fingerprinted, then was shackled and escorted to the Queens County Jail through the flashbulbs, crushing onrush, and screamed questions of what he would call "the war maneuvers of the great American Press."

Ruth, too, was astonished by the gangs of journalists, photographers, and gawkers who followed her and her police cortege into the Queens-Bellaire Bank to reveal the Prudential life insurance policies and the other contents of her two safety deposit boxes and then to the Waldorf-Astoria, where she claimed the couple's "honeymoon bag" and was recognized by the manager and staff as "Mrs. Jane Gray."

There were eleven major newspapers in metropolitan New York and each seemed to consider the evolving Snyder-Gray case the crime of the century. And each paper would see its circulation double when Ruth or Judd was featured. So there were installments each day for the next few months and regular items through January 1928, and anything about them, their families, their "sordid love," or their "brutal, cold-blooded murder" seemed a fair subject for discussion.

Even before Judd made it to New York City and then into the Queens County Jail, a news gatherer forced an entrance into Judd's mother's home in West Orange by claiming he was a Brooklyn homicide detective and boorishly demanding that a frail and frightened Mrs. Margaret Gray answer certain questions at once. Another journalist invaded the office of the principal of Washington Elementary School in East Orange on the 21st, insisting on an interview with Jane Gray, who was then ten. The girl was sent home without hearing why and found the family's brick house on 37 Wayne Avenue was guarded by a contingent of police who were holding off a wide gang of shouting reporters.

Isabel finally appeased them that rainy Monday evening with a terse announcement that she read aloud from the front porch, requesting civility and privacy for the family and seemliness from the press corps, and saying she would not believe "the wild allegations about my husband's treachery" unless he personally confirmed them.

She got the chance for that on the morning of Tuesday, March 22nd, when she visited Judd in the Queens County Jail. A Wednesday headline would read "WIFE AIDS KILLER." She was wearing "a beaver coat of inferior quality" and a turban hat "that was not smart." She seemed "cold and passionless" and "inclined to plumpness, not pretty, with no glamour or intrigue."

In jail, she glared at the handcuffed man and asked, "Bud, did you do those things?"

Judd frankly said, "Yes."

Isabel was steward to a jilted wife's agony for a minute, and then she asked, "Did you sign a confession?"

Judd nodded. "At four this morning."

"Were you pressured to sign it?"

"No," he said. "They have treated me like a gentleman."

She became conscious that a great crowd of onlookers was being held in abeyance by the jailers and she spoke more softly, but she was overheard telling her husband, "Don't forget all your friends are standing by you, even though we can't understand why this tragedy has happened. You must have had liquor."

Judd confided details to Isabel but he was aware enough of journalism to hide his mouth and hush his voice so he would be unheard.

After a while she stiffened a little and said in answer, "You asked me to see you. I am here. I intend, as your wife, to do my duty by you."

Holding her hands, he said, "You can see me every day."

She scanned the wolfish faces listening in and said, "That's impossible. I can't do that."

Judd hung his head, and when she stood, he stood. She suffered his kiss.

With tears, she said, "I can't understand it."

"I can't understand it myself."

"And then," it was written, "in an adjoining room, she gave herself over to his affectionate petting."

A few days later Isabel wrote him: *I cannot go out. I haven't the strength. I try to sleep, but that fails me and I stew and stew, hoping that my thoughts are just a nightmare. As I sit here the 91st Psalm is before me. Read it and you will know my thinking. I go over my life with you and look for any wrong that I have ever done. But there is none. I have tried to be a devoted wife and mother to you and dear Jane. And now I only have faint memories of the loving and kind husband you once were to me.*

Isabel was never on view again. Jane never again saw her father.

Haddon Jones had still said nothing to the police, but after an hour's grilling he was allowed to privately visit his friend in his jail cell. Crying, he asked, "Bud, did you do what they're saying?"

Judd answered, "Had, I did."

Haddon sighed with grief. "Oh, Bud. Why did you do it?"

And Judd said, "I don't know myself."

With the feeling that good old Judd would forgive him, Haddon then went to the district attorney's office and was forthright about what he told them regarding his high school friend.

On that Tuesday afternoon, Henry Judd Gray was herded through a formidable crowd for his preliminary arraignment in the police court in Jamaica's town hall. Hundreds jammed Jamaica Avenue and some onlookers ascended the scaffolding on a construction site to watch through the tall courtroom windows as the infamous couple entered their pleas to the magistrate.

Mrs. Ruth Brown Snyder was waiting there, in a green felt helmet hat, brown muskrat coat, flesh-colored silk hose, and green alligator pumps. She still wore her platinum wedding ring. With Ruth were some of the detectives who'd investigated the Sunday crime as well as her ill-matched defense team: Edgar Hazelton, a scholarly former municipal court judge with an interest in Republican politics, and Dana Wallace, a grandiose criminal attorney and confirmed alcoholic who'd studied drama at Yale. The lawyers soon grew to hate each other. Mrs. Josephine Brown had withdrawn ten thousand dollars from the bank for their retainer—her whole life savings—and she'd have lost it all if Wallace hadn't refused his half of the fee for Lorraine's sake.

Judd's attorneys would be Samuel Miller, a certified public accountant in his thirties, whose experience was in corporate and tax law, and the older William J. Millard, a Republican politico, former assistant U.S. attorney, and a close friend of the late president Theodore Roosevelt.

Since Judd and Ruth last saw each other less than sixty hours had passed, so when he walked up beside his lover in the courtroom he instinctively held out his hand to her. She took it affectionately and they exchanged fleeting smiles. But then both recalled the coaching from their attorneys and faced forward. They would never touch again.

Judd would have entered a guilty plea and been done with it, but he was being indicted for first-degree murder, for which a not-guilty plea and jury trial was required.

Ruth's side fervently contended that she was not guilty, that Judd Gray acted alone, and that, "She is being held on an alleged confession which she now repudiates on the grounds that it was made under duress and force."

A public viewing of Albert Snyder was held on the first floor of his home, just below his bedroom, on the night of March 22nd. Mrs. Josephine Brown took care of the arrangements. The shining coffin was made of dark oak; his facial injuries were concealed with cosmetics; his high shirt collar and tie hid the traces of his strangulation. Ruth said she was inconsolable over a judge's refusal to let her attend, but hundreds of others did go there, including the staff of *Motor Boating* magazine, the Shelter Island Yacht Club, the Queens Village Democratic Club, and his friends at the Flatbush Bowling Alley. The funeral eulogy that night was given by Reverend Everett Lyons of the Queens Village Dutch Reformed Church. Albert had dismissed churchgoers as hypocrites, but he'd vaguely known Lyons because Lorraine sometimes went to Sunday school there.

A half mile of cars followed the hearse on Wednesday morning when Albert Snyder's remains were laid to rest in the Schneider family plot at Mount Olivet Cemetery in Maspeth. Afterward, Albert's sisters Mamie and Mabel were interviewed and each talked about him as the soul of kindness. "He was always gentle and considerate. She wasn't of his class or educational level, but he loved Ruth so much that he protected her from everything, even the mildest criticism. And he never complained about her constant gallivanting." C. F. Chapman, the publisher of *Motor Boating* magazine, called Albert "one hundred percent he-man; quiet, honest, upright, ready to play his part in the drama of life without seeking the spotlight."

Judd seemed just the he-man's opposite as he was mercilessly described with variations on "a meek-looking Lothario," "a weazened little corset salesman," "an inert scare-drunk fellow," "a sissy," or "just a sap who was kissed and told on." There were articles that wrongly claimed Judd was raging in his cell, shouting out Bible passages, insanely striding from one wall to the other, or that, seeking to kill himself, he'd tried to inveigle a jailer into getting the "cough medicine" that was taken from him in Syracuse, only to be told the poisoned half-pint of rye whiskey had been locked away in the evidence room.

His face in a photograph was analyzed by the phrenologist Dr. Edgar C. Beall, who alliteratively noted that "the narrow temples declare he is neither methodical, mathematical, musical, mechanical, nor mercantile. To his mind, life is a lottery or a matter of chance. He is therefore, by instinct and habit, a gambler. Gray is a voluptuary, greedily drawing honey from the deep-throated calyx of illicit joy."

Of Ruth Snyder's photos, Beall wrote that "the element of conjugal fidelity is practically nonexistent. She is endowed with an exceptionally voluptuous nature, the demands of which are ceaseless, imperious, and utterly beyond control. A shallow-brained pleasure seeker, she is accustomed to unlimited self-indulgence, which at last ends in an orgy of murderous passion and lust, seemingly without parallel in the criminal history of modern times."

On the Wednesday afternoon of Albert's burial, Ruth held her initial press interview with three carefully chosen female reporters whose written questions where submitted to Edgar Hazelton hours earlier. Just before the overmanaged sit-down, some excluded male reporters strolling a hallway caught Ruth getting her picture taken and overheard the photographer offer sympathy for her loss. To which she shrugged with an "Oh well." And when he hinted that dabbing a handkerchief to her eyes would give the public fitting evidence of her grief, she grinned widely and then flirtatiously warned him, "Don't you dare get a shot of me laughing."

Edgar Hazelton had selected stunningly innocuous questions that Ruth could answer with a confidence and poise that finally seemed a kind of narcissism. Even then she was pretty, but she seemed rather dowdy in the jail's overlarge gray smock and with flyaway hair and purplish welts of sleeplessness under her crazily electric eyes. She spoke in that lilting, sexy, silken voice of a great variety of things: of Lorraine; of her canary, Pip, and her fondness for animals; of her intent, when freed, to become a stockbroker; and of gifts she'd been given at Christmas. The jail breakfasts, she told them, were oatmeal, prunes, toast, and black coffee. She hated wearing this unflattering jail gown; it made her look like a fat fishwife. She said she took up with Judd "only after Albert Snyder eliminated love from the house." About what had happened, she felt "terribly, awfully sorry." Of Judd, she said, "I love him still, in spite of all he has done." About confessing to murder, she said, "I don't know what I was saying when the police got that statement from me. I was so tired that I would say yes to anything they asked me. I deny absolutely any part in the crime." Contradicting herself just a little later, she added, "Any consideration, affection, or love I ever had for Judd Gray has turned to hate because of his cruel and barbarous murder of my poor husband and because he tried to entangle me in it."

She looked to Edgar Hazelton and asked, "Should I say that I'm innocent?"

His pince-nez shone white in the sunlight as he nodded.

She took a hundred words to say she was innocent, and she concluded, "I ask every mother, every daughter, and every wife to withhold judgment until she has heard it all, and I am sure they will find some sympathy, some consideration, some understanding for me in this terrible sorrow which is mine."

In fact, the judgment against Ruth as well as Judd only worsened. An editorial noted, "Lust—stark, blind, cruel lust in hideous form—was the motive for the shocking Snyder murder. No more heinous crime has occurred in the annals of American criminology." And Cornelius Vanderbilt III wrote the next morning: "The instinct of motherhood, the desire of a father to shield his child from harm, common sense, any feeling of decency toward a loving mate were all swept away before a wild surge of guilty passion."

Ruth was at first described as a "headturner," "a wowzer," "a beautiful blonde, five feet seven inches tall" with "China blue eyes crackling sparks." But almost immediately women loathed her and soon she'd even lost some attractiveness to men, becoming for journalists just "the faithless wife," "the blonde fiend," "the Viking vampire," and "the spider woman," or, in more highbrow publications, *"La Belle Dame sans Merci,"* "Mata Hari," and "the quintessential femme fatale." She was felt to have an air of "burning ice," "iron unconcern," and an arrogance that was masquerading as injured dignity. Damon Runyon, who covered the trial for the William Randolph Hearst paper *American,* called Ruth "a chilly looking blonde with frosty eyes and one of those marble, you-bet-you-will chins." One paper even preposterously stated that she was reading Nietzsche and Schopenhauer, "the philosophers blamed for so many student suicides."

Even after the damning interview was published, Judd defended Ruth, saying, "She is a pure woman, a perfect woman, and I won't say anything against her. She is a woman any man would like." Evidence of that came when Judd's attorneys found no less than fifteen mooning men, generally policemen or Coney Island "beach sheiks," who'd been in the gay and gorgeous Tommy's thrall, if not her arms.

Because most of those paramours were married, they never visited her in jail, and because Lorraine was underage, Ruth celebrated her thirty-second birthday on Sunday, March 27th, with just Josephine and her lawyers. Mrs. Brown had baked a twelve-egg, "heavenly angel food" cake that the jailers had ravaged with a pencil to ensure no tools of escape were concealed inside it. But even the butchery of a dessert delighted Ruth. She beamed and bounced on the jail cot like a child before shutting her eyes to blow out the flames on imaginary candles. Edgar Hazelton smiled and asked what she'd wished for, and Ruth said, "Liberty and justice for all."

Dana Wallace teetered as he squeezed up a ball of cake and filled his mouth and fell down in a hard-backed jail chair, intoxicated and tired.

Like a good hostess, like Emily Post, Ruth told Hazelton and Josephine, "Oh please, everybody. Eat up. Eat and be merry."

After coolly wishing May a happy birthday, Josephine felt permitted to scoop up a handful of cake, for there were no forks, then sucked the goo from her fingers. Hazelton slouched against the jail bars with folded arms and an ankle crossed, kindly evaluating his client.

She told him, "Al and I were going to have the grandest birthday party last night. Loads of company. Liquor already bought. Al was selecting his favorite music for the Victrola, but I insisted on some more popu—"

"Mrs. Snyder, please," Hazelton said. "I'm not the jury."

She stared at him with concerned innocence and for some reason she recalled heat misting the bathroom mirror as she lifted a tiny Lorraine from the sink, and carrying the towel-swaddled infant, fresh from the bath and fragrant, her small head bobbing against Ruth's brassiere and then finding a tiny thumb. And Hazelton was looking at her as she told him how she'd linger by Lorraine's bed and love her child as she slept. Tears rose in Ruth's eyes in a slow, tidal way, and then her face reefed and she folded over toward her gray-smocked knees and rocked as she cried, "Oh, why isn't my baby here? Don't they know how much I need her? Don't they see what I've done for her? She's my oxygen!"

Mrs. Brown softly patted her daughter's back in a *there-there* gesture but contradictory emotions would not let her speak.

Ruth bolted upright on her cot and fiercely shouted at Hazelton, "Cruel and unusual punishment, denying me Lorraine! You tell them! Cruel and unusual! I'm her *mother*!"

Hazelton tugged up Dana Wallace's left elbow and Wallace's head jerked from his doze.

She screamed, "Are you listening to me?"

Hazelton ignored her as he helped Wallace struggle up from his chair. "Well, we'll be going now. We just wanted to wish you the very best on your birthday."

"Are you representing Judd Gray?" she demanded.

"Emphatically no."

"You do as I say then."

And Hazelton smiled as he repeated, "Emphatically, no."

She wrote a poem:

> *Just a thought of cheerful things,*
> *Things I used to know.*
> *Joys that loving—mothering brings,*
> *Watching Lorraine grow.*
> *Years, Oh, ages—long ago*
> *Happiness was mine.*
> *Oh, I loved my family so,*
> *Now all I do is pine.*

With Mrs. Isabel Gray, Mrs. Kallenbach, and Jane all hiding out in Norwalk, Connecticut, the newspapers again sought out Judd's mother, Mrs. Margaret Gray, as the not-Ruth of the day. She was sixty but seemed much older, a frail, white-haired, cultivated, sorrowful woman whose selflessness, loyalty, and piety were treated as an instructive contrast to Mrs. Snyder.

Mrs. Gray invited a freight truck full of reporters out to Judd's sister's house in West Orange and gave them coffee and still-warm macaroons from the oven as she talked about how Buddy loved reading as a boy and was an excellent student and athlete who would have gone on to college and medical school were it not for the pneumonia he caught in high school. She petted her white Pomeranian Nicky in her lap as she spoke, also, of the jobs Bud had held, the good deeds he'd done, that "he was not what I would call a drinker." "Bud's home life was ideal," she said. "Isabel and he never quarreled. They had a fifty-fifty arrangement in which they were both equal in their home."

She was asked if she still loved her son and she said, "The Judd Gray of today is a boy I don't understand. But one I must help. He must be brought back. I am trying to reach through this strange personality and . . ." Quavering, her tragic eyes flooding with tears, she broke off that sentence and could not go on.

Quietly offering their sympathy, the reporters excused themselves from the home and only on the jouncing ride back to the City did one scour his notes and find that she'd referred to "Buddy" as "my son," "my precious boy," and "my darling boy." She said she'd urged Judd always to be manly, but she'd never once called him a man. And he was thirty-four years old.

Judd Gray was forced by his counsel to have an X-ray taken of his skull to see if there was a medical cause for the crime; then he was interviewed by a panel of four alienists to find out if he was sane. Included in their tests was his giving a vial of blood for analysis, walking a chalk line, and spinning until he fell. Psychiatry was still in its infancy. And then he was seated in a chair opposite four other chairs, and Doctors Cusack, Block, Leahy, and Jewett closely scrutinized the criminal. Judd chain-smoked as he was questioned and joked whenever he could, but after fifteen minutes he excited their interest by unself-consciously revealing that Ruth's nickname for him was Loverboy and his nickname for Ruth was Momsie, and that he felt hypnotized and helplessly dominated by her.

"Was there any pleasure for you in that?" one alienist inquired.

"How do you mean?"

"Having Mrs. Snyder in control of you? Compelling you one way or another?"

"I guess."

Another asked, "Why? Why do you guess?"

"Well, we were together for twenty-one months."

Three alienists made notations as Dr. Thomas Cusack inquired, "But what is it that interests or excites you in the opposite sex?"

Judd looked away and was silent for a long time, giving it so much rumination that the alienists weren't convinced of his candor when he finally said, "I am attracted to females not by their beauty or sheer physical enticements so much as by their neatness and intelligence."

A doctor jotted on his notepad, *Effeminate?* and another jotted underneath that, *Lying*.

Dr. Siegfried Block asked, "Tell me, in jail now, what are your fantasies?"

"Sexual, you mean?"

"Sexual or otherwise. You have so little to do, so much time on your hands. You must find yourself dreaming, remembering."

Judd exhaled smoke and crushed his cigarette out. "I haven't got much of an imagination."

Instructed to reconsider some childhood memories that night in his cell and to write an account of one that seemed to be recurring and important, he turned in this recollection: *I was just a child, about four. Awaking from sleep, I found myself on the sofa with my head in my mother's lap. A fly is whirring around my face and she chases it away. She strokes my hair with her gloved hand. If I raise my head, Mother fans me quiet with a cardboard fan that has a beautiful girl pictured on it. She has very red cheeks, blue eyes, and yellow curls, and I fancied she was eating a heaped up plate of ice cream. It's a hot day and my sailor suit is stiff. It pricks through my underclothes.*

At the end of the sessions, the panel voted that Henry Judd Gray was sane within the meaning of the law, but that liquor,

Oedipal conflicts, and the sexual novelties to which he'd been introduced by Mrs. Snyder had hampered his judgment of right and wrong. Dr. Siegfried Block said of Judd, "I feel so sorry for him," and Dr. Thomas Cusack commented, "If he'd just seen one of us for a while, none of this would have happened."

Seeing Mrs. Margaret Gray's interview about her son, Mrs. Josephine Brown sought to uphold her daughter's reputation by agreeing to have a few journalists to their spic-and-span corner house. She indicated Ruth's flair for interior decorating and handicrafts and forced them to note that the kitchen's white-enameled oven was so spotless it could have been new. "And you could eat off that floor." She took them down to see Ruth's neatly labeled fruit preserves and said, "Who puts up fruit anymore?"

Walking into the music room, Josephine said the upright player piano needed tuning and Ruth wanted to have it fixed, but Albert had raged, "You let that piano alone, you buttinsky!"

"She let it alone and stood back, trembling all over."

Josephine primly sat in the floral chintz armchair, illustrating, as one journalist wrote, "the humorous grimness of a kindhearted grandma." She recalled for them in her Swedish cadence, "Al did not like to laugh. He had a bad temper. He thought she was foolish to laugh and be gay. And he was always working on something—so intense always. He seemed to be too occupied to play."

She looked off at a photo of the pretty, tomboyish Lorraine. "I think their love really died after the baby came. Mr. Snyder, he said she was just a lot of sickness and expense."

The joint Snyder-Gray first-degree-murder trial was originally slated to begin on April 11th, 1927, but that would have meant holding the hearings during Holy Week, so Justice Townsend Scudder, of the New York State Supreme Court, delayed the initial interviews of prospective jurors until after Easter.

A Palm Sunday service for Protestants was held in the Queens County Jail on April 10th. Like Albert, Ruth was not a churchgoer, but with nothing much to do, she decided to attend, watching Judd throughout from the women's side of the chapel and sneering at his full-throated reverence as he sang: "'Lead, Kindly Light, amidst th'encircling gloom, / Lead Thou me on! / The night is dark, and I am far from home, / Lead Thou me on! / Keep Thou my feet; I do not ask to see / The distant scene; one step enough for me.'"

She'd brought out the best in the runt. And now he was Isabelling. Ruth then remembered a gay nineties song she'd heard as a girl—"She's More to Be Pitied Than Censured"—and she giggled so hard and distractingly that she was forced to leave the chapel, humming the tune as she went.

Yet she requested a visit from the jail chaplain that evening. The minister was home having dinner with his family, so she was sent the Roman Catholic chaplain of the Queens County Jail, Father George Murphy of the Brooklyn Diocese. He was an affable, overweight, fun-loving man with a gin-blossom nose and she liked him at once in spite of his off-putting black cassock and biretta. She wanted to tell him about her fresh discovery: that women gave men sex so they could get love, and men gave women love so they could get sex.

"Well, yes," Murphy seriously said. "That's something of an old saw."

"Really? I just figured it out."

"Oh dear," the priest said with a smile. "Too soon old and too late smart? We see that a lot in here."

"But also, men fantasize about sex all the time."

"Very true," he said, and winked. "In my confessional experience."

"And women fantasize about romance."

"Yes."

"And looking for romance will get you in just as much trouble."

The jolly man exclaimed, "Oh, but I wish you could preach!" And he stayed with Ruth in the cell for an hour that night, instructing a little and telling jokes and treating their meeting like a party. She felt girlish again and begged him to return, which he did regularly each morning after he'd finished with the jailed Catholics that he called "the brethren."

On Holy Thursday he gave her the gift of a jet-black rosary, which he called, romantically, "a garland of roses," and he included with the gift a folded paper on which he'd handwritten the words to the Our Father, the Hail Mary, and the Glory Be. But Ruth failed to make the connection with prayer and thought of the sixty strung beads as a pretty necklace, happily flaunting the rosary as the only jewelry she was allowed.

Even so, the murder trial that would begin on April 19th so unhinged Ruth Snyder that she ignored the legal advice of Edgar Hazelton and Dana Wallace and on the seventeenth, Easter Sunday, she issued a screed about Judd Gray to a friendly journalist from the New York *Daily Mirror*. She'd scrawled it in pencil on a child's school tablet, in handwriting so large she could only fit three or four words on each line. The journalist corrected Ruth's misspellings and inserted so many fillips of his own that she was forced to practice the recitation before Easter's pool reporters were invited to her jail cell.

Too jittery to sit, she tilted into the jail bars as if she would soon faint and with shaking hands, fluent tears, and a tremulous voice Ruth read aloud: "I know now that Judd Gray is a coward, a low, cringing, sneaking jackal, the murderer of my husband, who is now trying to hide behind my skirts to try to drag me down into the stinking pit that he himself willingly wallowed in; to brand me as a woman who killed her husband."

She flipped a page. "I am a mother! I love my child and I loved my child's father! God! Can you mothers and wives read this and appreciate the terrible, stifling ordeal I am going through at this time? Easter Sunday! Holy Week! I wish I was home with Albert and Lorraine. Oh, what a tragic difference a few months make."

With violence, she flipped another page. "Please, mothers and wives, abide with me in your thoughts. Do not think of me harshly. Your sympathy will not help me before the bar of justice, but it will comfort me to know that I am not an outcast in the eyes of the women of this world."

She closed the tablet and wrestled up a smile. "Will that do the trick?"

Six reporters were still jotting their shorthand when a quicker woman asked, "Are you aware that female jurors are not allowed in a murder trial?"

Half her face twitched. "You're kidding."

The pool reporter said she wasn't. New York law.

Ruth flumped onto her jail cot with a hand over her eyes as if she were full of woe, but she heard a tiny squeak and childishly beamed as she looked to a far wall where a gray mouse's head was dodging about in a food hunt. She kissed the air and the mouse cautioned forward to a smidgen of toast crust that she held out to him, even sitting back on his hind legs and craning his neck to get what she held just out of reach. Ruth smiled to the reporters. "My little pet," she said. "See how he loves me?"

ᕮ EIGHT ᕲ

THE WAGES OF SIN

Because Justice Townsend Scudder disliked the death penalty and the theatrical nature of criminal trials, he sought another judge to replace him when the Snyder-Gray case was put on his docket, but no one else with jurisdiction was available. Reluctantly, he took it on. Scudder was then sixty-one and a widower, a scholarly, patrician man with a European education and sonorous voice who'd graduated from Columbia University Law School in 1888, was elected to two terms as a congressman, and served thirteen years with the New York Supreme Court before returning to the private practice of law. In February 1927, his friend Governor Alfred E. Smith reappointed him to that court and Scudder was his first choice to succeed him in the governorship if Smith resigned to run for the presidency in 1928, as in fact he did. But ex-assistant secretary of the Navy Franklin Delano Roosevelt would insert himself into the governor's race, and Scudder would graciously step aside, retiring from the judiciary in 1936, exhibiting his prized cocker spaniels in international dog shows, and only dying in 1960, at the age of ninety-four.

The first interviews of jurors—called "talesmen" in New York—took place on Monday, April 18th, 1927, just four weeks after Judd Gray, with murderous intent, journeyed down from the Onondaga Hotel in Syracuse to the Snyder home in Queens Village. In heat that reached as high as eighty-six degrees, Justice Scudder eventually examined three hundred ninety men before he found twelve talesmen who didn't try to weasel out of jury duty with excuses like "dyspepsia" or "tenderheartedness" and could swear they weren't influenced by the one-sided stories in the press. Because the accusation was that there was a conspiracy to commit murder, Justice Scudder crucially decided that the defendants would be tried jointly; hence the trial was not just *State of New York v. Snyder and Gray* but also *Snyder v. Gray* and *Gray v. Snyder.* Essentially each of the accused would be prosecuted twice, but the joint trial was felt to be advantageous for Judd since no Queens County jury had ever sent a woman to the Sing Sing "death house" and he could perhaps piggyback on that reluctance.

In defending their client, Judd's attorneys would adopt the strategy of insisting that he was dominated by the hypnotic and overpowering will of a conniving, attractive woman who exploited his obliging nature, erotic desires, and other vulnerabilities; that she augmented her mastery of him by threatening to disclose Judd's misconduct to his wife; and that he killed Albert Snyder in absolute obedience to Ruth's wishes, a subservience born out of both infatuation and fear. Judd's attorneys would argue that it was she who planned the crime and he but carried out her orders, even to the establishment of an "ironclad" alibi that located him in Syracuse at the time of the murder. Court proceedings, it was said, would make it evident that Mrs. Snyder had everything to gain in getting rid of her husband, while Judd had nothing to look forward to beyond greater freedom in their trysts and lovemaking, which had never been interrupted and were not likely to be.

Ruth Snyder's defense was established by attorneys Hazelton and Wallace just two days after the crime: she recanted a confession coerced from her on March 21st after more than sixteen hours of police grilling in which she was denied sleep or solace after the shocking, bloody, and devastating loss of the deceased. She would maintain that Judd was intent on murdering her husband, that she'd allowed him access to the house only in order to have it out with him and finally end the affair, and that she'd accepted the sash weight from Judd in the restaurant to get it out of his hands. Ruth's attorneys would argue that she and Judd had often joked about her husband's up-and-down health and the gladsome possibility of his accidental death, but that the thought of a homicide was the farthest thing from her mind. She'd had a change of heart that Judd had ignored. She would contend that Judd deliberately, solely, and secretly hatched the plan to kill Albert Snyder and, having done so, tied up the corpse, counterfeited a burglary and assault by fabricated Italians, and threatened to murder Ruth with Albert's revolver unless she assisted him in the deception. She'd been scared enough to cooperate with Judd for a while, and then she cooperated with the detectives, giving them exactly what they wanted in the vain hope of being allowed to go home to a grieving nine-year-old daughter.

Judd Gray had lost weight and was almost spindly when he was handcuffed in his jail cell and huddled within a squad of bailiffs for the secret predawn walk to the courtroom. Earlier, Harry Folsom had brought him clothing from Judd's East Orange home, so he was, as always, a Brooks Brothers model in a fine, dark, tailored suit and owlish tortoiseshell glasses, his stern face soothed with Tabac aftershave and his ridged and furrowed walnut-brown hair gleamingly groomed with Brilliantine.

Looking up at the Queens County Courthouse from the sidewalk, Judd asked a friendlier bailiff about its architecture and was told the building was in the English Renaissance Revival style. But it was in fact a rather garish, four-story jumble of red brick and limestone, with paired Ionic columns holding up balconies on each side of its high, arched entrance. Inside, Judd and his squad of guards noisily trudged up a grand marble staircase with intricate black ironwork that zigzagged up to oak-paneled hallways. And then they were in a majestic, third-floor courtroom with a forty-foot ceiling, Jersey cream wall facings, heavy dark oak furniture and high-backed pews, and a magnificent skylight of green and orange stained glass that sketched a flaming torch and the scales of justice. Judd was told that Cecil B. DeMille shot the trial scenes for his 1922 movie *Manslaughter* there.

"Oh, yes, of course," Judd said. "Leatrice Joy starred in it, right?"

A bailiff seemed affronted by his calm. "You *do* know why you're here?"

"It's just that I was recalling how Miss Leatrice Joy began the bobbed hair craze."

Judd was escorted into an oak-paneled side room and given a doughnut and coffee. And his conversation shifted to other movies and musical revues over his nervous three-hour wait for the first session.

The Queens County courtroom was meant to accommodate two hundred fifty people, but even during jury selection there were half that many just in credentialed reporters, with fifteen hundred more viewers jammed in so tightly that the acoustics worsened, and so for the first day of the trial a Long Island broadcasting company outfitted the room with microphones and loudspeakers—the first time that had ever been done in a court.

Sitting right behind Judd and in front of the rows of journalists and the wide courtroom railing were the Gray family, including Judd's plump sister Margaret and her husband Harold Logan and Judd's mother, the haggard Mrs. Margaret Gray, who hitched her chair so she could fix a smoldering glare on Ruth. Also initially in the audience were his employers, Alfred Benjamin and Charles Johnes, and a few of their staff; Manhattan lingerie buyers; Elks club members from Orange; and friends from the Club of Corset Salesmen of the Empire State, plus Haddon Jones and Harry Platt, who would be witnesses for the prosecution. Isabel, Jane, and his mother-in-law stayed in Connecticut.

Mrs. Josephine Brown also was missing, having chosen instead to stay home with her granddaughter. But sitting behind Ruth in the courtroom were her familiars: Kitty Kaufman, Harry Folsom—still a friend to both defendants—and Ruth's frail, tubercular cousin Ethel, whose divorce from Patrolman Ed Pierson had been finalized in the Bronx Supreme Court. Kitty, Harry, and Ethel would never be required to testify since both the prosecution and the defense sought a tidy narrative with none of the puzzling contradictions and tangents of real life.

Ruth was no longer a sylph. Though some journalists would still write of her beauty and shapeliness, others exaggerated her ordinariness, for the inactivity of jail had caused her to gain weight, she'd not seen a hairdresser in a month, and she was forced to manicure her nails with matchsticks. She wore on the first day of the trial Shalimar perfume and the chic, all-black outfit she'd bought at Bloomingdale's for Albert's funeral: the patent-leather pumps, sheer hose, a Jeanne Lanvin silk dress, as well as the jet-beaded rosary with a silver crucifix that she wore as a necklace. Father George Murphy chose not to correct her and each morning as she walked into the courtroom he would wink or offer a thumbs-up to gladden her spirits.

Because of the risk of disorder and pandemonium in an over-burdened courtroom, off-duty policemen were given free admission, a lot of them still friends of Tommy, not a few of them drunk by noon. And there must have also been in that audience at least some of those satyrs who thought they knew what they wanted and sent the jailed dominatrix one hundred sixty-four proposals of marriage.

But the focus of attention was often on the hundreds of celebrities who attended the trial. It was a hot-ticket item and generally only the famous or connected got inside. The eleventh Marquis of Queensbury, in morning coat and spats, and his wife Cathleen were regulars. Composer Irving Berlin was there and was vexed to hear that Ruth and Judd had adopted his song "Always" as theirs. Arriving in a limousine from his mansion on Long Island was D. W. Griffith, the American director of more than five hundred silent films, including *Intolerance* and *The Battle of the Sexes*. Griffith thought there could be a thrilling melodrama in the trial, as did theater owner and producer David Belasco, who affected the soutane of clergy as the self-anointed "Bishop of Broadway" and thought of Ruth as "passionate and misunderstood and not nearly as bad as she's made out to be." The *Telegram* engaged Will Durant, the author of the surprising bestseller *The Story of Philosophy,* to contribute opinions because his book was, inconceivably, a favorite of Ruth's. The *Evening Graphic* ironically countered Durant with the sly humor of vaudevillian Jimmy Durante. Actress and playwright Mae West had just been released from ten days in jail for *Sex,* the risqué Broadway farce that was shut down for indecency, and now she was assigned to act as a commentator on the

Snyder-Gray case by the *National Police Gazette.* Short-story writer Fannie Hurst was hired for the length of the trial, as was Maurine Dallas Watkins, the playwright of *Chicago,* which was about two "jazz babes" who became murderesses. Accompanying Watkins was comedienne Francine Larrimore, who created the role of *Chicago*'s Roxie Hart, and stated in the play, "I'm so gentle, I couldn't harm a fly." In a pretrial interview, Ruth had stunned reporters with the variation, "Kill my husband? Why, I wouldn't hurt a fly."

The oft-married celebrity Peggy Hopkins Joyce wrote maliciously about Ruth and Judd for the New York *Daily Mirror,* as did Samuel Shipman, whose play *Crime* was still running and whose leading lady, Sylvia Sidney, joined him in the courtroom. The magician Howard Thurston was a continuing presence, as was Ben Hecht, the screenwriter and novelist who was called "the Shakespeare of Hollywood." Actress Olga Petrova generously posed for a host of photographers in front of the Rolls-Royce that oozed her there. Evelyn Law of *The Ziegfeld Follies* also found attendance a fine way to get noticed, as did so many other theater people that their general seating area was called "the Actor's Equity Section."

Wearing an odd Buster Brown necktie was the Reverend John Roach Straton, pastor of Calvary Baptist Church, the first hellfire preacher to broadcast his Sunday sermons over the radio and the man who would campaign against the Catholic Al Smith as the presidential "candidate of rum, Romanism, and rebellion." Revivalist Billy Sunday skeptically looked in on the trial one day, and in nightly columns for the *Evening Graphic,* evangelist Aimee Semple McPherson railed against "Sex Love," "demon alcohol," "red-hot cuties," and the multiple sins and vices on exhibit in the trial.

It was mid-April and getting hot in that third-floor room, but flashy ladies still displayed their sealskin coats and muskrat furs. They carried opera glasses. And though playwright Willard Mack would negatively review the trial—"The plot is weak. The construction is childlike. The direction is pitiful. The principals are stupid"—each performance was standing-room only.

Justice Scudder introduced the situation and accusations for the jury on the first morning, noting that the defendants were jointly on trial for the crime of murder in the first degree, that each was presumed to be innocent, that the burden of proof could never shift from the prosecution to the accused, and if the jury entertained a reasonable doubt of guilt, both must be acquitted. And then Justice Scudder critically indicated that "if two persons with malice afore-thought and with a deliberate and premeditated design join hands to kill a third person, and accomplish the act, the law does not con-cern itself as to how much of the act of inflicting death was done by either one; the fact that they both participated in any degree makes them equally guilty."

Stout, short, silver-haired Richard Newcombe calmly presented the government's strong case against the couple in just thirty min-utes, deftly organizing details and chronology and giving evidence that the murder was premeditated by noting that Henry Judd Gray initially intended to kill Ruth's husband on March 7th. "Whether it was an act of Providence that left that poor devil, Albert Snyder, to live a few more weeks I don't know, but the crime was not consum-mated that night."

Employment of that vaguely salacious phrase—"consummated that night"—was not accidental. Adultery and homicide were linked throughout the trial. One journalist quoted Shakespeare's *Pericles* in writing, "'One sin, I know, another doth provoke; murder's as near to lust as flame to smoke.'" Judd had admitted exchanging "caresses" with Ruth before and after she strangled Albert, and because a full three hours were exhausted between the killing and Judd's getaway, it was gossiped that they had engaged in congratulatory intercourse when Albert's body was not yet cold. The district attorney hinted at that in his opening statement by noting the three-hour gap and saying they could only have been filled with "planning and conceiving and scheming and God knows what else—I don't *want* to know."

Warren Schneider stated that the corpse he'd identified was that of his brother; Dr. Howard Neal of the medical examiner's office testified about Albert Snyder's cause of death; a toxicologist noted Albert's extreme drunkenness; the office manager at the Waldorf-Astoria testified that over fifty registration slips were signed in the names of "Mr. and Mrs. H. J. Gray"; and Leroy Ashfield, who'd justifiably lost his job with the Prudential Life Insurance Company, wanly maintained that there was no intent to deceive Mr. Snyder in having him affix his signature to a blank form that would result in a forty-five-thousand-dollar policy with a double-indemnity clause.

Confessions were read; Queens detectives and assistant district attorneys recollected their actions, observations, and conversations; a German waiter at Henry's said he'd frequently seen Ruth and Judd together there; Dr. Harry Hansen, the first physician at the homicide scene, said he'd found no injuries to Ruth's skull that would cause unconsciousness. And put into evidence were picture wire, a gold Cross mechanical pencil, Albert's handgun, the towel and necktie used in tying him, the blue cotton handkerchief soaked in chloroform, Judd's half-pint of poisoned rye whiskey, and the bloodstained pillowcase found hidden in the Snyders' laundry hamper.

It was ascertained that Judd was seen waiting for a bus in Queens Village on Sunday, March 20th, that a taxi took him from Jamaica Station to Manhattan, and that he was seen on the New York Central run to Syracuse that Sunday morning. Then Haddon Jones and Harry Platt were called to testify about Judd's prevarications that night. And suddenly, just after noon on April 28th, Richard Newcombe stood to announce, "The people rest their case."

Attorneys for the accused were so surprised that the state had halted its prosecution at that juncture that they sought, and were granted by Justice Scudder, time to stall, prepare motions, and organize their defense.

And then the fifteen hundred in the jammed courtroom, the vast majority of them women, finally were rewarded with the chilly testimony of Mrs. Ruth Snyder, the fiend they already loathed. Writing of her courtroom demeanor up until then, Damon Runyon noted, "Whatever else she may lack, which seems to be plenty, the woman appears to have nerve. She has never for a moment cowered like her once little pal of those loving days before the black early morning of March 20th. She has been cold, calm, contemptuous, gusty, angry, but never shrinking, save perhaps in that little walk to and from the court between the recesses. She then passes before the hungry eyes of the spectators. That seems to be her most severe ordeal."

She was called as a witness on the afternoon of Friday, April 29th, hastening to the stand with both hands clutching the front of her jet-black coat, a felt, brimmed helmet hat hiding much of her straw hair, and her frosty eyes avoiding all others.

Those hundreds who'd just been listening over the hallway loudspeakers outside all but rioted in trying to jam into the court-room, and policemen got out their nightsticks to force the onrush back.

When there was a little peace, Justice Scudder tilted left toward Ruth and in his rich, theatrical voice cautioned, "Now, madam, you are not required to take the chair as witness. The law privileges you, and you can testify only of your own free will and accord. If you do take the stand, you are subject to the state's cross-examination as is any other witness. The court now affords you an opportunity to decide whether you would prefer to avail yourself of your privilege."

"I'll take the stand, please," she said in that soft, velvety, affectionate soprano that few there had ever heard. Half the thousand in the room stood to see more of her and realized that she was in fact prettier than the venomous depictions of her in the press, with a face of luminous, ivory skin and riveting, starry, Delft-blue eyes. Some writers even compared Ruth to the shy, stately, tranquil women in paintings by Alessandro Botticelli or Jan Vermeer.

Edgar Hazelton began the questioning with some background on Mrs. Snyder's relationship with her husband, extracting from her that she and Albert were continually arguing within three months of their marriage and that whenever Albert got irritated with his wife, he contrasted Ruth with the late Jessie Guischard, "the finest woman he had ever met." His motorboat was even named the *Jessie G* until Ruth forced him to change it. She admitted she'd secretly undergone surgery in order to conceive a child, and that just angered Albert more, and he was nettled further that Lorraine wasn't a boy.

Ruth's mouth quivered as she mentioned Lorraine and she cried into her handkerchief, only recovering composure when Justice Scudder handed her a glass of water.

Hazelton established that she'd been a good wife and mother, teaching Lorraine prayers and hymns, sewing curtains and the baby's clothes, stocking the cellar with fruit preserves. And then he asked, "You were unfaithful to your marriage vows with Henry Judd Gray, were you not?"

She shied from his stare. "Yes."

"Was this the only man except your husband who ever knew you carnally?"

"Yes."

She said she did not drink much, she never smoked, she insisted on extra insurance only because Albert seemed so accident-prone: there had been incidents in the garage when the jack gave way and the Buick fell on him, or when the motor was running and the garage door swung shut. And he was sleeping on the sofa and she'd reached to switch the radio off and she'd accidentally kicked the gas pipe off its floor cock, then gone on an errand. She returned to find Albert was almost asphyxiated. She'd mentioned that in a letter to Mr. Gray, who shocked Ruth with his wish that Albert had died.

"Was that a typical response from him?"

"Uh-huh. Getting rid of my husband was a regular subject with him." She then said that was the reason she intended to end the relationship, but that Judd had warned that if she "ever stopped going with him he was going to tell the world what kind of shameless woman I was."

Hazelton then invited Ruth to say how she'd acquired the sash weight, and she told him that it was in a package Mr. Gray had given her at Henry's Restaurant. She'd thought the package contained just a rolling pin that Benjamin & Johnes was marketing as a flesh reducer, but she later found in it the sash weight and a note in his handwriting that read: *I'll be there Monday night to do the job.*

She'd hidden the sash weight in the cellar. When Judd arrived on the 7th, he'd said he was there "to finish off The Governor," but she'd objected, "Judd, you'll do no such thing!"

She said he'd then decided to return on Thursday, Albert's bowling night, "and get him in the garage," but Judd got cold feet and instead left on his sales route, heading first to Buffalo. She received a bulky letter from him with instructions to give Albert the enclosed sleeping powders before the Snyders left for the March 19th party at Milton Fidgeon's house. She washed the powders down the kitchen sink. But her worst fears were realized when she got home from the Saturday-night party and found Judd in Mama's room. She whispered that she'd see him later because she wanted to tell him their love affair was over. Waiting twenty minutes, until she was certain her husband was sleeping, she went back to Judd, who kissed her.

"I immediately felt the rubber gloves on his hands, and I said, 'Judd, what are you going to do?' And he became semi-mad to think that things hadn't gone as he'd planned."

"What did he say to you?"

"He said, 'If you don't let me go through with it tonight, I'm going to get the pair of us.' And he then had my husband's revolver, and he said, 'It's either he or it's us.' I grabbed him by the hand and took him downstairs to the living room."

She claimed they'd talked there for quite a while as she pleaded with him to get thoughts of murder out of his mind, "and in my excitement I said things that probably enraged him." She excused herself to go upstairs to the bathroom and then "I heard this terrific thud." She ran down the hallway and found Judd straddling Albert, hitting him with the sash weight.

Hazelton seemed honestly in suspense as he asked, "What did you do?"

"I ran in and grabbed Mr. Gray by the neck, pulled him off, and in wrestling with him he slugged me to the floor, and I fainted. I remember nothing else until I came to again and saw my husband lying there under a pile of blankets. I was hauling them off and—"

She stooped forward, shaking, and wept for a minute.

The courtroom went silent.

Judd fleetingly glanced up at her, then gazed at his shoes. A heavy old jailhouse matron walked up to hug Ruth into calm.

Justice Scudder watched Ruth and finally told Hazelton, "You may proceed."

"Yes, sir," Ruth's attorney said, and asked, "When you came to, was Gray in the room?"

She wiped her eyes with her handkerchief as she answered no. She was trying to pull the blankets off her poor husband's head when Judd came running into the room, shouting, "Are you trying to undo what I've done?" She was roughly hauled by him into Josephine's room and there he said, "I have gone through with it, and you have to stand just as much of the blame as I have." And then he told her, "We can frame up a burglary. We will both get out of it."

"I had no hand in that murder at all," Ruth told her attorney, "but I knew then I was in the mix-up, and I just had to sit and listen as he made up the lies I told the detectives all that Sunday."

"Were you afraid at that time?" Hazelton asked.

"I was heartily afraid. I saw what a terrible mess he had made of things and I couldn't see my way out other than doing what he asked me to do." She helped him to ransack the house and she let him gag her and tie her hands and feet with rope.

"Why did you let him do that?"

"Because I was afraid if I did not go in with what he asked me to do that he would finish me that night."

The court adjourned.

Reporter Damon Runyon wrote of Ruth that night: "In the main she was as cold and calm sitting there with a thousand people staring at her as if she were at her dinner table discoursing to some guests. She kept her hands folded in her lap. She occasionally glanced at the jury, but mostly kept her eyes on Edgar Hazelton. If she is the cruel and cunning blonde fury that Gray's story would cause you to believe, you would expect her to be calm. But if she is the wronged, home-loving, horror-stricken woman that her own tale would imply, her poise is most surprising."

Ruth's testimony took three days to complete and filled 345 pages of stenographic transcript as she was cross-examined both by Judd's attorneys and the attorneys representing the people of the state of New York. She stayed still and seemed relaxed, only toying with her rosary necklace or shaking her head when she answered "no," but otherwise seeming self-possessed and even graceful as she responded to the heated objections and hectoring of the lawyers.

She formally recanted whole pages of her March 21st confession. She said she'd kept the sash weight in the cellar because "I didn't want to have it anywheres around." She didn't throw it away "because I felt it should go back to Mr. Gray, inasmuch as he gave it to me." She didn't warn her husband of danger because, "I thought I could talk Judd Gray out of it." She left the kitchen door open that Saturday night because "I was going to have it out with Judd that I did not want to have him around me anymore."

She was fuddled or evasive about the insurance policies she'd taken out, but she smiled when it was determined she paid the premiums from a joint checking account that Albert could have examined at any time. She denied ever attempting to poison or asphyxiate her husband. She denied scheming to murder him. She went into her mother's room that Saturday night to simply reason with Judd Gray.

An attorney for the prosecution inquired, "And the first thing he did was to kiss you?"

"Yes."

"And you kissed him?"

"Yes."

"Knowing or believing, whatever you want to say, that he was there to kill your husband?"

"Yes."

"And knowing or believing that he had come to your house to kill your husband, you sat downstairs with him on a settee and you talked?"

"Yes."

She claimed she left Gray, with her husband's handgun on the piano, when she went upstairs to the bathroom. And even at the far end of the hallway, with the bathroom door closed, she heard "a terrific thud" as Judd hit, but did not fracture, Albert's skull. She herself did not strike her husband with the sash weight or pour chloroform on his pillow or strangle him with picture wire that she tightened with Judd's mechanical pencil. When she revived from her faint and saw what had happened, "I was too frightened to cry out."

"Did you administer any aid to your husband?"

"No."

"You did not know from any examination of your husband whether or not he was then dead or alive?"

She sizzled with contempt for the prosecutor but coolly answered, "No, I did not."

"And you remained with Gray in the adjoining room for how long?"

"For a couple of hours."

"And you gave him your nightgown and robe to burn?"

"Yes."

"You took your nightgown off in his presence?"

"Yes."

"You got some other clothing, did you?"

"Yes."

"You went into the room where your husband lay dying or dead to get that other clothing?"

"Yes."

"And still you did not look at him?"

"No."

"You did not touch him?"

"No."

"But you could have?"

"Yes."

She felt she was no longer playing or impersonating; she just *was*. Looking past the lawyers and jury to that huge crowd of excited strangers, she felt like a grande dame of theater bestowing a few hours of her celebrity on a grateful audience. There was petulance in her voice at times, she often glared, and she was forced to admit that she'd lied to whomever she spoke to on Sunday, March 20th. But Ruth guessed rightly that the examiners sought to stir up some vestiges of the fury and ferocity she'd used against Albert, so in the main she countered their attacks with stateliness and restraint. She recognized that she was telling of a night as it ought to have been, not as it was, but for Lorraine's sake she was clinging to that tenet of justice called "beyond a reasonable doubt." She was therefore as careless in her testimony as she was also honest and shameless, flaunting her disregard for her husband, serenely contradicting herself or insisting falsehoods were true, seldom reversing a statement when she was caught in a lie, letting inconsistencies grow wings and fly. She innocently communicated an outrageous version of events as though a jury of men would have to believe her. It seemed to outsiders that she did not recognize the jeopardy she was in.

But her attorneys did, so they called pretty, nine-year-old Lorraine Snyder to the witness stand, a girl without a father and, should the jury so choose, with a mother soon to die. Because of the jail's rules, Ruth hadn't seen her daughter since March 21st when she was arrested, and it was now May 3rd. She gasped with surprise when Lorraine's name was called and she was so pleased to watch her filing into the courtroom behind the bailiff that Ruth couldn't help smiling even as she wept. Ruth leaned toward Dana Wallace to say how pretty Lorraine looked in that wide-brimmed black hat and a just-bought black middy dress. And Ruth swiftly wiped her blurring tears away so she wouldn't miss a second of the child's testimony as Lorraine solemnly listened to Justice Scudder's instructions.

The court ruled that the girl would not be sworn, then requested she give her name and address. She avoided the faces of Ruth and Judd as she did so. Justice Scudder then said, "Just lean back in your chair and be comfortable and look at that gentleman at the other end of the table"—indicating Hazelton—"and do not look at anybody else. Just look right at him."

Hazelton strode away from Lorraine's mother as he asked, "Lorraine, do you remember the morning your mother called you?"

"Yes, sir."

"Was it daylight or dark?"

"Light," she said.

"And how long after she called you did you go for help from the Mulhausers?"

"Right away."

And that was all. She'd just been there to establish the existence of a child for the talesmen. Ruth ached for some contact with Lora, just the tiniest wave of hello, but not even a stray glance was exchanged as the nine-year-old was escorted out by the bailiff. She was not the only one in the courtroom crying when the door shut behind the girl and Samuel Miller interrupted the mood to say, "The defense calls Henry Judd Gray to testify in his own behalf."

Because of his wariness, his earlier slavish devotion to Ruth, his general neglect of the goings-on now, and his melancholy slump in his chair at the defendant's table, reporters had depicted Judd as "inert," "a scared rabbit," "a putty man." Playwright Willard Mack sneered that he was "a man, I am sure, who couldn't put up a croquet set without help." And Peggy Hopkins Joyce snidely compared him to "a bunch of dough that somebody forgot to knead." But when called to the stand, Judd went with confidence, a fast stride, and an officer's bearing. Well-tailored as always, he wore a dark, pinstriped, double-breasted suit, a white silk shirt, and a finely chosen tie. His face was jailhouse pale; his undulant, nut-brown hair was freshly cut; he surprised the courtroom with his baritone voice. Justice Scudder would much later reminisce that while Mrs. Snyder struck him as "frivolous and coarse," the ever-obliging Gray "gave off the appearance of a divinity-school student." Even cynical journalists soon were judging him as a pious and repentant gentleman, "well-educated, well-bred, well-mannered." And he was Ruth's opposite in that his testimony conformed not just to each item of his confession but adhered so closely to the police department's established facts that the district attorney hardly interrogated him.

Had it been possible to plead guilty, Judd would have done so and resolutely gone straight to the penitentiary, so there was no protection, censorship, or surprise in his recital, just minor clarifications, frequent forgetfulness, and an alcoholic's wakened consciousness of how crazily intoxicated he'd generally been. Singer Nora Bayes would note with amazement after he testified, "There's not that much liquor in the world!"

Within the afternoon Judd and his defense attorney had gotten to the murder, and Ruth held her face in her hands, crying, as Judd recited his account of that night, and he saw his mother crying, too, and then Judd was done for and fell apart, and Samuel Miller was forced to ask for a recess.

Even Willard Mack's negative opinion was altered. Holding forth on the courthouse steps, he shouted, "I say to you that if ever human lips uttered the truth, this was the time."

There was an announcement that the pathological details of Judd's sexual liaisons with Ruth were expected to be so shocking and revealing that ladies would be barred from the courtroom. But in a joint conference with the attorneys, Justice Scudder interrogated the relevance of that line of questioning, and there seems to have been an agreement, because in cross-examination the next day, Dana Wallace focused solely on the murder. Demeaning the codefendant whenever he could, Wallace even requested that Judd get up and demonstrate exactly how he'd held the sash weight high over his head in both hands in order to gash in Albert's skull. Afterward, Ruth's attorney noted, "You had not the same emotions just now as you had yesterday."

"No, sir," Judd said. "I don't think so."

"Was that because you were preparing yesterday under direct examination to be emotional at just that time?"

"It was not, sir, no."

"So the recital for your attorney brought tears to your eyes, but the actual enactment from your memory brought none, is that right?"

"I wouldn't say that, no, sir."

Wallace let that go and scoured his notes. "Will you tell us, so that we won't have to rehearse it all, when was the first time you heard Mrs. Snyder propose getting rid of Mr. Snyder?"

"In January nineteen twenty-six."

"And from that time on it was discussed very often, wasn't it?"

"A number of times, yes, sir."

"And in fact, to use your own expression, she kept hounding you with it, is that right?"

"That is true, sir."

"And told you of the attempts on his life that she made?"

"She did, sir."

"Although you have recited many attempts, as she told you, to destroy her husband, as a matter of fact Albert Snyder was alive up to the time when you first entered the room, wasn't he?"

"He was alive then, yes, sir."

"In other words, no harm came to him of a serious nature until you became an accessory, is that it?"

Wallace would continue along that line to illustrate that it was

Judd, not Ruth, who governed the relationship and sought the death of his rival, and it was he who orchestrated the particulars of the murder plot. But Judd did not veer in his testimony. Character witnesses then spoke on Judd Gray's behalf, including next-door neighbors and lingerie buyers—though no one from Benjamin & Johnes—and at five the court adjourned.

Sunday, May 8th, was Mother's Day, and so there was the inevitable photograph of Lorraine signing a card for her Mommy, and as the ever-solemn Mrs. Josephine Brown cooked dinner the reporters wanted her feelings about the probable outcome of the trial. "I have no idea what the jury will do," she said as she mashed potatoes. "Men are so strange."

Some journalists who'd sentimentally watched Lorraine testify at the trial felt they needed to nudge and nag Ruth about the anguish she must have been feeling in not having her daughter around for the grand occasion of Mother's Day. She said she'd eaten roasted chicken and spaghetti that she'd gotten from Roberto Minotti's Italian restaurant, which was in the neighborhood. She wouldn't divulge who bought it, and she otherwise gave them very little, just stayed on her cot and gently smiled when she saw her pet mouse scooting around, but she did finally stand at the jail bars to read aloud the telegram she'd be sending Mrs. Brown.

"'Mother's Day Greeting,'" she read. "'I have many blessings and I want you to know how thankful I am for all that you have done for me. Love to you and kiss Lorraine for me. Ruth.'"

"Anything else?" a reporter asked.

"Yes," she said. "Tell my jailers to have Kitty Kaufman here to marcel my hair. And I'd like a manicure, too."

Judd was just one floor away. Like Ruth, he stayed on his jail bed. Asked if he'd sent a card or present to Isabel, he said, "She's my wife, not my mother."

"So no?"

"So no."

"Then how about Mrs. Margaret Gray then?"

"I shan't repeat what I said in my note, but I did have sent an inspirational book: *When the Days Seem Dark* by Philip E. Howard. I found it . . . restorative."

A reporter shouted, "Have you thought about the verdict?"

"Well, I don't expect clemency."

"Are you going to the chair, you think?"

Judd shrugged. "I'm not at all afraid of death now. Ever since I confessed my story to the world from the witness stand, I have found a deep tranquility."

But his smile seemed more a wince.

On May 9th, the hot, seventeenth day of the trial, Attorney William J. Millard orated to the jury an old-fashioned summation in defense of Henry Judd Gray. With aching and melancholy, his hands in prayer at his chin, Millard gently regarded Judd, the courtroom, and the jury box. And then he gravely began to tell of the tragedy that had befallen "his friend," first praising Judd's biography, his happy life, his spotless reputation, and the "fires of the home hearth that were burning continually with love and devotion." But then "suddenly in the month of June, nineteen twenty-five, a sinister, fascinating woman came across his path. Oh, gentlemen, what a catastrophe!"

Elderly-seeming, Millard fully reached out his hand to wag a finger at Ruth. "That woman, that peculiar creature, like a poisonous snake drew Judd Gray into her glistening coils, and there was no escape. Why, gentlemen, it was a perverse and alluring seduction. This woman was abnormal. Just as a piece of steel jumps and clings to a powerful magnet, so Judd Gray was subjected to the compelling force of that woman, and she held him fast. This woman, this peculiar venomous species of humanity, was possessed of an all-consuming, all-absorbing sexual passion, a rapacious animal lust, which seemingly was never satisfied."

Ruth's eyes were shut and her head was resting on her right hand as she pretended to doze through his peroration.

"She gradually trained her victim," Millard said. "She employed every possible opportunity to satisfy his desires and ensnare him. And thereafter, after the indulgence which had been going on month after month, she held him enslaved, entrapped, her very own, as though she were acting through him, handling him like a human manikin. Whatever she wanted, he did."

She bullied the postman, he said; she conned the insurance agent; she made a slave of Judd. All of it had been asserted many times; his sole addition was a reminder of the half-pint of poisoned rye whiskey that was discovered in Judd's possession at his arrest. It was William Millard's contention that Ruth had intended that Judd drunkenly drink the poison that night and die there in the house so that the crime scene could be construed as a murder/suicide. She would not have needed to ransack the house or hide anything; just a very few lies would have been necessary, not the heap that she'd piled up.

Attorney Dana Wallace presented the closing arguments in favor of Mrs. Snyder and gallantly noted that she was a damsel sandwiched between two prosecutions: that of the district attorney's office and that of the attorneys for the codefendant, and she had been "put in one of the most unfair positions possible before an American court of justice." Wallace scornfully looked at Judd as he said, "This miserable filth of the earth is allowed to sit here and make his squealing appeal for mercy, hiding behind a woman's skirts to try to fool you." Eventually Wallace would add "diabolical fiend," "weak-minded," "despicable creature," "falsifier," and "human ana-conda" to his descriptions of the codefendant. But Judd just stared straight ahead as Wallace took three hours longer than Millard to say again and reiterate and hit twice more each point that William Millard had expressed in defense of his client, but altering the evidence to make Ruth, not Judd, seem the beguiled, helpless, infatuated victim of a criminal Svengali.

His defense failed to fit either the familiar history of the couple or the personalities that had been so vibrantly on display in the press and in the courtroom. And Wallace was so excessive in his demonstrations, even going so far as to jerk his coat off his shoulder and massage himself to imitate Judd soothing Ruth's sunburn with cream, that an overheated and hostile courtroom audience laughed in ridicule, and Wallace shouted at the crowd, "Your titterings bespeak vacant minds. Such people should never be allowed to pass judgment on a defenseless woman."

At no time did either defense team impugn Albert Snyder's character or try to excuse their client by indicating he deserved the excess and finality of his punishment.

District Attorney Richard Newcombe very briefly rehearsed the state's case against Mrs. Snyder and Mr. Gray, noting that it made no difference who invented the scheme to murder or actually committed the murder. They were equally and intricately involved. Even Judd's excuse of intoxication was insufficient since each of his actions seemed so fundamentally clear-headed and well recollected. Mrs. Snyder, he reminded the jury, had held to one story for sixteen hours until she told Police Commissioner McLaughlin that she couldn't lie anymore. She'd then made a confession in which she neglected to mention the extenuating circumstances she introduced in the courtroom, and now instead, under oath on the witness stand, she'd presented a third story, and it was this one she currently wanted the jury to believe.

"She, gentlemen of the jury, was like a wild beast in the jungle, crouching there and watching her husband sleep, waiting for the opportunity to strike with Henry Judd Gray. And together they came in and committed cold-blooded, atrocious murder. After Albert Snyder had been struck on the head, he rose up and there he saw in the act of killing him his own wife and her lover, Gray. God, gentlemen, think of that man's thoughts and his sudden realization that he was being murdered by his own wife and her lover."

Shortly after five on that hot afternoon, the jury was sent to a room where the twelve gentlemen slung off their jackets, hoisted the windows for air, and went over the judge's instructions concerning the various degrees of murder. There was a ballot that went ten for, and two against, the verdict of homicide in the first degree. The jurors were not intellectuals. The reasoning code they lived by they called horse sense. They jawed about the case for a little longer and another ballot was taken. And just before seven, less than two hours after the jury retired, the foreman announced to the court, "The jury finds the defendants, Mrs. Ruth Brown Snyder and Henry Judd Gray, guilty of murder in the first degree."

Ruth and Judd were standing, but Ruth immediately fell back into her chair in shock and hid her face in her hands as she arched over, shrieking and quaking with sorrow. Judd tottered with his fists clenched but stayed upright, then fuddled in his navy blue suit-coat pocket until he found and extracted Jane Gray's Sunday school worship aid *A Child's Book of Prayer*. He swayed as he quietly recited what he read.

There was pandemonium in the courtroom as fifteen hundred people sought to get closer to the condemned couple, yelling at them, screaming curses, inviting sentiments and opinions, wanting just to touch them as a memento. Justice Scudder hammered his gavel and ordered Ruth and Judd sent out to the jail, but it took ten minutes before police could form an alley wide enough for passage through the wild and raucous crowd.

The New York newspapers had prepared front pages for whenever the presumptive guilty verdict was delivered, and just minutes after seven o'clock that night newsies were hawking extra editions on the streets.

Ruth halted her exit from the courthouse so she could tell reporters she would instruct Wallace and Hazelton to appeal the verdict. Seeing a grieving George Murphy, the jail's Catholic chaplain, she lamented, "Oh, Father, I thought they'd believe me."

Although he opposed capital punishment, Justice Scudder was required by New York law to sentence Ruth Snyder and Judd Gray to solitary confinement in Sing Sing penitentiary and to execution in the electric chair. Entering the courtroom, both Judd and Ruth were cautious to face forward lest their glances collide, but as they waited Judd overheard her joke with the bailiff: "This is my worst Friday the thirteenth ever." And even Judd smiled.

Ruth took none of the sentencing seriously. She grinned at Justice Scudder's gloom when he announced the death penalty, and she tickled a jail matron's side as she was escorted from the courtroom. She told the *New York Times,* "This is just a formality. I have just as good a chance now of going free as I had before the trial started."

But Judd stood ramrod straight as he heard Justice Scudder announce the same sentence, and when his attorneys sought to console him he justified the extremity of his punishment by tranquilly quoting Saint Paul's "Epistle to the Romans." "You *have* heard, haven't you, gentlemen, that 'The wages of sin is death'?"

Walking back to 1 Court Square, he paused on the jailhouse steps for photographers and reporters to herd around him and then, so all could hear, shouted out his handwritten statement: "I am one of the sterling examples of what whiskey, lust, and sin will ultimately condemn one to. I have seen so many pitiful cases here as an inmate of this jail as to what liquor and improper intimate relations will exact in retaliation that it makes me more than anxious to urge my fellow men to see the shining light of God as our only true salvation."

Whether it was because of a religious awakening of her own, because of Father George Murphy's general friendliness to her, or because she was craftily alert to Governor Alfred E. Smith's Catholic faith, Ruth invited the priest to her jail cell, reminded him that she was a nonpracticing Lutheran, and announced her intent to convert to Catholicism.

Commenting on the public declaration for reporters later, Father Murphy said only, "I think Ruth has a deep and profound sense of repentance."

≈ NINE ≈

AND IN DEATH
I SHALL SMILE

The Great Mississippi Flood of May 1927, the greatest natural disaster in the history of the United States, affected three-quarters of a million people, but as comedian Will Rogers was seeking to raise funds for the victims, he joked that the flood was ill-timed since it was vying for headlines with the Snyder-Gray case.

There was no decrease in public interest after the sentencing, and Ruth increasingly displayed a peculiar sense of what was actually occurring. On Monday, May 16th, as she was escorted out to the seven-passenger Cadillac that would convey her to Sing Sing, Ruth asked the jail matron she was handcuffed to, "Could we stop along the way? There's a dandy roadhouse near Sleepy Hollow, and I'd like to order a lobster dinner."

The jail matron frowned. "And hurt the feelings of the prison chefs? They're probably cooking up a feast."

It would be pork and beans.

Judd was tucked into the long black Cadillac that was just in front of Ruth's. Sheriff's deputies got in, and six blatting motorcycles with sidecars and rifled policemen took forward and flanking positions for the procession north to Ossining. But five thousand onlookers, most of them wives and mothers with a loathing for Mrs. Snyder, surged around the cars, screaming invective and striking the curtained windows and hoods, until police horsemen with nightsticks scared and injured and collided with enough people to guarantee an exit. Eleven cars filled with reporters followed. The Cadillacs raced across the Queensboro Bridge at forty miles per hour but on the Manhattan side were slowed by the enormous crowds shouting catcalls or just waiting for glimpses of the murderers. Crawling through a chaos that a hundred traffic cops couldn't manage, the caravan eventually crossed Central Park and took Riverside Drive to the Henry Hudson Parkway.

Judd finished off a pack of cigarettes in the hour-and-twenty-minute journey north to Sing Sing and was relieved to hear he could buy more at the prison store. He still had the cash he'd stolen from Albert's wallet. Spectators and newspapermen were outside the south gate of the penitentiary, but the Cadillacs were waved through, and for the first time in almost two months Judd felt freed of the hordes. There were inmates who ran alongside the car to look in, but a greater number were just walking around in the sun or playing a baseball game. Judd was handcuffed to a deputy sheriff, who said, "I hope you make the team," and Judd told him, "Well, I was pretty good in high school."

But in fact there would be no mingling with other prisoners for him.

Cells for those condemned to die were located in a building that was just five years old, contained its own kitchen and exercise yards, and was called by convicts "the slaughterhouse." There were two wings of twelve cells each for men, a wing of three cells for women, an infirmary, and six cells in the pre-execution section that was called "the dance hall." Autopsies were performed in "the icebox."

Judd caught a fleeting glimpse of Ruth as she was received as the sole female prisoner at Sing Sing, and that was it. They never saw each other again.

She surrendered whatever she owned, including her wedding rings and Juicy Fruit gum; was watched as she took off all her clothing and showered; and then was weighed, measured, and examined by Dr. Charles Sweet, who certified that she was not diseased or contagious. Because shoes could function as weapons, she was given felt slippers to wear, and because she was the only woman incarcerated there, Warden Lewis Lawes supplied Mrs. Snyder with cotton stockings and calico housedresses rather than a prison uniform. Three matrons were assigned to guard Ruth in alternating eight-hour shifts. She was never alone. She'd written on a prison form that she was now Catholic, and Father John McCaffery was the first visitor to a cell with concrete walls, a washbasin and toilet, a plain table and chair, and a bolted-down cot with a straw-stuffed mattress.

McCaffery was contacted by a journalist later and asked what Mrs. Snyder was like, and he said, "Attractive, pleasant, and quite a cut-up."

She was told her visiting days would be Monday, Wednesday, and Friday, that she could go to the exercise yard for twenty minutes twice a day, that all mail would be screened, and that she could get writing materials but she'd have to return the pen to the matrons whenever she finished.

She cried, and to console her the Catholic chaplain said he'd work on Warden Lawes to permit Ruth to have the face powder and cold cream she'd requested, and that happened. She was no more than one hundred feet from Judd, but it may as well have been a continent. Each of them slept ten hours a day.

Judd had an easier time of it in the penitentiary. Even in solitary confinement, with other male prisoners within shouting distance he could converse about events in the world; read his Bible aloud for other hearers; call out his moves in a coded checkers game; consult on religious concerns with Reverend Anthony Peterson, the Protestant chaplain; and keep himself fit by playing handball with the priest in the exercise yard. Each night he wished "Good night" to the murderer in the cell next to him, and each morning he greeted him with a "Good morning." The inmate, a lifelong criminal who'd killed the proprietor of an ice cream shop, called Judd "a hell of a nice fella."

Each day Judd occupied himself with his voluminous correspondence: to Samuel Miller, the defense attorney who'd become a close friend; to Mrs. Margaret Gray; to Jane; to Isabel; to Haddon Jones; to high school classmates; and to members of his New Jersey country club, the Elks lodge, and the Club of Corset Salesmen of the Empire State. On June 2nd his wife visited him for the first time since his arrest. She would do so just twice more. On late nights in the fall, he began a penciled memoir, *Doomed Ship,* dedicated "To My Faithful Little Mother" and edited by his sister, a book that would run as a serial with the Famous Features Syndicate and would be published by the Horace Liveright Company a few months after his death. Judd wrote in it: *I cannot explain the mystery of being reborn in the Spirit. I can only tell you of the peace that surpasses all understanding. Perhaps you will say: how can a murderer expect to enter Heaven—one such as I am? Just by faith. I am a new creature—just-born again.*

In 1927, Philo Farnsworth transmitted the first experimental electronic television pictures; the Academy of Motion Picture Arts and Sciences was founded; aviator Charles Lindbergh flew the *Spirit of St. Louis* on the first solo, nonstop, transatlantic flight from New York to Paris, and an enormous ticker-tape parade was held for him on Fifth Avenue. The British Broadcasting Corporation was created, as was CBS. President Calvin Coolidge announced he would not run for a second term; Italian anarchists Sacco and Vanzetti were executed for murder; the first movie with sound, *The Jazz Singer,* premiered; the New York Yankees and a "Murderer's Row" that included Babe Ruth and Lou Gehrig swept the Pittsburgh Pirates in the World Series. Leon Trotsky was expelled from the Soviet Communist Party; the Holland Tunnel was constructed underneath the Hudson River, linking New Jersey to New York; the young Chinese revolutionary Mao Zedong and the newly formed Red Army failed in their "Autumn Harvest Uprising"; and after nineteen years of production, the Ford Motor Company scrapped the Model T to introduce the Model A.

And Ruth Snyder stayed in the headlines, ever increasing circulation. Reporters noted that she used peroxide to bleach her hair; she read true-romance magazines; she spoke in Swedish whenever Mrs. Brown visited Sing Sing; she wasn't allowed to wear the gorgeous dresses her mother brought from home, but she was allowed to "visit them" by hanging them in her cell; and that Ruth's fun-loving cousin, Ethel Anderson, was laid to rest in Woodlawn Cemetery after a death from tuberculosis that seemed to have been worsened by the strain of trial publicity.

At times Ruth seemed a madwoman, but she was examined and ruled sane by the Lunacy Commission. She rebelled and schemed and objected through her lawyers; or she fainted, she was hysterical, she fell into crying fits each night; or she giggled with the matrons, she received Holy Communion on Sundays, she was visited each day by the warden's wife and by Father McCaffery. She penned secret notes to the prison cook with each food tray return and he fell crazily in love with her, skulking by a kitchen window overlooking the exercise yard so he could kiss his hand and blow the kiss to her, ecstatic when she grinned and blew a kiss back.

Ruth inserted herself in the conflict between Albert's brother and Mrs. Josephine Brown over the custody of Lorraine. The little girl was overjoyed when Granny Brown succeeded. Ruth lost the case against the Prudential Life Insurance Company that would have awarded Albert's beneficiary ninety-six thousand dollars for his "accidental death." Instead the company sent a check compensating Mrs. Snyder for all the premiums she'd paid, but on the advice of counsel she refused to cash it. She won a stay of execution in June, but then, on November 21st, Justice Irving Lehman of the New York Supreme Court announced that the seven-judge panel saw no reason to grant a new trial, commute either Mrs. Snyder's or Mr. Gray's sentence, or delay the court-ordered execution, and there was nothing else for Ruth to do but, in fury, fire her lawyers. Whom she rehired a few days later.

Each weekend New Yorkers had been permitted tours of Sing Sing, but when the numbers swelled from half a dozen to three thousand because of the notorious pair, Warden Lawes halted the practice. Each Sunday in the summer and fall of 1927, Queens Village neighbors complained about the stream of motorists cruising by the Snyder residence, seeking a gander at Lorraine or her grandmother, some even installing themselves on the lawn with box lunches until police were called in. At last the throngs were too much and the house in Queens Village was sold at a loss to an old German husband and wife who were unaware of the property's infamy.

Lorraine would move with her grandmother to the home of Ruth's older brother, Andrew, in the Bronx and enroll in a Westchester County boarding school run by Ursuline nuns—exactly the school Albert had stolidly rejected in 1925. She would grow up to be a pretty young woman, happily marry at age twenty, and find a serene anonymity in her husband's last name. Judd's daughter Jane would do much the same. Each would live a very long and very private life.

The New York *Daily Mirror* ran a contest awarding "$25 each day for the best letter telling why Ruth Snyder should NOT be executed" and an equal amount for "why she SHOULD." Almost no men thought she should die in the electric chair. Almost all women did.

Although in November 1927 she was aged ten, Lorraine purportedly wrote a letter to Santa Claus, requesting that he "bring my darling mother home to me for Christmas. That's all I want. I'm so lonesome without her." Hundreds of wrapped presents from those who ached for the girl soon filled her room.

The Snyder case went to Governor Al Smith, who would not rule on it until January and whose reluctance to execute a woman was well known. Mrs. Brown surprised him with a visit in Albany, barging into the governor's office and begging for mercy not for Ruth but "for the child's sake." The governor was cordial and respectful but stated, "I feel for you with all my heart, Mrs. Brown, but we must remember that there are many other daughters, sons, fathers, and mothers in prison. All cannot be released."

Another avenue was taken by Ruth, who sought the outrage and sympathy of the general public, and financial help for Mrs. Brown, by slashing out a wild, disjointed, and schizophrenic harangue: *My Own True Story—So Help Me God!* The circulation of the New York *Daily Mirror* increased by one hundred thousand copies over each day of its serialized run. To establish authenticity, the editors photographed and reprinted the strange first page of the original manuscript that Ruth's mother had smuggled out, but that facsimile also illustrated the dash-happy, large-lettered handwriting of a crazed and fanatical woman who seemed on the verge of a nervous breakdown: "Judd Gray talks!—about 'the big brown bug'—he 'put out of its misery'—does (he)—J. G.—ever think back of RUTH BROWN'S BUG he 'put out of its misery?'"

Albert Snyder was a "brown bug"? That *helped* her cause?

The *Daily Mirror* finally tidied Ruth's prose for readability, but the excitement, confusion, and cockeyed view of what took place in the last year still screamed through: "Don't the 'outside' believe ANYTHING I tell? I did all in my power to stop J. G. without telling my husband."

She said Judd "would fall in love with anything he could use to advantage." She claimed, "In order to keep Isabel from telling my husband of our affair, I had to buy her luxuries her husband couldn't give her, including garments from his job, and because I couldn't supply her demands she was going to tell my husband!"

> *Oh God! Where is there any fairness? Where? . . .*
>
> *Even tho he confessed to the killing of my husband, why did the WHOLE WORLD believe EVERYTHING he told as "THE TRUTH"? I admitted "the truth" in my unlawful love affair, yet none DID believe me when I said, "I DID NOT KILL MY HUSBAND." Why was my word doubted? Why? Because J. G. handed the public the same suave talk that took me completely off my feet and fed me up on the biggest lot of bunk, yet we POOR FOOLS love them just the same. . . .*
>
> *I just had the misfortune to give my love to a cur—I was only as bad as he made me. . . .*
>
> *MY ADVICE TO MEN AND WOMEN, YOUNG AND OLD, IS READ YOUR BIBLES AND PRAYERBOOKS! . . .*
>
> *PRAY and have FAITH! For the reward of FAITH is the signature of the Lord Jesus Christ written in your hearts. For*

Christ's signature is recognized in the Bank of Heaven. You want to go there, don't you? . . .

[Editor: Ruth Snyder's mood suddenly changed at this point in the writing of her amazing narrative and almost as an anti-climax, she wrote the following:] *Please thank the kind people of the outside world for their beautiful cards and letters. Many beautiful books have come, too. Poetry—Elbert Hubbard's works—Bibles—prayer beads—hankies—many, many thanks.*

She also illustrated the damp wit of a vaudevillian, writing, "I always wanted an electric heater, but my husband was too stingy to buy me one. Now I guess I get my wish."

Researching the seven previous executions of women in New York, Ruth's attorneys discovered that all were married with children. The majority were hanged, but the first woman to die in the electric chair at Sing Sing, in 1899, was Mrs. Martha Place, who'd jealously hurled acid into her pretty stepdaughter's eyes, then suffocated her, and then stove in her husband's head with an ax. Theodore Roosevelt was governor then and rejected pleas for clemency by saying, "To interfere with the course of the law in this case could be justified only on the ground that never hereafter, under any circumstances, should capital punishment be inflicted on a murderess."

So Ruth's attorneys realized there were no precedents to help them when on January 5th, 1928, a clemency hearing was held in the executive chamber of Albany's Capitol Hill. Edgar Hazelton and Dana Wallace escorted Mrs. Josephine Brown into a formal room whose walls were faced with rich mahogany and the hanging portraits of New York's governors. Then District Attorney Newcombe and his assistants walked in, followed by Judd's attorneys, Mrs. Margaret Gray, and Judd's sister Margaret.

The governor sat behind a grand ceremonial desk, took off his glasses, and heard Millard's plea: "I am aware that the mob is calling for vengeance, the same mob that cried, 'Crucify him!' I know the yelping of these human coyotes will not affect your decision. I know you will treat this case with Christ-like sympathy and I beg you to commute the sentence of these two sinners to life imprisonment."

District Attorney Newcombe's rebuttal was little more than a jaunt through the facts as brought up in the trial, saying he'd conducted a conscientious examination of the case and found no extenuating circumstances, and that this "revoltingly brutal crime" was the result of connivance, premeditation, and wanton greed for Albert's insurance money.

A psychiatric defense was offered, but Governor Smith interrupted, saying, "There's something abnormal about anyone who commits murder. Stay off this psychiatric stuff. Stick to the law."

Quoting Saint Paul, Hazelton recited, "'The letter of the law killeth, but the spirit of the law giveth life.'"

"Well, the New York legislature says different," Smith said, "and that's a later authority than Saint Paul and the one which I am sworn to uphold." And soon after that the governor proclaimed the clemency hearing was over.

Warden Lewis Lawes announced the execution would be carried out on the night of Thursday, January 12th, and twenty journalists and four medical doctors were selected by lottery to act as witnesses.

Reporters went up to Norwalk, Connecticut, where Isabel and Jane and Mrs. Kallenbach were hiding out in the home of a wealthy banker and friend who held off the scribes by telling them, "Mrs. Gray has nothing to say. Her nerves are shattered, she is prostrate on a bed upstairs, and she has no desire to make any comment."

Mrs. Josephine Brown was treated to a restaurant dinner by a couple of reporters and she obligingly told them, "She knows she must die, that it's useless to hold on to hope any longer. Ruth is very blue, but she's taking it better than I would. She has been a very brave girl."

Even more journalists than were at the trial now headed up to Ossining to cover the execution. The one hotel there, the Weskora, had burned down just a week earlier, so they were forced to stay in the town's only boardinghouse, where the room rates were jacked up so high that some took children's bedrooms in homes or paid to sleep on a sofa. Extra telegraph wires were run along Dunstan Avenue from Ossining to the prison; a ramshackle hot dog stand near the main gate was rented for fifty dollars and changed into an office with its own wire hookup for the New York *Daily News*; office telephones in the town were leased for a dollar a minute.

Governor Smith's wife, Catherine, had collapsed with an appendicitis attack during their overnight at the luxurious Biltmore Hotel on Madison Avenue and 43rd Street, and reporters hung out in the lobby to harvest news about the illness. But instead, at six o'clock on Tuesday evening, they were invited up to the executive suite on the fourteenth floor and heard the governor read his decision on executive clemency. "The execution of this judgment on a woman is so distressing," he read, "that I had hoped that the appeal to me would disclose some fact which would justify my interference with the procedure of the law. But this did not happen. I have searched in vain for any basis upon which my conscience, in the light of my oath of office, can approve, that I might temper the law with mercy."

But he found he agreed with the twelve jurors and the seven justices of the court of appeals; hence he denied the application for executive clemency, held up his hand to avoid further questioning, and then left to see his wife in the hospital.

Hearing the news on Wednesday, Ruth emptied her Death House bank account and finished off five dollars' worth of chocolate. Toiling hard at signing her name on some legal forms, she said, "I'm a thirty-two-year-old mother in the prime of life and they're going to kill me. It don't seem right. Oh, I'll have to go. But I'm still so young and full of life, it's a shame."

Six signatures had been required on the forms and she was so adrift from her authentic self that not one resembled the other. Ruth's attorney told the press, "Mrs. Snyder looked like a dead woman. She touched my hand and she was cold as ice. Her face was red from crying. She had been lying down all day before I arrived."

Whereas Father George Murphy left the Queens County Jail for a final visit with Ruth in Sing Sing and told Mrs. Josephine Brown that he'd noticed the solace that was filling the erring daughter's soul and bracing Ruth for the ordeal to come. "Why, she even smiled when I left. The beautiful, spiritual smile of those who have made peace with their Creator."

She'd written him instructions about her funeral. "Remember—only the most simple burial, no Mass, no inscriptions, very plain. I want to go out of this world as I came into it—just a poor soul." She'd be buried in Woodlawn Cemetery in the Bronx, and her headstone would be engraved with her birth name: "May R. Brown." She asked Father Murphy "to just say a few prayers over me before my clay is laid to rest" and noted, "I offered my Communion for Judd last Sunday—I have no hate in my heart, and I don't think he has either."

Judd signed forms that finalized the transfer to Mrs. Isabel Gray of about seven thousand dollars in stocks and bonds and full equity in the house on Wayne Avenue. She would also be the sole beneficiary of his policy with the Union Life Insurance Company of Cincinnati and she would receive a check for twenty-five thousand dollars on January 13th. Isabel would stay on in Norwalk,

Connecticut, volunteering for the Women's Guild at Grace Episco-pal Church and dying in 1957 at the age of sixty-five.

Eight months of purchases of tobacco and incidentals had exhausted all but twenty-one dollars in Judd's Death House bank account; he requested that fifteen dollars of it go for a first-class chicken dinner with all the trimmings for the ten remaining inmates on death row, and six dollars were given to Dixie Baldwin, a Negro, because he had no friends or family or funds for ciga-rettes. Upon hearing that, Dixie wept.

Warden Lawes received twenty-five letters from women vol-unteering to die in place of Mrs. Snyder, a letter from a man who signed his name "The Jolly Roger" and threatened to kill Lawes if Ruth were executed, and another from a Washington group that called itself the Soul Mates' Union and wanted Lawes to permit Ruth and Judd to sleep together on their final night alive.

Judd woke at a quarter to nine, ate breakfast and read his Bible, and was examined by Dr. Charles Sweet. Since he seemed more reconciled and composed, Judd was told he would follow Ruth to the electric chair, the harder position. Judd wrote thank-you letters to those who'd helped him and eleven letters to Jane, one to be opened and read on each birthday until she achieved twenty-one. Hot tea was served as Isabel visited him; then Mrs. Gray and Mr. and Mrs. Harold Logan; and finally Attorney Samuel Miller. Arrangements were made for his burial in Rosedale Cemetery in East Orange, New Jersey. Judd's mother told reporters he was "the sweet boy he's always been. He's not a real criminal. Circumstances just got the better of him."

Walking to his pre-execution cell at the far end of the west wing, Judd was finally allowed to see and shake hands with the inmates with whom he'd shared eight months of incarceration, as at ease as a hard-used man finally heading into retirement. Some prisoners got misty-eyed, some bucked up his spirits. Even the guards had the husky voices of grim emotion when they spoke.

Judd played handball with Father McCaffery in the exercise yard and won three of three games. At six he ate chicken soup, roasted chicken, mashed potatoes, celery, stuffed olives, and vanilla ice cream—a dinner he didn't order; it was just the Death House "special." Judd reflected that nine months ago he would have had whisky or gin throughout the meal and a cognac afterward, but now he topped off the dinner with only coffee and a cigar.

A Mafia inmate named Vincent de Stefano, the prison barber, showed up to shave Judd's face and a three-inch circle on his skull where the electrode contact would be.

Judd asked, "Are you a drinking man, Vincent?"

"Well, not in here."

"Then when you get out have a drink for me," Judd said. "Raise me a jolly toast."

A prison attendant told the *New York Times,* "No man in the Death House has ever shown such quiet and dignified deportment as Gray."

Ruth woke at nine thirty that morning and was greeted with the erroneous gossip that a justice of the appellate court had granted a stay of execution so she could testify against the Prudential Life Insurance Company. She ate a hearty breakfast of oatmeal, orange juice, toast, and coffee, then was allowed to pace the vacant corridor for exercise, gladsomely singing popular tunes: "Ain't She Sweet," "My One and Only," "'S Wonderful," "Thou Swell." Dr. Sweet was examining Ruth when Warden Lawes visited the cell, meaning to tell her the gossip was false but losing heart when he saw how happy she was.

Mrs. Brown and Ruth's brother, Andrew, were introduced to the Death House cell for the first time that afternoon and there was giggling, the fond exchange of good memories, and motherly instructions for taking care of Lorraine. Mrs. Brown kissed her daughter's forehead with the expectation that she'd be released from the Death House soon. Ruth called to them as they walked out, "Look after my baby!"

Mrs. Josephine Anderson Brown would reside with Andrew for a while, then revert to her maiden name and find her own home on Mahan Avenue in the Bronx, where she died of heart disease in 1939. She was buried in Woodlawn Cemetery.

Lawes left it to an underling to tell Ruth the bad news that she was to die that night. She fell facedown onto her cot, howling with tears, and ate little of the Spanish omelet that was the general fare for that evening and, in her case, was coated with morphine, to calm her.

Hardly on speaking terms anymore, Edgar Hazelton and Dana Wallace were given the privilege of a final visit at seven that night. Hazelton was agitated later when he told reporters, "She is too far gone to know what she is doing. I never saw anything more terrible. I cannot describe her terror, her misery, her agony. I died a thousand times in the fifteen minutes we were with her. It was awful.

"We sat down beside her. She was sitting with her head in her hands. All of us felt so bad that we didn't say anything. Finally I said, 'Have you asked God to forgive you?'

"She said, 'Yes, I have and He has forgiven me. I hope the world will.'

"Then she put her head back into her hands. We sat there. Finally, embarrassed, she lifted her head and said, 'Well, good-bye.'

"What could we do? We got up and left."

Wiping off tears, Dana Wallace illustrated the gulf between the attorneys by interpreting the meeting differently. "She is bearing up and has made her peace with God. She is reconciled with the inevitable and said, 'I bear no malice against the world or anybody in it.'"

A matron was forced to shave a three-inch circle on the crown of Ruth's head and both of them wept at the violation. Ruth wrote thank-you notes to all the matrons who'd watched over her. One matron would later say, "She was always a perfect lady. She wasn't no trouble at all. She'd chat with us about our problems and such, acting like she had none of her own."

When Father McCaffery arrived she glanced at the clock, and he reconstructed their conversation in his own words, with Ruth telling him, "I have an hour and fifty-five minutes to live, Father John. I am terribly sorry that I have sinned, but I am paying dearly for it. Judd and I sinned together, and now it looks as though we'll go together. If I were to live over again, I would be what I want my child to be—a good girl, really making the commandments of God a guide to a wholesome life."

She then wrote a note to Judd Gray, its contents undisclosed. Judd was delighted and immediately wrote a farewell to Ruth. "I am very glad," he told Reverend Peterson. "I had hoped she would forgive me. I hope God will forgive the both of us."

Remarkably, Judd found the time to jot the final six pages of *Doomed Ship,* recalling much of what transpired that day and faintly hearing the inmates choiring for him "The Pilgrims of the Night": "Rest comes at last; though life be long and dreary, / The day must dawn, and darksome night be past; / All journeys end in welcomes to the weary, / And heaven, the heart's true home, will come at last. / Angels of Jesus, angels of light, / Singing to welcome the pilgrims of the night."

And at last I am sure of Christ, Judd wrote. *I will be free. I have bought this all with my own coin and paid with my body. Deep in my*

heart creeps in that peace of Eternity, that peace that only God can give.
It is like laying my head on a cool and restful pillow. And in death I
shall smile.

An old, cadaverous, white-haired electrician for the New York
State prison system was also, since 1926, its executioner. Robert
Elliott was famous enough to have been called on to officiate at the
Massachusetts execution of Sacco and Vanzetti, but he had never
electrocuted a lady and would have to watch her jerk against the
restraints as he regulated the voltage. Too little electricity and she'd
fry painfully but not die; too much and she'd hideously incinerate,
her brain as charred as a fist of coal. Elliott would be paid $150 for
the execution, but he'd told a reporter, "I hate like hell to do this
job. I hope it ends capital punishment in New York State."

Tabloids had contended that Ruth wanted to die in the black
silk lingerie she kept in Josephine's cedar chest and in the black
silk dress she'd often worn to house parties with Albert. But she
in fact wanted no reminders of the high and footloose times that
she felt had gotten her there. After arriving in the pre-execution
cell, she asked McCaffery to fetch the Blondex shampoo she'd left
behind, and then she was watched by a matron as she cried in the
shower and washed her hair. Ruth put on sky-blue panties, ink-
black hosiery, and a coarse green skirt that hung to her knees, but
she was instructed to have nothing on above the waist for facility in
listening for a heartbeat. She dipped her feet into felt carpet slippers, then got into a heavy black smock that was like the housecoat
she wore when she cleaned. The only vanity she indulged was looking into a rectangular mirror and raking her wet hair back with a
comb to hide the tonsure of an hour ago. She did not even put on
her Shalimar perfume.

Father McCaffery was in his black cassock when he was

invited back to the cell. Yoking his neck with a purple stole and sitting beside her on a cot, he hunched forward to hear Ruth's final, hushed confession of sins. The confessor was overheard saying, "There's nothing as lonely as dying. Even Jesus felt abandoned on the cross." Ruth was blessed in absolution and anointed with holy oil. She knelt to receive the Host of viaticum. And then McCaffery stood at the cell entrance to recite in Latin the Office of the Dead. Within a few minutes, John Sheehy, the principal keeper, was there to tell them, "The hour has come."

Ruth felt her legs weaken but she was held upright by the matrons. She hated it that she could not halt the tears. She was gently urged into the corridor that was called "the last mile," and she managed to stagger forward, saying over and over again, "Jesus have mercy on me." She cradled a large crucifix.

Even though it was cold and late at night and there was really no spectacle to witness, a great crowd had formed outside Sing Sing's main gate, where four rifled prison guards were stationed. Children straddled their fathers' shoulders; some teenagers shinnied up trees; journalists sat on the running boards of their cars, desultorily smoking cigarettes as they waited for the flare that would signal the first death. Some people tramped through a field of snow to watch ice float by on the dark Hudson River.

Zoe Beckley wrote for the same Famous Features Syndicate that was serializing Judd Gray's memoir, and she was the sole woman who'd volunteered to witness the executions. She told Warden Lawes she wanted ever so much to see Mrs. Snyder die, however she felt a conflict of interest concerning Mr. Gray. She therefore told the warden she would have to leave when Judd was escorted in, but Lawes wouldn't permit that, hence she was replaced by a man.

And so it was that when Ruth entered the execution chamber she was greeted by the silence and scrutiny of twenty male

reporters, four male physicians, some sullen prison guards, Warden
Lawes and his assistants, and with Father McCaffery still reciting Latin prayers beside her. All told, there were forty-one men.
Albert's sister had called Ruth "man crazy" and now she was overwhelmed by them, with only the matrons for sisterly company.

Oak church pews for the witnesses had been hauled up from
the chapel, but otherwise the wide room was stunningly white
except for some silver pipes and silver radiators. Six frosted wall
lamps increased the glare, so that Ruth was shading her eyes when
she finally noticed the wide oaken chair on its rubber mat. And
there was nothing to do but shriek in such a high-pitched way that
some reporters held their ears. She would have fallen like a child in
a tantrum without the matrons holding firm.

Saying, "Jesus, have mercy on me, for I have sinned," Ruth tottered forward as if she'd soon faint but was guided around and gently pushed down onto the rubber seat. McCaffery took the crucifix
from her and completed the rite of extreme unction as each upper
arm and wrist was buckled to the wooden chair with a leather
restraint. Ruth's black stockings were rolled down to her ankles
and each ankle was restrained. She was belted in at the chest and
waist. She wildly glanced around at a civilization frankly staring at
her fear. Waiting for her to die. She fought to breathe as a strapped
black leather mask with just a slit for the nose and mouth was fitted
over her face so her head could be fettered against a rubber head-
rest and so the viewers would not have to see her face in its horrible constrictions. A sea sponge that was soaked in salt water and
contained a circular mesh of fine copper wire was inserted into the
crown of a leather football helmet, Ruth's wet hair was parted to
expose the shaved occiput of the skull to the electrode, and the helmet was fitted on, the chin strap cinched. She softly said, "Father,
forgive them, for they know not what they do," and another electrode was attached to Ruth's shaking right calf to complete the
electrical circuit.

All the attendants stood back.

Cameras were prohibited, but an overly ambitious photographer named Thomas Howard, who'd lied that he was a journalist, was sitting in the front row with an Ansco Memo Miniature taped to his ankle. Raising his trouser cuff and gripping the inflated bulb for the shutter in his front pocket, Howard waited.

Robert Elliott stood in his alcove, his hands on the electrical controls, and looked through window glass at Warden Lawes.

Lawes was just watching an overhead clock until it was exactly eleven.

Ruth was praying, "Jesus, have mercy on me, Jesus, have—"

She could not finish the sentence because Lawes nodded and the executioner slammed the switch that closed the electrical circuit. Ruth's body heaved up but was held fast by the restraints. Howard snapped his photo and was paid an extra one hundred dollars. It would be headlined "DEAD!" on the front page and be judged one of the *Great Moments in News Photography*.

The high voltage instantly shocked Ruth into a coma and paralyzed her heart muscles, but Elliott maintained the current for five seconds more until he felt certain that the skin temperature had crossed the threshold of 140 degrees, when the central nervous system would be destroyed. Elliott shut off the current and Ruth's body relaxed. With folded arms, Lawes considered the floor.

Ruth's hands clenched in an involuntary muscular reaction. Ruth's flesh was fried a scarlet red.

Elliott forced up the switch again and two thousand volts coursed through Ruth, and again she surged up against the restraints. There was a crackling sound. Her hair caught fire and faint smoke trails floated up from the helmet. She relaxed when Elliott shut off the current, and then, erring on the side of caution, he hit her with the electricity again for a full minute.

Dr. Sweet went forward and took off the helmet and mask. Ruth had shut her eyes but the current had caused the rictus of a smile, and foam slid from a corner of her mouth. Sheehy held up a towel to hide Ruth's naked breasts from the witnesses as Sweet searched for a heartbeat with his stethoscope. Dr. Harold Goslin searched too and shook his head. Another doctor did the same.

Dr. Charles Sweet shouted out, "I pronounce this woman dead."

It was 11:04 p.m., Thursday, January 12th, 1928. A red flare was shot up into the heavens to alert the reporters outside the penitentiary.

Attendants walked forward to carefully hoist the electrocuted body onto the gleaming white enameled bed of a gurney cart. The housedress smock was not just for modesty; it kept the helpers from being burned by her scorching-hot skin when Ruth's corpse was lifted from the chair. She was wheeled into the white-tiled morgue, "the icebox," and Principal Keeper Sheehy went down to the west wing to tell Henry Judd Gray it was time.

Within seconds, it seemed, he was there, dressed in a gray, pin-striped suit and a tieless, unbuttoned white silk shirt. The flower of a mauve handkerchief bloomed from his left chest pocket. Like Ruth he shushed along in felt slippers. His right trouser leg had been scissored for the electrode and it flapped when he strode in, but he seemed otherwise organized, efficient, and formidable in spite of being the smallest man in the room. His tortoiseshell glasses were off, as they'd been whenever he made love to Ruth and when he went in to kill The Governor. The Protestant minister, Anthony Peterson, was helping Judd cope by reciting the "Blessed are" halves of the Beatitudes while Judd supplied the latter halves. But Judd, like Ruth, was distracted by the sheer number of people there to watch him die, and he hesitated in disorientation until Warden Lawes held a hand out to the oaken chair like an overtipped waiter, and Judd went directly to it, wiping hot tears away with his shirt cuff.

Judd flicked his trousers as if they were crumbed and was buckled down just as Ruth had been, and Reverend Peterson bent close to him to help in reciting the twenty-third psalm, cueing him with, " 'The Lord is my shepherd; I shall not want.' "

Holding his chin up to help the attendants affix the face mask, Judd overloudly responded, " 'He maketh me to lie down in green pastures: he leadeth me beside the still waters.' "

Reverend Peterson recited, " 'He restoreth my soul.' " The helmet was fitted on. And Judd said, " 'He leadeth me in the paths of righteousness for his name's sake.' " Sheehy cautioned Reverend Peterson to retreat from the rubber mat as Judd tremblingly said, " 'Yea, though I walk through the valley of the shadow of death, I will fear no evil: for—' "

And then, in midsentence, all air gone from his lungs so that they would not gurgle, the current shot through him with a sizzling sound, his body jerking up as if he could have flown had he not been belted. Elliott shocked him twice for a total of two minutes. His right sock flamed; his dark brown hair underneath the helmet sent up spirals of smoke. The face mask was removed. His eyes were half-shut and his mouth was wide, as if he were laughing.

There was still some buzzing from the transformer.

Dr. Sweet hunched over Judd's body with his stethoscope and officially shouted, "I pronounce this man dead!"

It was 11:14.

Warden Lawes hitched his head toward the door and the gentlemen witnesses saw it was time to go and filed out.

In the yard, an inmate yelled, "It's over! It's over!" and that heralded a ghoulish celebration that grew ugly and then just wearisome and finally caused the crowd to straggle off to their homes.

The final remains of Mr. Henry Judd Gray were hoisted onto a gurney and shoved into "the icebox," where his clothing was taken off, just as Mrs. Ruth May Brown Snyder's had been, for New York's mandated autopsy. As the doctors readied their trays and instruments, there Ruth and Judd lay, naked and side-by-side again, their arms hanging from the gurneys so that their hands almost touched. Calm now. Silent. Dispassionate. Loved.

ACKNOWLEDGMENTS

This is a work of fiction based on fact, and though I hew closely to the history of the events, the majority of the narrative is, of course, invented. My sources for this novel have principally been the New York City newspapers of the period as well as the following: the memoir *Doomed Ship* by Judd Gray, *The Trial of Ruth Snyder and Judd Gray* by John Kobler, *The "Double Indemnity" Murder* by Landis MacKellar, *Murderess!* by Leslie Margolin, *Trials and Other Tribulations* by Damon Runyon, and *My Own True Story—So Help Me God!* by Ruth Snyder. I would like to express my gratitude to those authors for their information and guidance. And finally my thanks to my lovely wife, Bo Caldwell, and my old friend Jim Shepard, the first readers of these pages, whose encouragement, aesthetic judgment, and editorial advice have been invaluable over the years.

This is Ron Hansen's eighth novel. He is married to the novelist Bo Caldwell and lives in northern California, where he teaches film, fiction writing, and literature at Santa Clara University.

A Scribner Reading Group Guide

A WILD SURGE OF GUILTY PASSION

Ron Hansen

INTRODUCTION

In a vivid, morbidly compelling novel of infidelity and deceit, Ron Hansen brings to life the actual events of the famed 1927 Snyder/Gray murder case—a lurid scandal that shocked a nation.

Trapped in a loveless marriage, the irresistible, reckless Ruth Snyder starts an affair with owlish Judd Gray, a lingerie salesman from New Jersey beleaguered by his own marital woes. What begins as a tryst quickly turns sinister, as Ruth and an enchanted, alcoholic Judd begin to plot the murder of Ruth's husband, Albert. From murder plan to police investigation to their murder trial, Hansen deftly re-creates this famous story with sultry prose—and shows just how dangerous desire can be.

TOPICS & QUESTIONS FOR DISCUSSION

1. What were your first impressions of the opening crime scene? Did you immediately expect Ruth's involvement? Why or why not?

2. Discuss the magazine-style narration of the novel. How did this affect your reading? What did you make of the

references to the future, post-trial? Consider Ethel's tuberculosis, Ruth's incarceration, and Judd's memoir in your
response.

3. Consider Ruth and Judd's "love," and how Ruth took
part in trysts with numerous men, while Judd's infidelity focused exclusively on Ruth. Do you think Ruth really
loved Judd? Did Judd really love Ruth? Was there something there beyond sexual infatuation and the promise of
Albert's disposal?

4. How were Ruth and Judd similar? How were they different? Can you identify any specific personality traits that
result in such a dangerous pairing? How did their respec-
tive backgrounds drive them to first an affair, and then
murder?

5. Was the author effective in painting a picture of New York
City during the Jazz Age? Discuss the historical specifics—
from actors to periodicals to shampoo brands—the author
used to illustrate the late 1920s.

6. Consider the role Ruth's and Judd's families played in this
reimagined account of history. How would you describe
Ruth and Albert's marriage? Judd and Isabel's? In your
opinion, who were the ultmate victims of this crime?

7. Do you agree with the tabloids that Ruth is the "quintessential femme fatale"?

8. When Father George Murphy visits Ruth in prison, she
tells him, "Men fantasize about sex all the time . . . and
women fantasize about romance . . . and looking for
romance will get you in just as much trouble" (p. 204). Are
sex and romance equally dangerous? Discuss their destruc-
tive natures in relation to Judd and Ruth's erratic affair.

9. Did you feel any sympathy for Albert? He was painted as a vile, abusive character—but did he deserve to die? Discuss the complexities of being trapped in an abusive marriage, especially during the time period of the novel, when it was difficult to divorce.

10. Do you believe, as the priest puts its, that Ruth arrived at a "deep and profound sense of repentance" (p. 233)? Consider Ruth's testimony during the trial in your response. Was she justified in lying to stay out of jail and with Lorraine?

11. Considering Judd's nervous, alcoholic nature, why do you think he was so calm during the trial and his sentencing? Do you believe he truly found tranquility in his renewed faith?

12. Did you find yourself hoping for an appeal of Ruth's and Judd's death sentences? Why or why not? Did you sympathize with either character?

13. Were you able to find any kind of poeticism as Judd's and Ruth's charred bodies lay almost touching on the gurneys? Was it just another case of what "whiskey, lust, and sin will ultimately condemn one to" (p. 233)?

Enhance Your Book Club

1. Since *A Wild Surge of Guilty Passion* is based on real events, research the actual happenings of Ruth and Judd's trial. How do they compare to the novel? Can you find any facts left out or altered?

2. Ron Hansen includes a long list of references to late 1920s music, fashion, movies, and culture, such as the films of Mae West, F. Scott Fitzgerald's *The Great Gatsby*, and Irving

Berlin's "Always." Sample some of these other mediums and reread your favorite passages from the book. Does it help to better place you in the time period?

3. Read another historical fiction novel and compare it with *A Wild Surge of Guilty Passion*. Consider Joseph Kanon's *Stardust*, Matt Bondurant's *The Wettest County in the World*, or one of Ron Hansen's previous novels: Are there similarities in the devices used to convey the mood of the period?

Turn the page for a short story from
Ron Hansen's new story collection,
She Loves Me Not: New and Selected Stories,
coming from Scribner in Fall 2012.

THE SPARROW

by Ron Hansen

She'd been flying a Cessna, shooting practice takeoffs and landings
with a flight instructor at an Omaha airstrip that was just a wind
sock and one lane of unnumbered concrete runway veined with tar
repairs. Richard Nixon was president, the month was September,
the temperature was sixty degrees, and she was Karen Manion,
mother of two. The flying lessons were a gift from her husband
for her fortieth birthday. The flight instructor was a gruff, retired
warrant officer named Billy who claimed he'd flown everything
the army had, from fixed wings to Chinooks. Within a week
Karen would take the flight test to get her private pilot's license,
and she'd told her husband a night earlier that Billy was trying
to prepare her for it by pulling stunts that some examiners were
known to do, hiding flight plans and cross-country maps, or forcing
the plane too steep in its climb so that the horn warned of a stall.
Yesterday Billy had watched Karen's face with a confident smile
as she recovered from a hammerhead spin. And now as she ran
the Cessna up to sixty-five miles per hour, eased back on the yoke,
and felt the plane lift up from the runway, the front window would
have filled with skies that were the blue of old jeans, nothing more,
and she probably glanced at the vertical speed and turn-and-bank
indicators before she noticed that Billy's hand was on the plunger

throttle and suddenly jerking it back, cutting the power. Karen was supposed to immediately push down the nose to maintain air speed, but she may have glared with shock and insult at Billy or screamed a question about what he thought he was *doing,* and in that hesitation the Cessna fell forty or fifty feet. The stall horn would have blared and Billy would have lunged for the control yoke as he hurriedly said, "I've got it," giving the plane full throttle as he tilted the nose down. But they'd fallen too far and they would have seen skid marks on concrete rushing up into the front window fast as the Cessna crashed into the runway, very hard.

Karen's son, Aidan, was twelve years old and he was at home hitting a shag bag of golf balls into a peach basket with his father's chrome-bright sand wedge when he heard the kitchen telephone and ran inside to answer it. "Oh, Aidan," Kelli, their neighbor, said, not sounding right. She paused and with some strain asked, "Is Lucy there?"

Lucy was fifteen, his older sister, so he first thought his mother's friend was hunting a babysitter. "She's at a friend's house," he said.

Kelli seemed to be crying. A hand seemed to clench her throat. "Would you go get her, honey? And then I'll come get you both."

"Why?"

She told him there had been an accident and his mother was at Immanuel, nothing more.

Aidan found Lucy four houses down the street. She and Molly were lying on the floor of the yellow living room, Lucy's head pillowed by Molly's stomach as she read aloud from Dylan Thomas's *Adventures in the Skin Trade*. Wildly giggling at the prose, Lucy tried to go on, but Molly's stomach bulged with laughter too and Lucy yelled in pretend anger, "You're jiggling the pages!" Molly guffawed, rolling away and holding her waist with both crossed arms, and Lucy caught sight of Aidan in his loneliness of grief. She got up on an elbow and she quieted as she stared. "What's happened?"

"Mom's hurt," Aidan said.

Kelli drove them to Immanuel Hospital. She told them their father had been contacted at work and he was already there when he phoned her. The flight instructor had been killed in the accident.

"His name was Billy," Aidan said.

Kelli looked at him in the rearview mirror and said, "Billy. Thank you." She tried to give them further information, but she ran out quickly; there was too much she'd only be guessing at, and so she just held on to the steering wheel tightly as she raced through yellow lights. Aidan sat in the backseat, mutely watching as tears trickled down Kelli's cheek and she wiped them with her palm. She blurted an embarrassed laugh as she said, "I'm such a rock."

Lucy reached across and gave a sisterly touch to her hand. "That's okay."

Kelli was driving them through a cathedral of shade made by stately elm trees. Aidan looked outside at a boy half his age wobbling down the sidewalk on a bicycle too big for him. And there on a porch a mother was watching, too, a hand to her mouth, imprisoning her warnings. But still the boy did not fall.

At Immanuel, a nurse told Aidan and Lucy that their father had gotten there in time to accompany the gurney as their mother was rushed upstairs into surgery. Mrs. Manion was in a coma. The head and chest wounds were "traumatic." Kelli went down the hallway to the banks of telephones and Aidan and Lucy sat next to each other on hard plastic chairs in the uncoziness of the waiting area, saying nothing, staring at the floor. Aidan's thoughts were discontinuous, furious, forlorn, like a child's Crayola scribble on the wall, and when he heard Lucy whisper, "Are you praying?" he felt convicted.

"Uh-huh," he said.

"Me too," Lucy said, and she surprised him by holding his hand in hers. "She'll live," Lucy said. "She's got to."

He was shocked that he hadn't yet considered the fact that his mother could die from the injuries. With great urgency, Aidan silently recited the prayers he'd memorized in religion class, prayers he'd say hurriedly, his heart hammering, whenever he woke up from a nightmare. But he was convinced more was expected now, some plea, some contract, a way of prevailing against the grim odds with earnest promises that he'd be good, say a rosary every day, even become a priest, if only God would let his mother live. *Please, God,* he prayed, *don't let my mom die. I need her.*

And then they saw their father at the far end of the hallway, walking toward them in hospital scrubs with a friend who was an orthopedic surgeon. Aidan got up from his chair just as his sister did, but when he saw Lucy freeze and fail to run forward, he stayed as he was, too. He took it as a good sign that there were no bloodstains on either of the men, but he noticed their solemnity. Dr. Welter's stare drifted from Aidan's to the floor. When their father was a few feet away, he quietly said, "Hi, kids." Lucy forgot her pretense of calm and flung herself into him, her face in his chest as she screeched her misery. Worn-out, red-eyed, seemingly lost, Emmett Manion held her and kissed her head as she wept, then petted her hair and said, "Shh now. Shh."

Lucy screamed, "I don't want to shh! I'm *sad*!"

Their father looked at Aidan and held out his left arm. Aidan fitted himself under it and his father kissed his head, too. The hospital scrubs smelled of medicines, like a bathroom cabinet. The wing tip of his father's left shoe shone with a coin of moisture. His strong chest swelled as he forced himself to inhale. "She's gone, kids," he told them.

Lucy fell to her knees on the floor and wailed. And Aidan felt childish and empty and impossibly stupid, for he'd at first thought his father meant she'd gotten well and left the hospital. But he hadn't said "dead," he'd said "gone." Wouldn't he have said dead if she was dead? She wasn't, maybe.

Kelli had found cold cans of Coca-Cola for them and was strolling toward them in the hallway. But Aidan saw her halt when she saw his father. His face must have communicated with a great deal of accuracy, for she sank into a chair and folded over and cried.

The funeral was hard, but harder were the sentiments afterward as swarming people tried to console them. Either it was a touch of assurance and a sighed confession of mystery, as in "His ways are not our ways," as if with fathomless ulterior motives God coldly intended the crash; or they'd pat Lucy's or Aidan's hands while confiding in faith that much good would come from this, as if their mother's death were a lesson they would not have learned otherwise.

Classmates stood far away from them, hollowed and ill at ease, as if death were contagious. Even lofty, fearsome Monsignor Florio fell out of character, his soft handshake holding fast to Emmett Manion's as he instructed, "Saint Augustine wrote, 'Non enim fecit atque abiit,' meaning, God did not just make us and go away. We have a personal relationship with Him. Whatever happens to us, good or bad, it is equally as important to God."

Aidan's father shamed his son by weakly answering, "Thank you, Monsignor," seeming no older than twelve himself.

But hours later he found Aidan in his room and a football in the crook of his arm. Emmett worked up a smile as he asked, "How about throwing the oblate spheroid around?"

There was a competition over their father for a while. Kelli kept showing up with her little children and a casserole, a pan of fudge, a lasagna, and Lucy fumed, wordlessly ate, and afterward referred to Kelli as "The Divorcée." Even in her embarrassment at vying for their father's attentions, Kelli would find a reason to stay around until Emmett got home, and then they would drink Chardonnay in coats on the patio as Aidan whacked his Wiffle ball against the garage door and Lucy played desultory games of Candyland inside with the children.

But then there must have been an earnest nighttime conversation that Lucy and Aidan didn't hear, for with fall's unleaving Kelli stopped stopping by.

Still his sister cried for hours on end. Wherever she could in her room, Lucy hung old photographs of Karen from high school yearbooks, from the scrapbook *Our Wedding,* from the obituary in the *Omaha World-Herald.* She researched her mother's injuries and hung up a framed poster on *The Anatomy of the Brain.* She reread her mother's handwritten sentiments in the birthday cards she'd collected over the years and constructed a kind of shrine around a snapshot from her mother's fortieth birthday party; the one where Karen Manion smiled as she held up a small plastic Cessna airplane in her right hand, and in her left a gift certificate for flying lessons. Wedged in a corner of the photograph was a slip of paper on which Lucy had written: "I will not leave you orphaned . . . John 14:18."

Lucy lost weight. She forgot tests and homework. Wouldn't answer Molly's phone calls. She confided in her father, shared errands with him, and flew into his embrace when he got home from work, as if she'd been storing up those tears. She said she often dreamed about her mother and gladly reported the dreams at breakfast, but neither Aidan nor her father could invent the correct reply. Out of the blue she told Aidan once, "She wants you to sign up for sixth-grade basketball. She says you'll be good at it." And then she wept and fell into him and Aidan held her as his father did, patting her jerking back awkwardly, but not saying "There, there."

Their father was stoic about it. Strong for them. Each Sunday evening Emmett wrote out the week's schedules and chores. Listed grocery store items, his obligations at work, things that still needed to be done. Everybody was very careful with each other and avoided any harsh words. They were responsible for their own laundry now, shared the dishwashing chores, and once there was a rigorous inspection of their rooms, but he forgot to continue most of the other programs he established.

Aidan once wandered into the bedroom he still thought of as his mother's though only his father slept there now. Nothing had changed since September. His mother's clothing still hung in the closet—a faint hint of her sweat in her gardening shirt, a faint trace of Chanel in a cocktail dress. And hair was still in her hairbrush; her creams, conditioners, and cleansing lotions were like a cityscape on the mirrored counter in the master bathroom.

Was that healthy, having her present like that? Lucy was continually emotional, but Aidan noticed his father's grief only once, when he woke up in the middle of the night and saw him out in the late November cold of the backyard, coatless, facing nothing at all, and weeping so like a child that Aidan himself wept with him.

Some friends from Emmett's office visited the house in December to toast his promotion. Each was introduced to the children, but Aidan remembered only the pretty secretary's name: Gayl, with a *y*. His jealousy confused him. His father cooked rib-eye steaks on the outdoor grill as fat snowflakes fluttered down and decomposed on the patio bricks. Everyone seemed too loud. Homework took Lucy and Aidan up to their rooms after dinner, but Aidan came out after an hour and crouched on the landing, his knees in a hug, to listen in on the conversation. Only Gayl had stayed and she was contrasting their father with her ex, lavishing praise on Emmett, telling him how crucial he was to the company, what a pleasure it was to watch him succeed, and how much his friendship meant to her. Could he see how lonely she'd been?

Aidan's father said nothing.

And then she asked, "Are you aware I love you . . . passionately?"

Sheez, who talks like that? Aidan thought.

Emmett flatly told her, "Yes, I know how you feel."

Aidan held his hands over his ears as he got up to go back to his room. But then he saw his sister standing there behind him, listening too, and far more interested than Aidan in whatever happened next. She chose to defend her father in advance, whispering to Aidan, "He's human, you know."

Aidan entered his room, shut the door, and, just in case, tuned his radio between stations so he couldn't hear anything but a hissing, crackling noise, like tires on their cinder alley. A half hour later, however, he rose above the white forest of frost on his window to see Gayl hurrying to her Volvo with her face in her hands, as if she were holding it on, and he wasn't sure how he felt about that.

The assistant pastor in their parish was Father Jim Schwartz. He was handsome, humorous, in his late twenties, and all the schoolgirls got desperate and dreamy looks whenever he was around. Aidan's father said of his preaching that "He really gets you thinking," but the tone was that of a criticism. And Aidan's mother once joked that he was "Father What-a-Waste." Aidan misunderstood until she told him she meant it was a shame Father Schwartz could never marry. "The good husbands," she said, "are always taken."

Aidan had never visited the old rectory, no one his age ever did. It was like tempting the porch of a haunted house. He was an altar boy and one morning had to go to the kitchen door to get a cruet of wine from the old Belgian cook, and he'd seen the wide back of Monsignor Florio at the kitchen table, his black suit coat off and his trousers held up by crossed suspenders as he smeared jam on a slice of toast. Aidan was shocked by that secret look, his violation of the fathers' hard-won privacy, and the cook shooed him away as soon as she'd poured the red Cribari wine.

And yet one afternoon after sixth-grade basketball practice, his hair still wet and stiffening in the cold, Aidan went to the front door of the rectory and Father Schwartz himself answered the four-toned bell. Without his Roman collar and in his sneakers and jeans and Creighton sweatshirt, Schwartz could have been the high school senior who coached them. Smiling as if he'd just heard a joke, Schwartz said, "Hi."

With hesitation Aidan asked, "Could I talk to you?"

"Is this a confessional matter?"

Aidan wasn't sure and said no.

"It's my day off," the assistant pastor said, but he invited him in. "I'm trying to remember your name."

"Aidan Manion."

"Oh, right. Let's go to the parlor."

Schwartz strode jauntily to a hot, musty front room that was wallpapered in shades of lavender and was congested with ornate furniture that seemed at least a century old. He fell nonchalantly into an overstuffed chair and Aidan put his gym bag on the floor as he sat on the edge of a plush sofa cushion. Schwartz crossed his ankle-high black sneakers on an ottoman. "You're a fifth grader, right?"

"Sixth."

"Sister Josefina?"

Aidan nodded.

"So what's up?"

"You knew my mom died?"

"Oh gosh, I forgot. I'm so, so sorry, Aidan. I was racking my brain."

"That's okay."

"Is that what this is about?"

"She was really nice," Aidan said. "She never did anything wrong." Sins of his own started vagrantly populating his thoughts.

"And you're wondering why she died?"

"Sort of."

The priest's right elbow was on the arm of the chair and his right cheek was against his knuckles, as in a book jacket photograph illustrating wise consideration. "The psalmists asked it long ago," he said. "Why do the evil prosper? Why do the innocent suffer? Why, when a loved one is dying, doesn't God intercede? Those are philosophical questions and they fall under a category called 'theodicy.'"

"I'm just twelve," Aidan said.

Even in winter there, sunlight hurled itself through the southern windows and formed hatchings of shadow on the floor. Aidan's right shoe was untied but he didn't fix it. Schwartz linked his fingers on top of his head. His hair was Christ-long, the fashion then, and Aidan had heard older parishioners joke about it. Schwartz gazed outside at huddling girls scuttling against the wind as he told the boy, "There was an eighteenth-century Scottish philosopher named David Hume who said that our experience of the world contradicted our conception of God, because if God allowed evil to exist, He was not all good; or if evil was loose in the world and God was unable to counteract it, He was not omnipotent. Evil, for Hume, demolished God, and he became an atheist. But he raises good questions. Because sometimes it does seem God has lost interest in us. Children starve. Wars rage on. Illness goes the wrong way too often. I get a phone call and a lady says she's gotten a death sentence from her doctor and she cries, 'Why me?' I just look at

Jesus hanging there on the crucifix and want to say, 'Why *not* you?' Are you following me?"

"Sort of," Aidan said, even though he was lost. Each sentence seemed less like a window and more like a shutting door.

"We have to let God be God," the priest said.

The conclusion felt overly routine. *It's my day off,* he'd said. "But my sister and my dad and me. We ache."

Schwartz's head jerked as if he'd been insulted, but his frown gradually soothed. "Hey, I'm sorry, Aidan. I was off in systematic theology and you're there with a cosmic knee in your gut. I'm no help at all, am I?"

"You helped."

"Really? How?"

His question felt intentionally difficult and unfair, but his face was sincere. "I guess just talking," Aidan said. "Hearing about other people."

"So you don't feel so alone," Schwartz said.

"Uh-huh."

"Are you feeling responsible—that she died?"

Aidan felt accused. "Why?"

"Sometimes people do."

Aidan gripped his gym bag and stood up. "Is your mom still alive?"

"Yes." Schwartz stood, too, seeming puzzled. "Are we finished?"

"I have a long walk home. And it's getting cold."

Classes started again in January. Each week that year the sixth graders had been visited by parents in differing occupations for their "What I Want to Be" project, and now Emmett Manion was there to explain accounting while Sister Josefina hunched at a back desk correcting their English homework.

The clanging radiators in the old brick grade school were

generally too hot in winter, and on that near-zero afternoon there was a kind of sauna in their second-story classroom. Sister Josefina noticed aloud that the children were becoming dull, and Aidan's father opened the upper half of the four tall windows with a long, hooked pole. Waterfalls of cold air poured in.

Aidan's father returned to the accounting lesson, chalking a ledger page on the blackboard and printing in capitals "DEBITS" and "CREDITS." But then a sparrow flew in through one upper window opening, wildly looping around overhead like a frantic bat so that Aidan's classmates ducked down and covered their hair with their hands. One girl squealed, and Sister Josefina held her textbook overhead and swatted at the bird, trying to shoo it toward the window opening. But still the sparrow insanely circled and veered and swooped, hunting a way out, bashing into windowpanes, increasingly harassed and scared by every screech and waving arm.

At last, Emmett Manion told the class, "Let's try this, kids. Why don't we all quietly leave the room?" And staring over their heads at the thrashing bird, he held the door open in an official way as the class and Sister Josefina filed out. When the thirty of them were in the school hallway, Aidan's father let him and a few others look through the window in the classroom door.

Aidan watched the sparrow flapping its wings in a panicky swirl, but as quiet took over the room, the sparrow calmed and cruised the four corners of the classroom until it felt the chill from the foot-high opening in an upper window and with a sudden swerve was flying into the immensity of outdoors.

Emmett Manion said nothing as he softly stared out at nothing at all, but Sister Josefina smiled and said, "Let us resume."

Aidan filed back inside with the others. His father never mentioned it, and Aidan didn't tell Lucy because he wanted it for himself: that feeling of friendship with the silence he had been hearing but had not understood.